More
Scary
Kisses

More Scary Kisses

Edited by
Liz Grzyb

T℥
p℥   Ticonderoga
publications

To Debbie and Taz,
who have been my romance book-swapping
partners for more years than we want to count.

The editor would like to thank Russell, Mum, Shane, Angela, Kate, Kate, Andrew, Matthew, Debbie, Jacinta, Ambre, Michael Kylie, Mel, Mel, Phil, Ruza, Lina, Nikki, Andrea, Angie, Fee, Jane, Lynne, Jane, Dionn, Clare, Anne, Meredith, Genevieve, Suad; and all of the fabulous More Scary Kisses *writers: Felicity, Dayle, Carol, Amanda, Frank, Nicole, Eric, Roxanne, Fraser, Kirstyn, DC, Donna, Annette, Liz, Jason, Heather, Martin and Talie.*

Contents

Introduction

OWHEN I set out to put together an anthology of "paranormal romance with bite"—the first *Scary Kisses*—I was looking for stories which had the elements of the romance genre I loved: the heady tension between the main characters; the resolution of their relationship in some way, and also the paranormal: the interactions between humans and those not so human.

A lot of paranormal romance out there I've read, especially the early stuff, usually involved a human female becoming involved with a male who was not so human. This became pretty boring pretty quickly, not to mention the interesting ideological implications of always showing a "pure" female and a "savage" male character! The only real alternative in what I was reading seemed to be having a predatory villainous female: not always the most sympathetic of protagonists. So when I was looking for stories for *Scary Kisses* and again with *More Scary Kisses*, I wanted something a little different. There needed to be some form of romance, a paranormal element, and also had to be fresh and interesting. A big ask in under 8,500 words!

I was amazed at the breadth and depth of the submitted stories. There were stories from all over the world, from women, men and young adults who were all interested in taking a new look at the genre. It was very difficult to narrow the stories down to the seventeen excellent stories I've included.

Between these covers, you'll find stories that explore the paranormal romance idea in very different ways. There are happy endings and those which are bittersweet, tales from times past or set in a present we may not immediately recognise. The stories you read might not all be sugar and spice, but they might make your heartbeat quicken and your toes tingle. There is a mix of genre influences, from gritty urban fantasy, through horror and the grimmest of fairy tales, to humorous, historical and fantastical romance.

Paranormal romance is, quite simply, a lot of fun. I hope you find *More Scary Kisses* an enjoyable read, and that it whets your appetite for more.

LIZ GRZYB
JANUARY 2011

More
Scary
Kisses

Berries and Incense

Felicity Dowker

ROWAN ran the cobblestones of the night in a ragged purple dress made of hope. Her red foliage hair, long and dotted with berries that glowed like coals, rustled and shed pieces of itself as the wind plucked at it with sharp fingers. Waxwings and thrushes raced each other in the starlit sky, marking her passage on the earth below, their beaks snapping in anticipation of her soft fruit. She knuckled her white flower eyes with bark fingers, wiping away the pollen tears that dusted her stiff cheeks.

Oh, but she hurt. She hurt *so* much.

She took huge gulps of air as her wooden legs pumped. Her lungs burnt and her muscles ached and her chest pounded like a drum being beaten from the inside, but still she ran, screaming wordlessly into the dark. The birds above her shrieked back, delighted.

Finally she reached the ornate bridge that straddled the banks between Here and There. On the peak of the bridge, suspended in the aether, was where Rowan wanted to be. That place was Nowhere, a platform cushioned by the splayed tail feathers of sleeping peacocks and lit by winged yellow lanterns. There she could let Mother Bear lick the sap from her wounds with ancient tongue.

She climbed the bridge, digging her twig toes in for purchase, singing, as one always should when going Nowhere. Mother Bear waited for her, massive arms outspread, warm paws waiting to hold her tight. Rowan ran into the Bear's embrace with a dry kindling sob, pollen exploding from her eyes in earnest. Mother Bear held her and let her cry, the Bear's own beady eyes moist, a protective growl rumbling in her throat.

Eventually Rowan was hollowed out and done, and Mother Bear released her.

"Why don't you visit me more often, Rowan child?"

"I would if I could, Mother. I've tried. But I can't find my way here, save for times when the pain becomes almost enough to destroy me. I wish it weren't so."

"Well, what is, is. Tea?" The Bear pulled a red teapot from one of her many furry folds. Rowan nodded, as she always did, and the kettle steamed and whistled on cue. A waxwing alighted on her leafy hair, dipping its head and taking a berry in its beak before she shooed it away.

"What flavour tonight, Mother?"

"Salty mountain ash, the desiccated remains of a tree-girl's broken heart, mixed with sweet glass, the preserved lies dripped from a lover's tongue, served cold and bitter in an empty cup, the discovery of a lover's betrayal most foul."

The bear handed Rowan her tea, and Rowan cradled it, sipped, sighed. Peppery spices filled her nose and tingled on the back of her throat, their taste muted by Rowan's lack of a sense of smell, an absence she'd carried with her as long as she could remember.

"Drink it all. Let it sit heavy like a glacier in your belly."

Rowan did as she was told and handed the cup—which had always appeared empty, but was lighter now—back to Mother Bear. She clambered onto the peacock's feathers, lying on her back and staring at the stars, brilliant green fireballs in the dark sky.

After a while, the feathers whispered against each other as someone lay beside her.

"Delight of the eye," he said, his voice like boiling honey.

Rowan gasped, turning her head to see her visitor.

"Don't look at me," the voice said quickly. "At least, not just yet. I don't want you to see what I am and spurn me before I've had even the slightest chance."

Reluctantly, Rowan obeyed. She hungered to hear that smooth, warm voice again.

"This is my place," she said.

"Yes, yours, Rune Tree, Quickbane, Thor's Apple. You beautiful thing. You don't know how special you are. How exalted, throughout all places and all times."

"Nobody thinks I'm special. They call me dogberry. They threaten to burn me. They laugh. They desert." Except for Crow, poor pitiful fellow slave, and, like Rowan, she counted for little.

"They're fools." Rowan felt him rise to his feet, the weight of him gone from their shared featherbed, leaving her too light, untethered, addled. "I love you. I loved you before, and I love you now, and I'll love you after. I love you Here and I love you There. I love you Everywhere and Nowhere. *Don't* look at me," he added as Rowan began, again, to turn her head.

"You're leaving," she said.

"Yes. I'll be missed, and so will you, and this is not my place, as you pointed out. It's hard to leave so soon, but harder still to stay—impossible, in fact. I followed you here, this once, after many failed attempts. But this place is wise to me now, and I can never enter again."

Mother Bear snarled, a low, deadly sound, emphasising the visitor's words.

"I will come for you, Rune Tree."

"Wait!" Rowan cried, looking despite his admonitions, but he was gone.

Nowhere remained undisturbed, which was of course the charm it had always held for Rowan. Wind chimes tinkled. The water frothing under the bridge made pretty sounds. Mother Bear relaxed into slumber, and she and the peacocks snored. The winged lantern's flames sputtered and crackled, high in the air where their fire posed no threat to Rowan.

This was her lullaby and her medicine, and despite herself, Rowan was soothed. Soon enough, her own snores joined Nowhere's song.

. . . . .

You've got to stop running away at night." Crow held out a guano bowl to Rowan, waiting as Rowan snared a few warm berries from her hair and dropped them in. "It only makes the Seamstress angrier at you. She threatened to take your hope-dress from you, and make you new clothing, of fire and pesticide! She threatens your death, Rowan." Crow put the bowl of berries on the counter and added a pinch of spices, plunging her talon-fingers into the mix, piercing the berries and swirling the juicy mess around. Her beak opened and shut in small, pathetic movements on her otherwise human face, giving away her constant hunger, as if her emaciated frame weren't hint enough. It was torture, pairing her with Rowan, tempting her with fruit she could never touch. The Seamstress had Crow's droppings checked regularly for evidence of berry consumption, and her punishment was worth starving to avoid.

"I don't care what she does to me. I'm already dead." Rowan fingered the hard lines of dried sap that gnarled the bark of her arms, scars left by the Seamstress' needle fingers.

Crow cawed, the sound loud and harsh in the small, musty kitchen.

"You must care. We belong to her. The sooner you accept that, the better."

"I don't belong to anyone!"

"You can rage against it as much as you like, but the fact is, the Seamstress bought us, and that makes us her property. She can destroy us and it won't bother her or anyone else one bit. She can find more of us. We're just Wyrd Women, Rowan, offensive to the eye and worth nothing. We don't have any valuable skill or purpose to redeem us, like the Seamstress does. Just do what you're told, and don't run off, and the best you can hope for is to be fed enough to continue your sad life. Where do you go when you run, anyway?"

"Nowhere."

"Fine. Don't tell me. But I know you met with a man last night. You smell of his smoke. Surely that's too dangerous for you? Taking up with one who burns?"

The yellow centres of Rowan's flower eyes widened. "You can smell him? He smells like . . . like smoke? What does that smell like?"

"Charred sandalwood, drifting patchouli, the glowing embers of a stick of finest vanilla cinnamon. He is strong flavour that is eaten by the nose. He reeks of the incense makers."

Rowan closed her eyes. Nothing could be done, then. She was wood and leaf. He—whoever he was—was fragrant flame.

"Here." Crow shoved the bowl into Rowan's brittle fingers. "You take it to her. Throw yourself flat before her, grovel and weep, make your most poetic and moving apologies. She may take pity on you."

"There's no pity in the cold stuttering engine that is her heart. It beats only to remind her to beat *us*," Rowan muttered, but she went to the Seamstress' chamber. Tears would come easy to her today, thinking of the molten voice of her forbidden visitor. It was ridiculous—she'd not even seen him, had heard only a smattering of words from him—but all the same, the pollen flew from her eyes.

Maybe Crow was right, and that would be enough for the Seamstress today. Maybe she wouldn't require sap as well. For once.

. . . . .

*S*tupid, diseased little dogberry. Weed, pest, unpretty unwanted creeper!" The Seamstress shoved Rowan's berries into her mouth, her rows of needle teeth mutilating the fruit as its red juice trickled down her chin. "Your *ex*-lover whispers tales of your inadequacies to me as he kisses my lips, licks my throat, and moves inside me! Such a poor boy is he, but handsome, and he brings me riches of amusement at your expense. We laugh about you together. That's when he can even remember you at all, which happens less and less often. Not surprising—he's certainly traded up. You're nothing, aren't you, Witch Wood? A dirty thing crawling with stinking mildew and sightless grubs! Be thankful that you're designed so you can't smell anything, for I assure you, your own stench would slay you where you stand!"

Rowan pictured herself safe on the tail feathers of the Nowhere peacocks, and swallowed her rage as if it were Mother Bear's tea. "Yes, Seamstress," she said.

"'Yes, Seamstress'," the Seamstress mimicked in a high, cruel voice. "You speak like a snot-stuffed mutant child with gangrene of the nose. How ugly you sound. And where were you last night, my useless shrub? Where are you *every* night?"

"Nowhere, Seamstress."

"Don't defy me, girl. I'll score your bark until you scream for mercy." The Seamstress threw the unfinished bowl of berries aside and rose from her seat, looming over Rowan on her eight needle legs. "Get down on your knees and put your face to the floor so that I don't have to look at it."

Rowan did as she was told, grateful for the reprieve from the blank glare of the Seamstress' eight black thimble eyes.

"Now, I'll ask you once more. Where do you go at night?"

The truth wouldn't do. Not the small portion Rowan was willing to surrender, anyway. She thought quickly. "I go to the incense maker's den."

"What—madness! Why?"

"I . . . " Rowan hadn't thought quickly enough.

The Seamstress sneered. "Either you're lying to me, in which case I believe I'll claim one of your gormless eye buds, or you've been meeting with a new lover there, being that it's the place you're least likely to be discovered, in which case—"

"In which case *what*?" Ah, a voice like that could not be mistaken or forgotten. Rowan's breath quickened, her hands trembling where they lay splayed in supplication on the floor. She kept her forehead pressed to the ground, not trusting her limbs to support her weight if she moved.

The Seamstress yelped at the unexpected intrusion. "Who are you to enter my quarters, uninvited and unannounced?" She sniffed. "Aha! Incense! Well, that is altogether *too* coincidental. This virulent weed cowering here on my floor must have spoken the truth for once in her—"

"Enough." The voice moved closer, until it was right next to Rowan. "I didn't come to listen to your histrionics. I'd tell you that you're repulsive in your cruelty and arrogance, but there's little point, as you're incapable of understanding, let alone changing. So I'll tell you the one thing that will get through to you: I'm here to give you a lot of money."

"How *dare* . . . what?"

"There's the bobbin dropping now. Yes, money. A great deal of it."

"Why?"

"Because you're going to sell me your two Wyrd Women, Rowan Redberry and Crow Blackbeak."

Silence stretched like gum until tension forced it to break.

"Leave us, Witch Wood," the Seamstress barked. Rowan rose to her feet.

"Don't look at me," the visitor murmured as Rowan's leafy head lifted, but he needn't have bothered. She didn't want him to rush away this time, didn't want to botch the miraculous deliverance he seemed to be offering. Her eyes remained fixed on the floor as she exited the room. Her dress itched against her prominent shoulder blades and ribs, the hope-threads ablaze for the first time in the years Rowan had worn the thing. It had, after all, been just another perverse amusement the Seamstress had dreamt up to toy with her two playthings—hope, the eternal punishment.

Crow waited in the tiny kitchen, agitated, her beak agape, her clawed fingers in the black feathers of her hair. "Is it true? Is he here to save us?"

"I don't know," Rowan said, but she took Crow's quivering hands in her own, held them to her chest, and squeezed.

"I can smell him. He smells like jasmine, pine, and musk. He smells like love. He's your burning man, isn't he?"

Rowan didn't answer, for she didn't know what to say. It was answer enough. They stood, entwined, listening. But the visitor and the Seamstress talked in low tones now, their words no longer audible.

Eventually, Crow pulled her hands away from Rowan. "Best get on with the day's chores." The thrill had already faded from her voice, the reality of years of hunger and pain drowning it out. "Who knows what comes."

Rowan nodded, took up her bucket and scrubbing brush, and went outside to clean the marble courtyard. It was a lengthy task that needed repeating every day. The Seamstress' silken webs hung from the walls surrounding the courtyard, her sought-after wares dangling on the gossamer strands. Below the webs lay the gelatinous waste the Seamstress secreted from her fat arachnid body as she sewed. It gleamed in the magenta sunlight, thick puddles of it everywhere Rowan looked. Sighing, she once again got down on her hands and knees and did what she had to, grateful that the stench couldn't touch her.

. . . . .

Crow tumbled out of the kitchen door into the courtyard, landing hard on her hands and knees, beak agape, the nubs on her back where the Seamstress had long ago torn off her wings twitching wildly through her threadbare dress. The Seamstress appeared at the door a second later.

"You're dismissed from my service," she said through gritted needle-teeth, and was gone.

Rowan helped Crow to her feet, tutting at the pinpricks of blood where the Seamstress' fingers had punctured Crow's skin beneath her feathers.

Then *he* entered the courtyard, and this time, Rowan looked at him.

Prismatic smoke rose in a constant hazy stream from black hair, ashen skin, and clothes that burnt like the sun. He was tall and thin, with fine features and long, articulate fingers. His eyes blazed orange, surrounded by sooty lashes. Tiny balls of flame rolled off his tongue as he spoke.

"Rowan Redberry and Crow Blackbeak. Will you come with me?"

"Where?" Rowan was glad she couldn't smell him. The sight and sound of him was overpowering enough. He smiled at her voice, and she smiled back.

"You, Rune Tree most divine, will accompany me, if you are agreeable, all the way to my home—to the incense maker's den. You, Crow Blackbeak, I will take to the smithing district. There are metals that can only be hammered into shape by beaks such as yours, and tools that can only be made from the guano of your kind. I know this, because I've seen another Blackbeak there. Does the name Macaw mean anything to you?"

Crow's eyes moistened and her beak gaped open. She crossed her hands over the ruffled feathers on her chest and cooed.

"My mother," she said. "I haven't seen her since I hatched."

"Well, you shall see her by this day's end," the burning man said. He bowed low before them, sending the smoke that surrounded him into frenzied eddies. "I have been remiss in not introducing myself. My name is Incendere Resin. I am a Libanomancer. This is the highest art of the incense makers, and I am well paid. Money opens doors, and it has allowed me to walk through one such door today, to stand before you and offer betterment to both your lives."

Crow looked from Rowan to Incendere and back again. "However you came to be here today, freeing us, I am—we are—grateful," she said.

"I'm not entirely freeing you. I can't change our society's culture, or its attitude to your . . . uniqueness. But I can offer greater comfort for you, and," he stood from his bow and looked at Rowan. "Higher purpose."

Rowan inclined her head in a slight nod, and followed Crow and Incendere to the incense maker's flame-powered coach. They rocketed through the streets of Here, the townspeople leaping aside, shaking their fists and cursing as the incense maker and his Wyrd cargo shot past.

It was nightfall before they reached the smithing district, and Rowan was exhausted. Her petals rolling with fatigue, she embraced her longtime slave-sister and watched Crow rush from the coach into the brightly feathered arms of a large bird-woman who could only be her mother. A heavyset man, with a face both stern and kind, approached the coach and handed Incendere a hessian bag tied with twine, coin clinking audibly within. Incendere nodded at the man, who returned the nod before walking away, ushering the two bird-women inside with him.

Rowan was fast asleep when the coach finally reached the incense maker's den. Incendere reached to wake her. Rowan's bark skin blackened and blistered under his touch, her eyes flying open as she recoiled. The Libanomancer looked horrified. Rowan waved a twig-hand at him. She was well accustomed to pain.

But as she staggered tiredly into the den, the air heavy and mysterious with incense smoke, her skin throbbed and complained at the memory of Incendere's scalding touch, and pollen dusted her cheeks.

. . . . .

Incendere worked from sunrise to sunset each day, locked away in a cavern of the den, while Rowan was free to wander, her duties so light as to be ridiculous—dust an earthen ledge, polish a brass doorknob, fluff a velvet cushion. She was not permitted entry to Incendere's Libanomancy cavern, and she still didn't understand exactly what he did. Whenever she asked, he would laugh, flames spurting from his lips, and smile indulgently at her. "The nuts and bolts would bore you," he would say, and he'd point out another wonder of the den to distract her—a whorl of pulsating smoke in the shape of a heart, a net of dreams to capture the odours of life, a Dragon's Blood joss stick as tall as a man smouldering ruby-bright in a corner of the den.

Incendere forgot time and again that Rowan couldn't smell the incense, and after a while, she stopped reminding him.

Their kisses were painful and infrequent, always initiated by Rowan. Incendere would kiss her back for a time, but all too soon the sound of bark popping and sizzling would become too insistent to ignore. He would cry out in dismay and shove her away, but too late—her lips would already be swelling and splitting. She would smile sadly as he commanded another Wyrd Woman—Aloe, a healer—to apply soothing balm to her wounds. He would stride away, head bowed, but Rowan could still see the tears that rolled in tiny fireballs down his cheeks.

Love should not hurt, but in Rowan's experience, it always had. This time it hurt her more than usual, and more visibly, but surely that only meant it was stronger, and more honest?

Rowan slept in a large soil-filled cot, the dirt cool and black and comforting around her. Incendere didn't sleep, but he would enter Rowan's bedchamber and sit—at a distance, of course—and tell her fascinating stories, about oracles, scented altars, scrying shapes in rising smoke, reading signs in the crackle of incense on coals. In this way she pieced together the meaning of his work, the uses for what he created—what it was to be a Libanomancer—but she still knew nothing about the practicalities of the work, the nuts and bolts that he insisted would bore her.

And it became too much, this unsatisfactory endless talk, this gaping space between them. The burn was worse when he *didn't* touch her.

. . . . .

When Incendere entered Rowan's room one gloomy Saturday evening—the rain hammering at the little stained glass window over her bed, the air damp and cold—she was ready for him. She threw herself into his scorching arms, and he held her for a moment as he always did. But this time, she would not allow him to discard her. She fell backwards, and dragged him with her. They tumbled together into the chill dirt of Rowan's bed. Incendere propped himself up above her, his hands planted in the soil, his orange eyes searching her face for acquiescence even as he shook his head.

"Wait! See?" she said, lifting clods of dirt in her twig fingers and smearing them on her lips before she kissed him again and again.

"The soil cools your kisses enough for me to take them without too much pain, certainly without burning beyond repair. We can be together, here, in the dirt. *Fully* together, for the first time."

Incendere murmured protests, whispered fears and doubts, but his hands were at her bodice, ripping and burning, and his lips remained pressed to hers. She rubbed gritty soil over both their bodies, and soon enough the Libanomancer's words were dampened to moans. Smoke rose around them in thick clouds as they rolled and twisted together. Soon the only sounds were the rasp of flesh on bark and the hiss of burning wood tempered with soil.

· · · · ·

I have a favour to ask of you." Incendere trailed a finger through the air above Rowan's foliage hair, a painless gesture of affection, though some of her berries still withered from it. As the lovers talked, Aloe slathered Rowan's skin with balm, as she did every morning after the burning man and the tree-woman had lain together. Some of the deepest burns on Rowan's bark skin would not heal, and left deep black craters that oozed sap. Aloe packed these with a soothing poultice. It was all that could be done. Rowan didn't even flinch anymore as Aloe's fingers dug into her wounds.

"Then ask," Rowan said.

"I would like you to help me with my work."

Rowan opened her mouth to respond, but Incendere held up his hand.

"Don't say yes yet," he said. "There is much you must know. I don't want to lose you. I am only able to keep you here because you are valuable, my love. It is because of your value that my masters, who own this den, have provided the funds to allow us to be together. I wanted it to be forever, but if it can only be for now, then I want that, too. I have searched for another way. I cannot find any."

"Stop, you make it all sound so dire!"

"But it is." Incendere waved Aloe away. The healer left quickly, as if relieved.

"Then don't tell me."

"I must," Incendere said, hot tears blazing forth from his eyes. And the Libanomancer told the Rune Tree a tale, just as he had on countless nights before.

Once, a burning man saw a beautiful Wyrd Woman buying supplies for her mistress at the market, a tree-girl with hair of red leaves and berries, and eyes of soft floral beauty. He'd never seen such a thing, and he was spellbound. He asked about her, and learnt of her plight. He watched her from afar, saw her run the night streets in pain as birds trailed her through the sky, witnessed her climb a bridge and disappear at the peak, appearing hours later from Nowhere and running back to her cruel mistress. After many nights, he finally managed to climb the bridge himself, to lay with her, briefly. To whisper kindnesses to her and caress her with his voice, though he wanted far more than that.

And finally, the burning man hatched a plan. His work had led him to discover the secrets of a powerful divination incense, one that had never successfully been made before, one that would be worth an inestimable fortune to whoever produced it. His masters were hungry for fame and riches, and they commanded the Libanomancer to produce the divination incense, at any cost. The key ingredients were difficult to obtain, but he gathered them all—except for two. The berries and sap of a tree-girl. This wouldn't have been difficult if any tree-girl would do, but they wouldn't.

It had to be a Rune Tree. It had to be Rowan. This was good, because it led to a way for the burning man to have her. But making the incense would require *all* Rowan's berries—her beautiful crowning glory—and a *ll* her sap.

"But I'll die," Rowan cried, for surely Incendere didn't know. "My berries you could take, and I would give them to you freely, but my sap is my life. I can't survive without it."

He only looked at her sadly, and she realised—had realised long ago, if she was honest with herself, had known this moment was hurtling toward them—that he understood the price he was asking her to pay very well. She wept yellow pollen tears and shook her head, back and forth, unable to stop her negation.

"I love you, Rowan. This is the only way for us, however short our time may be. What is your alternative? Another Seamstress, a life of pain and starvation? I would be gentle, oh, so gentle. I would take only a little of you at a time, so carefully you wouldn't even notice, and we would make something magical in the process. Isn't that truly love? The fruit of our union would last forever."

Incendere reached for her, but she shrank away, lost to her weeping. He gazed at her for a moment, and then stood and left, wisps of dark smoke trailing in his wake.

. . . . .

*R*owan was pulled from the agony of her dreams by a gentle hand on her shoulder. She opened her eyes to see Aloe kneeling beside her dirt bed.

"You're not the first," Aloe said. Her voice was cool and soft. Rowan had never heard her speak before, had assumed she couldn't.

She sat up, frowning. "What do you mean?"

"There have been other great and secret incenses that Master Resin has been compelled to make, other essential ingredients, other girls he has immortalised through his work."

"You shouldn't be here. And you're wrong. He loves me, and I love him. This is torture for us both."

"Oh, yes, he loves you. I don't dispute that. Master Resin loves deeply, and often. And all of his love goes up in smoke."

"No. You're infatuated with him. Or you're misguided, thinking to help me, when I don't need your help. There is a way out of this, and Incendere and I will find it together."

Aloe shook her head, and beckoned for Rowan to move away from her bed. Rowan did, stepping out and standing over Aloe, who, still kneeling, leant forward and began to remove handfuls of moist soil.

"What're you doing? You're destroying it, stop!" Rowan reached for Aloe's arm, but the girl shrugged her off, digging at a furious pace. Within moments a hole several feet deep gaped. Rowan leaned down to look. The soil thinned until what Aloe pulled out wasn't soil at all but skulls, ribs, teeth, and fistfuls of ashes, amassing the charnel wares into a pile that grew until Rowan could bear no more. "Stop!" she cried. "Please, stop. Leave them alone. Cover them."

Aloe did, replacing the remains and swaddling them in dirt. She wiped her hands on her thin dress and stood. "He has me bury them, and the new one always sleeps atop them. I try to heal them after death, every time. And every time, I fail."

"I love him," Rowan whispered, knowing herself for a fool even as she also knew the truth of her words. He'd coupled with her, there atop the buried tower of his murdered lovers—Wyrd Women, like her, all of them. Like Crow, and Aloe. How deep did the mass grave go? "I love him!"

Aloe stood, her face close to Rowan's. "Love should not hurt! It should never take everything from you, never steal your light and demand your life. And if it does, well, then, where are you, and what have you got? It is far better to be nowhere, with not even the clothes upon your back, than anywhere near *that* kind of love." She shook her dirty finger in Rowan's face. "I will not bury you, Rowan Redberry. I will *not*."

"We're Wyrd, Aloe. Offensive to the eye and worth nothing. We don't have any valuable skill or purpose to redeem us, like Incendere does. We're lucky someone like him wants us."

Aloe gaped. "Do you think me without skill or purpose? How much pain have I eased, how many wounds have I healed? I'm still alive because of my convenient value to his ongoing 'work'. Rowan, you're the most beautiful creature I've ever seen. Your sap contains the secrets to life itself. You reek of magic, so much so that I need to breathe through my mouth when I'm around you, lest I be overpowered. Why do you suppose you can't smell anything yourself? Why do you think those who claim to own you are so eager to convince you of your worthlessness, but so reluctant to part with you?"

Rowan squeezed her eyes shut, rubbing the bridge of her nose with one trembling finger. "It doesn't matter. Where can the Wyrd go if we run, anyway?"

"Nowhere," Aloe said. "A place that, as you know, isn't as frightening or desperate as it sounds."

Rowan knuckled her eyes. "I'm tired. I need to . . . to sleep, to think. Please . . . I'm grateful for what you've shown me, and I appreciate your words and your care, but I need to be alone."

Aloe touched Rowan's arm as she passed. "Remember: I won't bury *you*," she said. Her careful emphasis was not lost on Rowan, who sank to her knees and stared at her dirt cot as Aloe left, closing the door softly behind her.

. . . . .

The night stretched on forever, as nights full of loss and confusion tend to do. By luck or fate or sheer mindless coincidence, Incendere didn't visit Rowan's bedchamber. She lay on the floor, facedown, her head cradled on her arms. If her thoughts were blood, then the hours that she'd passed tonight in this way were drenched in gore, exhausted half-dead things that staggered ever onward, defeated again and again by paradox and snare.

She loved Incendere, but could not stay and let him kill her. Nor could she leave and let him kill others. And, selfishly, she could not live without him if he lived without her. What was more, she cared for Aloe, and could not leave the healer to this endless dark cycle. Nor could she ask the healer to kill for her, or to clean up afterward even if she could bring herself to kill Incendere—which she couldn't.

Round and round the cogs of her mind spun, crushing her rather than carrying her forward, getting her . . . nowhere.

A place that was not as frightening or desperate as it sounded.

. . . . .

*R*owan ran the cobblestones of the night, naked, all hope left far behind her. Her foliage hair hung brown and wilted without her berries to offer it colour and radiance. No birds shrieked above her, swooping for her fruit. She ran alone and in peace.

She had passed through the smithing district on her long journey, and had seen Crow through a candlelit window, her head resting on her fluffed up feathers, her eyes closed in peaceful slumber, her mother stroking her beak, as the stern but kind man smiled at them. That picture had been true love. Stopping, Rowan had plucked a single petal from her right eye—*she loves me*—and dropped it on Crow's doorstep, knowing her slave-sister would understand.

"Live long and be happy," she'd said, and ran on once more. Her flower eyes were wide and dry, no yellow pollen dusting them now, though sap leaked in a thin amber runnel from the space where the missing petal had been. Her bark skin was ghost gum in the moonlight, Wyrd and strong.

She hurt, oh, she hurt so much, but she did not weep.

She ran faster than she ever had before, but her breath came easy, her heart troubling her not at all despite her exhausting pace, for she had left that behind, too, and found she could live without it. Eventually, she reached the wrought iron bridge, cherubs and serpents smiling at her from the railing, the water beneath burbling its delight at her return. She sang as she climbed the bridge, her voice broken and raw—but *there,* not lost, surrendered, or stolen. The lanterns nudged her head, their wings landing butterfly kisses on her cheeks. The peacocks snored, glossy tail-feathers twitching in dreams. And waiting with arms outstretched was Mother Bear, tears streaming down her fuzzy cheeks, giving Rowan's pain a face.

Rowan smelt it all. Tallow, feathers, fur, and so much more. The scents flooded her. They'd been here all along, waiting for her to claim them. In time, she would be ready to face her own scent, too.

"Welcome home, our darling," the Mother Bear said. "How long will you stay this time?"

"I'll never leave again," Rowan said, falling into the Bear's arms.

"You never really did, child," Mother Bear said. "But you know, there's a price that must be paid to stay here. It requires a selfless sacrifice and a selfish solution. Nobody has ever stayed, because until now, the toll has been thought impossible. How find *you* this toll, my beautiful daughter?"

Rowan pulled away and looked up at the Bear's face. "Are you hungry, Mother?"

The Bear smiled with shark-teeth. "Always. I am a Mother, but I am also a Bear."

Rowan nodded. "Plant his remains deep in the soil bed in my room, which you will know by its smell. I've left him a gift, the last and greatest one I could offer, a shining red pile of myself. Place it atop his grave, which was always the only place berries and incense could ever be together anyway. And he'll lie there with the others, which, if they feel as I do, may please them, though for different reasons."

With a roar, the Mother Bear charged off the bridge, disappearing into the aether. Rowan lay on the peacocks' tails and hugged herself. She watched the implacable stars wheel overhead and when sleep called to her, she sang herself toward it with gently murmured truths.

"I loved him before, and I love him now. I love him Here and I love him There. I love him Everywhere but, most of all, forevermore . . . I love him Nowhere."

Matchmaker

Dayle A. Dermatis

I LOOKED up hopefully when the bell on the door jingled, but it was only a particularly vicious gust of wind. Dusk had already fallen. Abandoning Facebook, I got up from the small desk and peered out through the glass. Streetlights were on, and the dusting of snow we'd received earlier in the day swirled and eddied. I shivered, wishing I could afford to put the heat higher.

It had seemed like the perfect business to open. I even had the perfect advertising pitch: "What does a computer know about love? Have an authentic Gypsy Matchmaker work her magic instead!" The matchmaking magic was passed on through each generation, and my gran, who had raised me from a toddler after my parents died, certainly had the talent.

It wasn't her fault she'd forgotten to tell me I was adopted. (Well, yes, it was. But I'd forgiven her for the oversight.)

I sighed. Thankfully, she had passed on before she could witness my dismal failure. Unless something amazing happened, I would be filing the bankruptcy papers next week.

At least I hadn't made the mistake another matchmaker had, promising "Satisfaction guaranteed!" The divorces haunted her bank balance years after the matches had been made.

I glanced down the street, but it was deserted. Nothing amazing was going to happen tonight. I turned around the "Closed" sign and was sliding the bolt home when a loud *crack!* outside shook the windowpanes.

I hastily turned the sign back and opened the door to admit the two visitors. They were from Aibara, home of Ali Baba and his forty thieves, of the tales of a thousand and one nights. The flying carpet hovering outside was a dead giveaway.

Aibara had been discovered five years ago by an amateur spelunker who fell through a cave floor right into the land of legend. Of course, faster than you can say "Abracadabra," we had established trade agreements and exchange programs. Aibara was now the hottest vacation spot around, where you could live out your Arabian Nights fantasies. The Aibarans were still wary of our machinery and technology, but had made the stock market soar with their desire for whitening toothpaste, baseball gloves, and disco balls. There were a few cultural differences that were still being ironed out, but nothing that either reality couldn't handle.

The man was slightly rotund and, I judged, middle-aged, but beneath his small fez his hair was still shiny black. He swept off his long woollen cloak to reveal traditional Aibaran clothing: flowing yellow silk trousers, turquoise silk shirt with an open vee neck, and heavily embroidered vest and slippers.

His companion, who was much younger, also had silky sable hair, except hers slithered down to her waist, with two plastic daisy clips pulling it back on one side. The rest of her dress was also modern—leather bomber jacket, crisp new jeans, Green Day t-shirt. Her only concession to her heritage was her shoes, which were red satin encrusted with tiny mirrors and turned up sharply at the toes.

"My name is Muqallad. We are looking for the matchmaker," the man announced, his voice deep and commanding.

"And you have found her," I replied. "Please, sit down." I indicated the two mismatched straight chairs in front of the desk. The woman gave a moue of distaste and brushed her hand across the seat before perching on the edge of it. I wished I still had a receptionist, but I'd had to let her go a month ago.

"Sir, I'm flattered that you have sought my services," I began, the patter falling easily. "But certainly a man with such obvious attributes doesn't need the assistance of—"

"It is not for me," he interrupted. "It is for my daughter."

That surprised me, but I recovered quickly. "A young woman as beautiful as this indeed cannot be in need of—"

"No!" he bellowed. He was taking a breath to continue yelling when the daughter whined, "Dad*dy*," and he seemed to remember that rich, powerful Aibarans were frowned upon when they tried to intimidate those in the Earth reality.

He took a calming breath, placed his be-ringed fingers on the desk for support, and said, "Begging your pardon. Let me explain. I do not need you to find a match for my daughter. She is already betrothed."

"I am *not*," she said. "You can't *make* me."

"Halima, my treasure, Bahir is a nice boy."

She wrinkled her nose. "He's *boring*. He spends all his time racing those *stupid* horses of his and he *smells* like them."

"I made this arrangement with Bahir's father when you were children."

"And you *can't* make me marry him." She sounded so petulant that I swore she stamped her foot. "You *can't*. As long as I go to school here, I'm under Earth law, and you can't force me to marry anyone I don't want to."

I was finally beginning to understand the problem. Many Aibarans saw it as a privilege to send their children to school in Earth—it was something like the old trend of sending your children off to a Swiss boarding school. If I weren't mistaken, Halima had the look of Wellesley, or maybe Sarah Lawrence.

"You see my problem," her father said to me, spreading his hands in supplication. "Such a stubborn child. My wife died when Halima was very young and I indulged the child too much."

"I'm *not* a child," Halima interrupted. We both ignored her. I sympathised with her situation, but I was getting tired of her whining.

"You must make her fall in love with him," her father said.

"Mr Muqallad, I don't think I can help you," I said, even though the words made my heart sink. Rich paying customers or not, I still had to be cursed with an honest heart. "My business is matching up people who are looking for partners, not matching up people who already know each other."

He reached into his vest, brought out a bag, and dropped it on the desk. The coins were so heavy that I swore the laminate dented.

Aibarans were still wary of paper money. Of course, every bank here was more than willing to exchange their currency.

"I ask only that you try. If you do, the money is yours."

My heart leapt. Just for trying.

"Very well, but one final thing," I said. I was probably shooting myself in the foot, but that much money kicked my honesty into overdrive. "I just want you to know that . . . the matchmaking talent didn't quite follow the lines in my family."

He grabbed my hands and looked deep into my eyes. His irises were so dark that they seemed to merge into his pupils.

"You are my only hope," he said.

Flattery, I confess, will get you everywhere with this girl. I couldn't say no.

I led them into the back room. Muqallad had come well prepared. He had brought a complete history of the prospective groom, right down to his medical records. It would have been infinitely preferable to have Bahir present, but Muqallad didn't want Bahir or his father to know that Halima was so vehemently against the arranged marriage.

I read over the files quickly—the details weren't as crucial as the overall *feeling* I got from him—and spent more time studying his picture. Young, dark-haired, a haughty gaze and sculpted café-au-lait features. He was quite handsome, really. Most girls would have considered him a real catch.

Not Halima, obviously. She answered my questions with bored detachment, and didn't even lean over as her father did eagerly when I breathed on the crystal ball to bring it to life.

I tried, I really did—and more out of compassion for Muqallad than for the bulging purse on the desk. His earlier bluster had given way to a nervous twisting of the ruby and diamond rings on his fingers. I'd heard that Aibarans were honest to a fault, and guessed that for him to break the contract with Bahir's father would be to violate his own honour.

It was all over in a few minutes.

"I'm sorry," I said, feeling truly wretched. "Everything I'm getting says that they're not compatible."

Halima yawned and rolled her eyes at her father in an "I told you so" fashion.

"Are you sure?" Muqallad asked.

"Everything points in the opposite direction to them ever finding happiness together," I said.

He moaned softly and put his head in his hands.

Halima opened her Gucci purse and pulled out a pack of cigarettes. When I pointed at the No Smoking sign, she screwed up her face at me, announced that she was going outside, and left the back office.

"I'm sorry," I said again. "But please realise that I'm not as good as—"

He took my hands again. I noticed how smooth his were, and again how intensely his sable eyes bored into mine.

"We in Aibara have no liking of your technologies," he said. "I could not go to—what do you call it?—a dating service. I have more faith in a bad magician than a good computer."

"I do appreciate your faith in me," I said, giving his hands a squeeze. "I only wish there were more I could do."

He sighed. "I don't understand it," he commented as he rose. "My wife and I were arranged, and we hated each other at first." His smile was a bright flash in the gloom of my office. "I remember the time she threw that lamp at me . . ." He touched his temple where a faint scar still showed. His smile faded, leaving us in shadow again. "I know it is not the way of your culture, but we have found it can work. My wife and I grew to love each other deeply." He turned to go.

"Maybe that's it," I said.

He turned back, face expectant.

"It's just a thought," I said quickly, to forestall false hope. "Maybe they simply need to spend more time together—get to know each other. If you could throw them together for a bit—"

"That is brilliant!" he cried, snatching up his cloak. I heard the bell on the front door jangle as he left me alone with his payment and a strangely unsettled feeling in my stomach.

. . . . .

I had never been in a police station before, much less to bail someone out. (Thank goodness I hadn't spent the sack of coins yet.) Luckily, by the time I got there, Halima had decided to drop the false imprisonment charges and Muqallad was free to go.

Halima had stormed off on the carpet, so I bundled her father into my car and took him home with me for a nice comforting meal of goulash. The one thing Gran *did* manage to pass on to me successfully was her skill in cooking, along with all her traditional recipes. And I enjoyed it, too.

"When I said you should find a way for them to spend time together, I meant invite Bahir and his parents over to dinner when Halima would be home," I said as I chopped the beef into small chunks. "I didn't mean lock them in a room together until they decided to like each other. That's illegal in our society, and since Halima is a student here and over eighteen, she was within her rights to complain."

"Things were much simpler in the old days," Muqallad mourned.

"More barbaric, you mean," I said, stirring the potatoes with enough force to send water hissing onto the stove.

"In what way?" he asked, looking around the room. "I don't see the presence of a man in your house."

"That doesn't mean I necessarily need or want one," I snapped. "And if I did want one, I'd find one on my own, thank you very much. I don't need anyone to choose someone for me."

"An odd statement coming from a matchmaker."

"I told you I wasn't very good," I muttered, tapping in the sweet paprika.

He sniffed appreciatively. "It is my guess that if you did that as well as you cooked, you'd be an expert."

I snorted and turned down the heat to let the goulash simmer. As I carefully turned the pages of Gran's recipe book to find the one for rhubarb pie, a piece of yellowed paper fluttered to the floor. I tucked it next to the basket of fresh bread to file in the cookbook later.

It wasn't until after the pie was in the oven and I'd turned down Muqallad's offer of more gold in thanks for the meal he'd eaten with gusto that I looked at it again. In Gran's firm, bold strokes along the top, it said, "Just in case."

"Well, I'll be," I said.

"What?" Muqallad asked, surreptitiously sliding the bag of coins across the kitchen table at me.

I slid it back, firmly. "This fell out of my grandmother's recipe book. It's a recipe for a love potion. Gran must have charmed it to be found when I started talking about . . ."

I fell silent and looked at Muqallad. The thought in my mind was echoed in Muqallad's sloe-eyed look.

. . . . .

So that's how I got an all-expenses paid trip to Aibara, complete with the vacation resort Muqallad owned to stay in as long as I liked. Which was awfully nice, considering I never could have afforded it otherwise. The only requirement was that I concoct the love potion for a formal dinner that Muqallad was arranging for Bahir's parents, which, of course, Bahir and Halima would also be attending.

Obviously, I wasn't allowed to go: if Halima saw me, she'd be suspicious. Until she showed up for the dinner, however, I had free use of the resort, which included Muqallad's palace and grounds. Muqallad and I rode some of Bahir's father's horses—something he and Halima apparently used to do when she was little—explored the nearby market, and enjoyed opulent dinners; and each night I fell asleep on a mound of silk-covered pillows.

And it was *warm*. No snow. Bliss.

After several experimental batches, I was sure I had the love potion right. It was added to Halima's and Bahir's couscous before the dish went to the table. I watched from behind some flowing curtains, out of sight.

Instead of observing the youngsters, however, I found myself regarding Muqallad's dinner companion, a woman wearing an scarlet silk caftan-type robe that should have been shapeless and unflattering, but on her only served to emphasise her lithe form. Perhaps it was the illusion that the gown was sheer, even though the silver-and-gold embroidery and the strategic undergown brought the outfit into the realm of politeness. Or maybe it was the multiple loops of necklaces, the glittering rings, the ladders of bracelets up her arms. She was exotic—and I, kitchen-flushed, felt anything but that as I peered from my hiding place like a curious servant.

Muqallad had told me that the woman had been one of his concubines before his late wife had insisted he give them all up; Halima had the same opinion and he continued to respect it. He and the woman weren't in a formal relationship, although I suspected she wanted them to be.

I glanced at Halima. Despite the fact that we were from different generations and different worlds, I did feel a certain kinship with her: she'd lost a parent; I'd lost both. She was lucky, though, to have such a devoted father. Muqallad couldn't be blamed for being what my society's standards called archaic, because he was a product of his own world. And to his credit, he was honestly trying to understand and learn. I respected that.

Did *she* respect him? I wondered, looking back at Muqallad's companion. My stomach clenched and I averted my gaze again, not knowing why. It didn't matter if she did or not; he had chosen her, so he must enjoy her company.

The only other place to look was at Halima and Bahir, and that made my stomach hurt more. According to Gran's recipe, the love potion should have worked by now. Halima was pointedly snubbing the handsome young man by chatting with Muqallad's date (apparently former concubine was still preferable to despised fiancé) and Bahir had given up any attempt at conversation with Halima and was now wolfing down his food.

Damn.

At least he was enjoying it, but still. Damn.

I felt more despondent than usual at my failure, and at first I couldn't figure out why. I drifted back into the sanctuary of the kitchens and thought hard. I truly felt bad that I had let Muqallad down. He'd had such faith in me from the beginning, and yet I kept falling short. Now I'd go back to my world and never see him again, and he'd continue dating his former concubine, and that would be that. Which made me feel worse.

Holy Spice Road—I was jealous!

How ridiculous was that? Muqallad and I were too different—from different worlds. Literally.

I laughed at myself. It was a typical reaction. Seeing Muqallad interested in someone else simply triggered my jealousy and made me *think* I wanted him.

And then it hit me.

. . . . .

" What if Halima thinks that Bahir's unavailable? That he's not an option anymore?" I tried not to sound too excited, in case I was off base yet again.

"I don't understand," Muqallad said. It was late. The dinner party was over; the guests were gone, Halima was asleep in her bedroom and would return to college tomorrow, and Muqallad had removed his turban in preparation for retiring. His thick, dark hair was tousled, and I was struck with the urge to smooth it off his brow.

I focused on the issue at hand. "If she thinks that Bahir has fallen in love with someone else, she might get jealous and want him for herself. She'll see what she's missing out on. It's the thrill of the chase. We have nothing to lose. What's the worst thing that could happen? She might get him and then change her mind. If so, you'll have to tell Bahir's parents the truth. If not, you'll still have to tell them—unless you have another plan."

I threw it out as a challenge, and Muqallad, sighing, agreed that the love potion had been his last resort.

The plan, as we hammered it out, was simple. The following morning, Muqallad would tell Halima that after she'd retired for the night, he'd had a long talk with Bahir's parents. It seemed that Bahir fancied someone else, and the arranged marriage had been cancelled. Then, we'd wait and see how Halima reacted.

· · · · ·

*H*alima was ecstatic at the news. After she practically skipped out of the room (after hugging Muqallad and I both), I stood.

"I suppose that's it for me," I said. "Will you send word if it works?"

He caught my hand. I was aware of the soft, yet strong, grip of his fingers, of the intensity in his dark eyes.

"No," he said. "Do not go, not yet. Halima may want to come to you for further guidance."

I already felt guilty about being part of the deception. Halima had said she trusted me because I was a modern, independent woman who believed in finding one's own destiny, and because at the very beginning, I'd been honest with Muqallad about my abilities rather than being swayed by his very impressive sack of money.

I told myself it was a white lie, a harmless falsehood. We couldn't force the two to fall in love. If this didn't work, it didn't work; if it did and they discovered our subterfuge, it would be a delightful story to tell their grandchildren.

"Okay," I said. "For a few more days."

I liked Aibara—the exotic smells, the sensuous silks, the spicy food I was learning to make—so I was glad for the excuse. Plus

I enjoyed spending time with Muqallad. As friends, I told myself firmly.

. . . . .

Our plan worked like a charm—if we believed in charms by this point, that is, and we didn't. Halima proved ecstatic at the news, but a few days later was showing a marked interest in horse racing.

Because of the hats, she said. Aibarans had recently learned about the British obsession with wearing ridiculously fancy hats to Ascot and other such events.

But she also went and cooed over the horses, particularly Bahir's (after all, she said, she loved riding as a child, and was thinking of taking it up again). Bahir didn't stand a chance. When he won his race, he announced she'd been his inspiration and presented her with the enormous bouquet of roses that were part of the prize.

The rest was history. My own guilt was assuaged.

As Halima and Bahir's relations improved, so did my prospects. Halima asked me to provide the resort's chef with her favourite Earth-world recipes for the nuptial feast, and how could I say no? Then the owner of a neighbouring spa hired me as a consultant in his acclaimed restaurant, having been present at the previous banquet and tasted my couscous (the secret is corriander, which they don't have in Aibara, but I'm not telling anyone that just yet.)

I've destroyed the recipe for the love potion. It was Gran's special gift for me, plus I've given up on the matchmaking for good. I now firmly believe in letting nature take its course.

On that subject, Muqallad has asked me to be his date at Halima and Bahir's wedding. I resisted at first, but that just made him more insistent. I agreed, only to save my hay fever from the bouquets of flowers he kept sending.

That's what I told him, anyway.

Snake Charmer

Carol Ryles

THE stranger stepped out from the marri trees and onto the track three metres ahead. A man. A tall, pale man with the kind of spiky, black hair that looks more at home on a brushtail possum. His amber gaze was fixed on my ankles. "Don't move," he said, his voice smooth and musical. "Whatever you do, don't . . . move . . . an . . . inch."

Until he'd appeared, the thought of moving hadn't crossed my mind. After hours of hiking, I'd stopped to rest on a fallen tree trunk. I'd wriggled my rucksack from my shoulders and was about to break into a packet of trail mix when he arrived, wearing that dusty oilskin coat of his.

This man is trouble. *Run.*

He held up his hand. "Don't move."

"My friends aren't far away," I said. I held his gaze so he wouldn't see the lie. I remembered my boyfriend telling me I shouldn't hike alone and how I'd laughed and told him that women were safer in the bush than on the street. I held my breath, hoping I wasn't about to prove myself wrong.

At that moment, something quick and legless slid through the leaf litter between my feet. There was no need to risk moving my head to look at it. I'd heard that sound more than once, but never so close, and certainly never in winter.

"It's a beauty," the stranger said slowly. "A big brown. If you stay like that, it'll leave you alone."

I let my breath out, heartbeat-by-heartbeat.

The stranger stood motionless, looking much like a snake himself, poised to strike. With both hands level with his chest, he began tracing two slow figures-of eight. I was tempted to remind him of the wisdom of holding still, but then I could see the snake sliding away from me, its scales glistening a spectrum of browns.

It was the meanest thing I'd seen outside of a zoo. And it was heading straight for the stranger.

My mind raced. I could throw a stick and try to distract the thing, but that could end up with it striking out at either of us in panic.

The stranger made a low shushing noise in the back of his throat. He leaned backwards slightly on one leg. With hands still tracing figures-of-eight, he lunged.

The snake reared into an 'S' and hurled itself forward. Before it struck, the stranger swooped and caught it with both hands behind its head. Then, instead of holding it away from him, he threw back his head and pressed its opened jaws against the side of his throat.

Fangs sank into the stranger's flesh with all the ease of needles sinking into butter. The snake writhed in his grip, and then stilled. Fang by fang, the stranger pulled it free. Two bloodless punctures stood out like red weals over his carotid.

He lowered the snake to the ground and stroked the length of its body, his hand undulating as if snake and man were partners in some exotic dance. The snake slid soberly away.

The stranger stood and fixed his amber gaze on mine. At first I felt trapped in it, as if I, too, were a snake and now it was my turn to be summoned forward. As I stared, wondering if the stranger would die quickly like snake-bite victims in the movies—or slowly like text books suggested—the weals at his throat began to fade. Within seconds they shrank to the size of pinpricks. A moment later, they disappeared.

Not human, I thought. *This man is not only trouble, he is not human.*

I dropped my packet of trail mix. Now was not the time to think. I let my instincts kick in and took the only course of action worth taking. Leaving my rucksack on the tree trunk where I'd wriggled out of it, I fled.

"Hey, wait," he called out. "I won't hurt you."

I kept running, knowing that if I stayed on the track, I would make it to the other end where it joined the main road. The hill climbed gently upwards. Now and then, I glanced over my shoulder to see if he was behind me, but saw only the pale, grey trunks of jarrahs, their branches twisted in snake-shapes and man-shapes and everything in between.

A kilometre later—or maybe two—I arrived, puffing and sweating, at a fork in the track. I stopped to get my bearings. Even before I reached for my back pocket, I knew it would be empty, but I checked it anyway, just in case. Nothing. Not even my mobile phone. That, too, was in my rucksack with my map and compass.

I tried to think. *Should I take the right fork or the left? No time, no time. Which way?*

I decided on the left because it was downhill and I remembered that somewhere ahead I was supposed to cross a creek bed. First the creek and then the hikers' hut, where I'd planned to spend the night. *Ten kays after that*, I told myself, *the road.*

A soft mist of rain began to drift down from the treetops. I swore under my breath. The morning's forecast had said it would rain tomorrow, not today.

A golden whistler whip-called from above, urging me forward, reminding me that my best defence was to keep running.

. . . . .

Three kilometres later, or maybe four, the creek bed was not where I thought it would be. The track wound downhill, uphill, and down again. Rain fell in short bursts, and then eased as the clouds grew darker and heavier. Thunder grumbled a dire warning, promising a night best spent undercover.

By dusk, I could not tell which part of the forest I had stumbled into. My clothes were wet through. Occasionally I heard the whine of a distant jet, reminding me that help was less than a horizon away. *But which way?* In the fading light, everything looked the same. The track was nothing like I remembered from the map.

At least I hadn't seen or heard the stranger. I tried to comfort myself with the thought that if I died of exposure, at least it would be on my terms and not his.

The smell of rain closed in. Thunder drew nearer. I kept pushing onward, mostly to keep warm. When I slowed, giving in to fatigue and hunger, I heard the unmistakable crunch of a footfall from somewhere close behind. I swung around in time to see my rucksack thud to the ground an arm's length away. The stranger slipped out from between the trees and stood on the track behind it.

"You'll be in for a bad night without your pack," he said. He lifted his chin and sniffed. "In fact, we're in for a downpour at any moment."

My legs were shaking and I couldn't tell if it was from cold or the prospect of what I had yet to face. I stood my ground. "Who *are* you?"

"Do you want the truth or the sanitised version?"

In all honesty, I wanted neither, but I was through relying on instinct, so I said, "I want the truth."

Even in the waning light I saw his amber eyes twinkle. I imagined myself being found months later, a decomposed body at the foot of a ravine. I wondered if I'd make the evening news. I looked around frantically for an escape route, one last-ditch effort to get away.

"I'm really not going to hurt you," he said, softly. "And to answer your question, you can call me James."

"*What* are you?" I asked, shivering.

That twinkle again, and a brief, uncertain smile. He looked skyward. "It's going to rain. Do you have a tent in that pack?"

I shook my head. "No."

"A bushwalker out alone without a tent? Do you have no sense of self-preservation?"

"I would have been fine if you hadn't chased me."

"I didn't chase you. You ran, remember? After I saved you from being bitten by a big brown, which had venom enough to kill a whale. You didn't even thank me. You simply fled."

"Why didn't it kill you?"

"That is a very personal question." He put his hands in his coat pockets. "There's an old gold panner's hut about a half an hour from here. I suggest we seek shelter there."

I picked up my rucksack. As far as I could tell, he hadn't opened it. The buckle straps were tied together exactly how I'd left them. My mobile was still in the side pocket, and so was my wallet.

He gave an exasperated sigh. "Look, if I wanted to hurt you, I would have done it by now. The hut's dry and has a fireplace. Tomorrow when the storm's passed, I'll show you the way to the main road." He held out his hands, palms up. "Deal?"

"How far away is the road?"

He shrugged. "Two leagues. Six miles. Nine and a half kays. Too far to walk in this weather."

He may as well have said a hundred kays. Even a half hour stroll seemed impossible. A soft wind started up, chilling me through my layer of wet thermals. I unzipped my pack's lower pocket and took out my raincoat and put it on.

"Here," he said, holding out his hand. "Let me carry your pack. You look exhausted."

As he took it from me, his hand brushed mine. Only for a second, but long enough for me to feel it was uncommonly warm. I was tempted to ask him if the snakebite was causing it, but not now. Not while he was already tramping ahead of me, carting my rucksack with abnormal ease. I struggled to keep up with him, and stumbled on tree roots rendered invisible in the starless night. When I asked him to stop so I could get my torch, he said, "No time. The rain's about to bucket down any moment."

He took hold of my hand and slowed his pace a little. At first I wanted to pull away because the warmth of his skin against mine was too personal and too comforting. I wasn't ready to accept that kind of help from a stranger, regardless of whether he was entirely human or not. But then the clouds lit up with sheets of lightning and all thoughts of protest were forgotten. I picked up my pace, and let him guide me.

With my hand in his, I did not stumble.

．．．．．

We arrived at the hut with boots sodden, faces and hands slick with rain. I wanted to believe he wouldn't hurt me, but didn't want to fool myself. I hesitated inside the doorway, pulling the door to without shutting it fully. He lit some fat, homemade candles, and then lit the fire.

Light flickered over the earthen floor, a table and stools that looked a hundred years old, and two crude stretchers strung side by side on wood frames beyond them.

"You're letting in the cold," he said.

I took a deep breath. "Yeah."

"You shouldn't stand there wet like that"

"No."

"You have spare clothes?"

"Yeah."

"Well, what are you waiting for? I'll get some more wood."

Rain rattled on the roof. I watched him go out and close the door behind him. Shaking and fumbling, I changed into my tracksuit and dry thermals, and then hung my wet clothes on the hooks by the door.

When he came back, he dumped an armload of ragged, dry wood by the fireplace—thick branches that looked like they'd been broken up by hand. He said, "I'm afraid I have no food to offer, or even drink, apart from water. But I can heat up whatever you've brought for yourself."

I huddled on a rickety chair close to the fire, still shivering, still cold to the core. He brought me what looked and smelled like an old horse blanket and draped it over my shoulders.

"There's a packet of freeze dried curry," I said through chattering teeth. "And a billy with some tea bags and biscuits. You're welcome to share."

He chuckled. "I do not eat. Venom is enough for me."

"What are you?" I asked. I kept my voice soft because I did not want it to sound like a challenge. I'd resigned myself to trusting him. After all, he hadn't hurt the snake, merely milked it.

"You still want the non-sanitised version?" he asked.

"Is it that bad?"

"Maybe. Maybe not. Depends on your definition."

I shrugged.

"Promise you will not interrupt me," he demanded. "Let me tell it from start to finish. And then you can judge me."

"Okay," I said. "Go for it."

He rummaged through my rucksack and found the food I'd mentioned. He read the instructions on the foil curry packet, and then set about preparing it, first putting the water on to boil and then opening the foil packet in readiness. He sat on his haunches and rubbed his hands in front of the fire. "I'm not as sensitive to the cold as you are, but the comfort of a good fire is a pleasure I have yet to grow out of."

I closed my eyes and waited.

"I was born in England in 1456," he said. "The son of a locksmith."

I snapped my eyes open. "What?"

His face was serious. He shushed me. "You promised you wouldn't interrupt."

I bit back a snort of disbelief, and remembered the way the puncture wounds had healed at his throat.

He stared into the fire. "I was apprenticed to my father and earned my place in the guild a year after coming of age. Four years later, vampires claimed our village, so I set about crafting a vampire-proof lock. It was too complex to be opened by any man, woman or child caught under a vampire's charm. Potential victims could no longer be lured beyond the safety of barred windows and locked doors.

"When the vampires learned of my audacity, they used my own locks against me, and then slowly and callously turned me into one of their own."

James stoked the fire, adjusted the pot of water. The flames lit up the spiky tips of his black hair and flawless, pale skin.

"I dare say you've read stories of our soulless existences," he said. "Of the blood feasts and cruelties. Well, let me tell you this. It's all true, every damning word of it."

By then, I had stopped shivering from the cold, but his story made me start up again. I drew the blanket to my chin and covered my throat.

His eyes focused ahead to somewhere distant and painful. "Our vampire clan was forced to move from village to village, but the locks always caught up with us. Years passed, decades, centuries. We still found blood enough to revel in—still caused death enough to amuse ourselves—so I grew complacent. I was stupid enough to think the clan had forgiven me about the locks. But they were simply waiting for the right punishment to present itself. When it did, I was the last to know.

"Using my own famous locks they sealed me in a coffin, and wedged it deep inside the ballast hold of a convict ship bound for

New Holland—Australia—here. I knew my imprisonment could not last forever, so I resigned myself to a voyage in hibernation. When at last I awoke, it was to the agony of the sun's first rays on my exposed face and hands. I was washed up on a beach. Wood and flotsam from the wrecked ship was scattered around me. I fled to the cover of trees." He chuckled. "At last I was free again—a free vampire in a land full of prisoners."

The water boiled. He made me a cup of tea, poured the rest of the water into the packet of freeze-dried curry and folded it closed. He proffered the tea with both hands. "Careful," he said. "I can't tell if it's too hot for you or not. I don't want to burn you."

I took the cup, grateful for its warmth. "What happened next?" I asked.

"There were so many throats that offered themselves to me willingly, and so many who did not understand what they were offering until it was too late." He paused, stoked the fire. "There was something else too. Something I had not felt before. I smelled it in the air, felt it through the pores of my skin. It wasn't until I saw a snake kill a man, that I understood what it was."

"What?"

"Venom. I'm only guessing here, but unlike blood, which is full of life, snake venom is full of death . . . with a good smattering of life on top of it. I could not help but wonder what it would do to the living dead."

"What did it do?"

"Venom is everything that blood is not. It gave me warmth. It reconnected me to my soul. It allowed me to face the sun. It gave me life. Not just a semblance of life, but the real thing."

"And you do not drink blood any more?"

"I do not."

"But it doesn't make sense," I pursued. "Vampires are cold blooded and so are snakes. Two negatives do not make a positive. Where does the warmth come from?"

"Ah, I knew you'd ask that. Remember, it's not about blood any more. It's about venom."

"Well that's a comfort," I said, sipping my tea.

He smiled, a disarming smile I could not help returning. "I hope I have not put you off your food. Your curry is ready," he said.

He unwrapped the packet and handed it to me along with my plastic fork. It smelled perfect. "So, tell me," I said. "Is it really true that you no longer drink blood?"

His eyes twinkled. "It's really true."

"And when you killed, was it because you had lost your soul?"

"It was."

"Well, I'm glad you've found it again," I said.

He smiled and looked like he was blushing. I blamed the fire and told myself that a six hundred year old vampire wouldn't blush at something *I'd* said. To stop myself from following up with something equally stupid, I scoffed the curry. When he merely sat staring into the fire, I broke open a packet of trail mix and scoffed that for dessert.

The storm hit, rattling the roof like a barrage of ball bearings. Wind blasted through the gullies. The little hut shook. I climbed into my sleeping bag on the stretcher, while he lay on the other one beside me, wrapped in his horse blanket.

"Do vampires sleep?" I asked.

"Only if they want to?"

"Do you?"

"In this racket?" He laughed. "What do you think?"

We lay in the dimness next to each other, listening to the rain. I was tempted to reach out to him, just to feel the warmth of his hand against mine. There was something about it. Something beyond the need for comfort and beyond the sensual that made my skin burn just remembering how it felt.

When the rain eased, he asked, "Do you always go walking alone?"

"Only when my partner backs out at the last minute."

He turned his face to me, eyebrows raised.

I shrugged. "I couldn't see why I had to spoil a good weekend because he wanted to do something else."

"You're betrothed, then?"

"Betrothed?" I laughed at that, and then regretted it because it sounded forced. "Not likely."

"Why? Is he not a suitable partner?"

"Not suitable?" I scoffed. "He's a jerk."

Lightning flashed, followed at once by a crack of thunder that made the tin roof resound like a drum. It occurred to me that the hut did not smell unused and musty like a deserted hut should. "Is this where you live?" I asked.

"Sometimes. Every few years." He paused, "Every seven years, in fact. I live here for one week in every seven years."

"Where do you live the rest of the time?"

He rolled onto his side, propped himself up onto his elbow, and looked me in the eye. I felt his breath against my cheek. Warm breath. Living. "That is a very personal question, and another story altogether."

He lay down again.

My cheek felt hot where the touch of his breath still lingered. I felt snubbed. He sat up and blew out the final candle. The room glowed warmly in the light of the guttering fire. I closed my eyes, listened to the storm, and wondered if snake venom had given him a heartbeat as well.

. . . . .

I awoke to daylight. It was still raining. The fire was lit and James was gone. I wriggled out of my sleeping bag and leapt from the stretcher wondering if I'd ever see him again. It occurred to me that there was no way of telling because, apart from his blanket, rickety furniture and candles, there was nothing in the hut that belonged to him. Only his scent. I hadn't noticed it before, but now he was gone it was obvious.

I held the blanket to my face. Beneath the smell of age and disuse there was an earthy scent that was both sweet and comforting. I wrapped the blanket around my shoulders and sat on the stool by the fire, convinced he had left without saying goodbye. I stared at the flames and tried to tell myself I had no reason to want otherwise.

When he returned, his coat dripping with rain, his arms loaded up with dry wood, I almost whooped for joy. He put the wood on the floor by the fireplace and hung his coat on one of the hooks by the door.

I stood. He crossed the room. "You're crying," he said.

"Am I?" I hadn't noticed. When he wiped my cheek with his thumb, it came away wet. My skin burned where he'd touched it.

"It's my fault," he said. "It's the venom. It's making you bond with me. When you go home, the attachment will be broken and you'll look back and wonder what all the fuss was about."

"Fuss? I'm not making a fuss, am I?"

He smiled. "Of course not. But if you stay too long, you will not want to leave."

I took a deep breath and drew as much of his sweet scent into me as I could.

"You shouldn't do that," he said in a low voice. "It will make it hurt all the more." He took a step backwards, so I caught hold of his hand.

He brushed the back of his other hand down the length of my cheek, leaving a trail of delicious heat in its wake. I snagged his fingers with my free hand and pressed them to my face. "Hurt? How?"

"You shouldn't do that," he said.

He leaned towards me, as if to kiss me, and paused. I couldn't bear it. This wanting and not wanting. Slowly, so as to make the moment last, I lifted my face and touched my lips to his.

His breath was sweet and warm, as I knew it would be. He drew me close and returned the kiss. Our desire quickened, caressing us, submerging us. I could feel his heart beating, but his heart was no longer enough. I wanted his soul, and I wanted him to have mine.

Abruptly, he pulled away, crossed to the stretchers and sat down. His amber eyes blazed. "This is not how it should be," he said.

I remembered what he was, but was no longer afraid of him. "It doesn't matter."

He smiled, that disarming smile that made my heart skip. "I do not wish to flirt with a woman who would call me a jerk merely because I did not explain." The look on his face was comical. I couldn't tell if it was intentional or not. Even so, I was in no mood to laugh.

"Listen," he said softly. "The venom only allows me to be human for seven days." He paused. "If I do not feed on venom, I die. If I do, I become a snake, but only for seven days more. And then I disintegrate, become dust. As such I remain, not quite alive, but not quite dead either. A kind of sleep I suppose you could call it. The equivalent of a seven-year sleep. At the end of it, I become human again and the cycle restarts. It's a messy form of immortality, but it's a small price for demanding both life and soul at the same time."

I stared at him, at once unable and unwilling to fully comprehend. "How long have you been human for this time?"

He grimaced. "This day is my seventh."

"And soon you will be a snake?"

"At the setting of the sun."

"And I will not see you again for seven years?"

He looked at me long and hard. "You will not."

He got up, put some wood on the fire and stoked it. I knew I should rage at him for letting us get this far, but I couldn't.

"Seven years is a long time," I said.

He winced.

"And when I go home, our bond will be broken?"

"If we do not seal it first."

"How do you know? Has this happened before?"

He shook his head and looked away. Swallowing, he met my gaze again. "I've always stopped it before it got this far."

"Why didn't you stop it this time?"

"Because I've never wanted it this much before."

I hadn't expected that. I had thought he wanted 'me', not 'it'.

"Look," he said, unbuttoning his shirt. "It's starting already." Fine black scales ringed his collarbones, glittering amber as he swivelled into the light.

I stared, wondering why I saw them as beautiful. "You should have told me last night."

"I did not want you running out into the cold again." He paused, held my gaze. "And I do not enjoy spending my human nights alone."

"So you kept me here for your enjoyment?"

He glared. "I thought your kind would have grown tolerant enough to understand by now."

Outside, the rain eased to a gentle patter. "I'll walk you to the road," he said. "I know where there's a bus stop. I'll wait with you until you're safe."

"If that's what you want."

He looked at me, his eyes dull, but said nothing.

While I repacked my rucksack, he brewed me a cup of tea. I sipped it and nibbled on trail mix. To avoid causing a fuss, I took out my map and concentrated on working out the exact location of the hut. But there seemed to be no huts on the edge of a gully where this one stood.

I asked James to point it out. He shrugged. "It's not on the map. I prefer to keep it that way." He turned away, hesitated, and turned back. Pointing to a spot about ten kays from the main road, he added. "But for the record, we're here. You can't see the hut from the track. That's why it's forgotten."

I studied the map, memorizing every fork in every track within a ten-kilometre radius. When I looked up, James was holding my mobile phone, punching the buttons, his face a mask of concentration.

"Hey, give that back," I said.

"These things. They get more complex each time I see them. Seven years ago, they were merely for talking to others. Now they talk to you." He pressed a button and played a recording of his own voice. *Now they talk to you.*

"How did you figure that out?"

His eyes twinkled. "I'm the locksmith who invented the vampire-proof lock, remember? It's in my nature to figure things out."

He flipped the phone closed and tossed it to me. I slipped it into my rucksack. While I was there, I checked my wallet. It was untouched.

He stared at me, scowling. "Shall we go, then?" He gestured for the door.

Despite what had happened, I still did not want to leave, but clearly he did not want me to stay.

On the walk to the main road, he offered to carry my rucksack, but I didn't let him. A breeze gusted, showering raindrops from the branches above us. He walked ahead of me, sometimes stopping to make small talk about the forest regrowth and the occasional rare bird he caught sight of. His words were polite, noncommittal. Each one cut into me.

At the bus stop I told him he didn't need to wait. I couldn't bear his coldness. Although it was he who was the stranger, it was I who felt like the intruder. He inclined his head graciously. Stepping backwards, he merged into the trees like a sliver of shadow.

I missed him already. My hand where he'd held it last night, felt empty, dead.

. . . . .

Home had never felt so comforting before. It had never felt so hollow either. I stood under the shower until the water ran cold. Then I cooked an omelette and escaped to bed with the electric blanket set on high. The following evening, Mike rang and apologised for letting me down. When I told him I went hiking without him, he offered to make it up to me over dinner. I told him not to bother, and hung up. Compared to James, his lovemaking had felt more like a repertoire of pre-arranged movements, something we did before he got dressed again and went home.

But James had never made love to me, anyway. So why does it hurt so much when I try not to think about it?

Work distracted me with its continuous flow of meetings and proofreadings and calls. By Sunday—almost seven days since I'd left James—I felt clear-headed again. I no longer pined over lost opportunities. I no longer cried when I saw my hiking gear still unpacked in my closet. I realised that whatever had happened to me in the forest was nothing but a dangerous encounter. Such things led to either escape or entrapment.

I'd been lucky. I'd escaped.

With renewed energy, I set about tidying the apartment. I decided to replace my dying herbs by the kitchen window with new ones. I was about to get dressed to go shopping, when my mobile pinged—the calendar—reminding me of an appointment.

An appointment on Saturday? I couldn't remember typing it in.

I flipped my mobile open.

Three words. Three words and one letter . . .

I love you. J.

In my mind's eye, I could see him in the hut, holding up the phone. *Now they talk to you.*

I held my fingers to my cheek. I could no longer feel the burn of his breath, or the hot trail traced by his fingers, but when I reread what he'd written, I whooped for joy.

I pulled on my clothes and hiking boots, and shrugged into my backpack. As I drove to the hills, I reminded myself I hardly knew him. What I was contemplating was irrational. No matter how many times I said it, I could not convince myself it was true. In those few moments we'd kissed, we'd fitted together, utterly.

I will not lose him, I told myself. If seven days every seven years were all I could give, I'd willingly give them.

. . . . .

I reached the hut an hour before sunset. The fire was cold. His blanket was folded neatly at the end of his stretcher, along with his oilskin coat, moleskins, shirt, boxers, socks and boots. They were all he owned. This hut and these clothes were the only possessions he needed.

I dropped my rucksack, unfolded the blanket, draped it around my shoulders and immersed myself in his scent. The hut felt more familiar to me than my own apartment. Outside, the air had never seemed clearer. I sat in the open doorway and looked across the bracken into the gully and waited.

He arrived in much the same manner as he'd left. A snake now, he slid through the marri trees as if he were part of them. I knew it was he by the blackness of his scales, and the deep amber of his eyes. "I love you too," I said. "If I'd known you loved me, I would have stayed."

He made a soft shushing sound in the back of his throat and slid towards me. I froze, suddenly unsure if his promise to not hurt me extended to his snake form.

His body was double my length and thicker than the big brown he'd saved me from the week before. When he reached my feet, he raised himself up, his face level with my hands. He nudged my fingers. His scales felt surprisingly soft and warm. They made my skin burn.

At that moment I would have done anything for him. "Seven years," I said. "I'll wait for you for seven years. And then seven years after that and seven years after that."

He blinked as if he understood. I held out my arm and he wrapped himself around it. When he reached my throat, he rested his head in the space between my collarbones. His tongue flicked in and out, caressing my skin, reminding me of the way his human thumb had once brushed tears from my cheek.

I cupped his chin and kissed the top of his head, letting my lips linger.

"If I could, I'd become a snake too," I said. "I'd wait out the seven years with you."

I saw his heartbeat quicken beneath the skin above his ribcage. He uncoiled himself from my arm and slid his head into the palm of my hand. His amber gaze fixed itself onto my throat.

I knew then exactly what he wanted. I knew that he meant it.

Carefully, so as not to hurt him—hesitantly, because I was afraid—I raised his head to the side of my throat. When he opened his jaws, I pressed them against my carotid. His fangs sank into my skin painlessly, just as he'd promised. His venom flowed into me like the softest, warmest silk.

At first my skin burned only at my throat. And then it burned all over and my bones ached and throbbed. I couldn't breathe. I feared that he'd poisoned me and I would die. I tossed and writhed and threw off the blanket and fell onto my side into the dirt. My breath came again, in long, laboured gasps. My bones shifted and my joints cracked. It felt like hands pulling me from two different directions, stretching me out of my skin. My arms began to shrink, and I could do nothing but stare at them dumbly, watching my fingers contract inch by inch. A fierce burning tore through me. My legs lengthened and fused.

James coiled himself around me, holding my head steady, keeping it from banging on the ground when I shuddered. He peeled my clothes away from my body so they would not smother me. I knew he would love me, not just once in every seven years, but in all the days between, and all the hours and minutes between them.

When it was over, I lay shivering, my scales bristling against the cold night air. James remained coiled around me, warming me. Together we rolled over and over, around and around, over leaf litter and stones and gravel, down into the gully. His scales were a thousand hands caressing me, loving me in a thousand different ways, imprinting themselves into my soul. With all the inquisitiveness and shyness of a woman discovering her lover for the first time, I imprinted myself into his.

We came to rest at the bottom of the gully under the protection of a rocky overhang. "Seven years is a long time," he whispered.

Our entwined bodies were already disintegrating, sinking into the ground, turning to dust. "Seven years is a very long time," I agreed, but I no longer cared. I already had what I wanted. Compared to eternity, a seven-year sleep was nothing. Not really a sleep at all.

Philomena and
the Blond God

Amanda Pillar

LONDON, 1815

LADY Philomena Pilkington was in love with a vampire.

She hadn't intended for it to happen—quite the opposite, in fact—but the emotion was there; strong, pure and worst of all, unrequited. It was also complicated. She counted the reasons silently: one, she wasn't meant to *know* he was a vampire; two, she wasn't meant to be in love with him, which went counter to three, she was meant to kill him.

Life was, quite simply, unfair.

"Philomena."

Blinking slowly, the bright, swirling colours of Lord Kipling's ballroom came into focus. Mina turned and smiled. She had to look down to meet Lord William Grenville's gaze—she was a maypole, according to her brother, Edward—and she fluttered her blue lace fan gently. She loved the Brussels' lace swirl of flowers. It had been a present from her uncle, a bribe, but she didn't care.

"Good evening, Uncle." She kept her voice low and pleasant. Lord William was a stout man, with the tendency to look like a flustered peacock. Tonight he was a peacock who'd somehow managed to fall into a tin of puce paint.

"How's the ball going, my dear?" He stared at her for a moment before flicking his gaze across the ballroom and the sea of brightly garbed *ton*, to the blond god, Lord Ashton Moreton, the Earl of Kent. The Earl was standing with lazy elegance by a palm and was surrounded by a bevy of Incomparables, all fluttering their fans and giggling. Lords, Sirs and Misters clung to the outskirts of the group, ready to offer ratafia, champagne and a body to dance with when the Incomparables realised they needed to find partners other than the Earl.

"The same as ever," Mina replied, then realised her eyes had followed her uncle's. She forced her gaze back to his ruddy face.

"Ain't right," her uncle muttered.

"What isn't?"

"That a damn leech is an Earl. I'm just a Baron and he's an *Earl*."

"Uncle, it's not like he had a choice."

A warm, sensual laugh wafted across the air and she felt her gaze drawn back to the blond god. She shivered with delicious titillation.

"I wouldn't bet on it."

She stopped shivering. "Why would anyone *choose* that?" Gah. Having to drink blood? Losing your soul? They were high prices to pay for beauty and immortality.

"You'd be surprised."

"He's very popular. Didn't anybody notice the change?"

"Change?" Her uncle was frowning, his thick, caterpillar brows almost touching.

"Becoming so beautiful." Her mouth snapped shut with a *thunk*. *Stupid Mina*, she berated. *Why don't you just tell Uncle William that you want to run your hands over the Earl's broad chest, down his stomach . . . and . . .* she narrowed one eye. Mina wasn't sure what would happen after that, but it would be delicious, whatever it was. She shivered again.

"Beautiful, eh?" Still frowning, he flicked his narrowed gaze to the Earl. "He's always looked like that. I don't think anybody noticed he'd been turned. It must've happened between Seasons, but there you go. And I wouldn't say he's beautiful—men ain't beautiful—his pretty face is just luck."

"Luck?" He was naturally that wonderful to look at *before*? But that made her sound shallow. She loved the Earl for more than his face, she really did.

"The change don't change 'em—not their looks, anyway."

Oh.

A woman with steel grey hair dotted with ostrich plumes, who was wearing a violet gown that exposed more than it hid, descended on them from behind a group of garishly dressed dandies. "Willy!"

"Matilda! What jolly good luck!"

Matilda was Mina's aunt, the much older sister of the Duke of Somerset. While Mina's maternal uncle had the fashion sense of a peacock, her paternal aunt had one that would have better suited a magpie.

"I was just saying to Philomena that she needs to dance with that young lad over there." Uncle William nodded at Lord Kent.

Her aunt came to a standstill amidst a fountain of purple silk. "Kent?"

"That his name? Well, never mind. Philomena should dance with him."

Mina stared at her uncle in horror.

Aunt Matilda was looking at Mina like a cat watches a large, bouncing bug. "Mina?" Matilda flicked her gaze to the god and back to her niece. Her expression didn't change.

"I say, Matilda, what's wrong?" Uncle William peered at her. "You look funny."

"Philomena is, well, she's—"

"A maypole." Her brother Edward appeared at her elbow. He was wearing a sour look, his regular expression whenever he was around her.

Mina glared at her brother. His brown hair was carefully arranged in a style to make it appear like he hadn't arranged it, while his clothes were a mishmash of blue and orange. Her family's fashions so far this Season had been an endless assault on her senses. Her first Season. And probably her last, the way things were going.

"Now, now, Eddie, Philomena is just . . . stately." Her uncle patted her on the arm.

Edward should have been initiated into the Brotherhood of Wood, rather than Mina. After all, it was a *brotherhood* . . . but

Uncle William had refused. "How can a turnip kill a vampire?" had been his argument. No one had really known how to counter that, and so Mina had taken her brother's place.

"She's a maypole. No self-respecting man would stand next to her, let alone dance with her." Edward shrugged.

Mina kept her face carefully blank. "You're standing next to me," she pointed out.

Edward hated her, and she wasn't exactly sure why. He didn't like Uncle William, so it wasn't jealousy over the fact that she was clearly their uncle's favourite. Maybe it was just the fact that while she was so horribly tall for a woman, he was, well, short. Edward barely came up to her shoulder.

"That is quite enough," Aunt Matilda huffed. Quietly, she said, "She isn't the usual sort of gel that Kent would dance with, Willy."

"Pish, he'd be silly not to."

Something in her warmed, even though she knew why Uncle William was trying to foist her on the Earl. It made her happy to know that he didn't think there was anything unusual with her dancing with the glorious Earl of Kent.

"He's the only fellow in the room taller than her," her uncle pointed out. She felt her cheeks redden. Sadly, it was true.

Matilda sighed and wiggled her fingers at Mina. "Come on, then."

With quiet dignity, she followed her aunt as she started across the jammed ballroom. "You didn't ask Willy to do this, did you?" Aunt Matilda said quietly.

"No."

Relief skittered across the older woman's face. "Good. Nothing wrong with you, but you're just not in Kent's league."

Trailing her aunt, Mina barely managed to forge her way through the crush of people. She wondered what that league would be. The league of vampires? The league of impossibly beautiful men? The league of—

"Kent! What a wonderful surprise!"

Blinking, Mina found herself within the crowd of Incomparables. She tried to hold herself still and attempted to blend in, but it was like putting a Clydesdale in a paddock filled with thoroughbreds. The other women stared at her in wide-eyed horror and the men were tugging at their collars, probably counting the inches she hovered over them. Her aunt, a solid purple rudder, had steered her way into the depths of the crush and was now gesticulating at the Earl.

"I've been here the whole evening, and we've already exchanged greetings. Is your memory failing, Maddie?"

"Oh, you are such a wit!" Her aunt batted the Earl's arm with her fan. Hard. Mina didn't see what was witty about his comment, although his voice had been simply divine. "You've met my niece, haven't you? Lady Philomena, this is Lord Kent." Aunt Matilda tugged Mina forward.

Extending her hand, Mina forced a smile. As the Earl took her hand and bowed over it, she realised she was staring at the godliness of his features and was lightheaded. He tugged her and she moved closer.

His voice was soft, almost inaudible, "Remember to breathe, sweetheart."

She gulped a lungful of air and blushed. He straightened and let go of her hand before looking her right in the eye. He seemed surprised for a moment. "Would you care to dance?" he asked.

The women in his crowd tittered and she could hear murmurs of, "He's taken pity on the giant", "Isn't he so kind?", "What a gentleman, look at that hair". She stopped listening.

"That would be lovely." Her voice came out smooth and calm and she extended her hand to him once more. Placing it on his forearm, he led her to the dance floor. Pulling her close, he placed one hand on her waist in the preparation for a waltz. He was at least two inches taller than herself, she decided, staring in awe at his nose.

She remembered to breathe.

"It is so unusual," he murmured. She waited for him to continue, but the music began and he swept her into the dance.

"What is unusual?" she asked after a few heartbeats.

"To not have to tilt my head to talk to a lady." His moss green eyes twinkled. He didn't look like an evil vampire, just a fun-loving rake. If only she hadn't been hiding in the Duke of Richmond's library, watching him as he'd fed on Lady Constance Meadow. If only her uncle hadn't found her there afterwards and told her that she had to kill the Earl before he murdered someone . . .

"So that was *you* in the library that night."

Mina blinked, stumbled, and stood on his highly polished Hessian. "Excuse me?"

He executed a deft turn. "I wondered who had been in the library that night, when I was with Connie."

"Did I miss something?" Mina asked.

"You know what I am—which no one will believe if you decide to tell anyone other than that silly uncle of yours, by the way—but you don't know I can read minds?"

"Oh." Oh, Good Lord, no.

"So . . . you think I look like a god?"

Her cheeks flushed. His green eyes were arrested. "You are lovely."

Mina tried to pull away from him.

"Your heartbeat is alluring, your skin soft and your blood is . . . tantalising. Blushes become you."

I am not having this conversation, she thought. *This is a dream, it's not happening, he can't read my mind.*

"Yes, I can."

It wasn't a dream; it was a nightmare.

She blurted, "You can't think I am lovely."

"What makes you say that?" He smiled then, showing straight, white teeth. She couldn't see any fangs; they must retract. His grin grew. He was just, well, mesmerising. "Why can't I?" he prompted.

Where could she begin? "One, I'm too tall."

"It's perfect. My neck feels positively wondrous, talking to you." He rolled the body part in question, "See? No cricks." He was still smiling. "Two?"

"Two, my hair is horrid." It was too curly and refused to smooth down into an elegant bun. And blonde was the fashion, not brown.

"Your hair is wonderful: a soft brown with hints of red—and those curls!"

Alarm bolted through her. "There's *red* in it?"

He smiled again. "It gives it character."

"I don't want character; I want to be *blonde*!" she wailed. Red was even less fashionable than brown.

"We all want what we can't have." The Earl said ruefully as he spun her around in a well-executed turn. She felt like she was flying. "So, what's number three?"

"Three," she said slowly. "Is that I'm me."

Mina sat in her bedroom the next evening, pretending to have the headache. She was the worst kind of coward, but she was already well-aware of that particular personality trait. So much for her so-called love, she thought. The first time she'd had a real conversation with the Earl and it had gone to pieces. He was so used to charming women that the lies dripped off his tongue like honey.

Rather than going out to face the music—or the Earl at a music recital, as the case may be—she was slumped in an un-ladylike manner on the window seat, watching the lights of Vauxhall Gardens in the darkened distance.

How on earth was she ever going to find the will to stake him?

And why did she even have to? As far as she knew, he'd never murdered anyone. He just had the occasional drink from a beautiful woman, and the one Mina had seen hadn't seemed to mind at all.

She wouldn't mind.

She frowned at herself. Yes, she would, she decided. She didn't want to be thought of as lunch.

Not that he'd *want* to bite her.

Feeling morose, she slithered off the window seat and climbed into bed. Sleep, she thought. Things always improved after a decent night's slumber.

. . . . .

Mina awoke with a start. She lay in the stillness, pulse pounding in her ears and breath coming sharp and fast. Had it been a noise that had awakened her?

Opening her eyes, she searched the shadows, but she couldn't *see* anything. Darkness, greyness and more darkness. A light blossomed on her bedside table, blinding her.

"This might make things easier for you," someone said. A male someone. A male someone with a voice like music.

Oh, *no*.

Blinking away the light-blindness, she scrambled upright, clutching the blankets around her.

"What a charming nightgown," the Earl of Kent said.

He stood near the open window, arms crossed against his chest as he leaned against the wall. Her hand flew to her bosom, pulling the covers up protectively.

"*You*," she said.

He grinned and pointed at himself. "Me!"

"What are you doing in *my bedchamber?*"

"You wouldn't come out and play, so I thought I'd come find you."

"I beg your pardon?"

"I had such fun talking last night," he said, moving away from the wall and coming into the soft spread of light. He was dressed in full evening attire, from his black superfine jacket, snowy white cravat, down to his polished Hessian boots.

"I'm glad one of us did," Mina muttered.

"Come now, sweetheart, didn't you have fun? Your heart was pounding in such a delightful manner, and your cheeks were blooming."

Blooming? More like red-faced idiocy.

"Why are you here?" she asked again.

"I already told you." He was now standing next to her bed. In the dim light, he looked like a fallen angel.

She straightened, fingers still clutching her blankets. "No, you made up some rubbish. Why are you here?"

"It is so wonderful to find an intelligent woman." He sat on the edge of her bed. She scooted away from him under the covers and stared at him.

"Fine," he said and folded his arms, charm leaking away. "I want to know why you think you have to kill me."

Mina shrank back.

"Well? I'm being honest. Now it's your turn."

Behind the protective layer of blanket she blurted, "You're evil."

"Really? And why is that?"

Thank the lord he hadn't asked why she was so madly in love with him if he was evil. She saw one golden eyebrow jerk right to his hairline. He can read your mind, you idiot, she hissed at herself.

Her thoughts scurried like rats in a mound of food scraps, so she said, "You're a vampire."

"Clever girl!" He started clapping.

"*Sssh!*"

"No one is around," he said, but he stopped. "Why does being a vampire make me evil?"

She stared at him like he had lost his mind. "You *eat* people."

Maybe she *was* just in love with his godlike visage. And his charm.

And his kindness. He was a vampire and that might make him evil, but he did give to charities and actively helped his dependents. She'd done her research.

"I don't *eat* people," he replied, affronted. "I drink their blood."

A part of her wanted to giggle at his pronouncement.

"It's true. And it doesn't harm my, ah, dinner."

"You're drinking their blood! People need blood to live!"

"Yes, but not all of it all the time. They can produce more. And I don't take more than the body can replace, and I don't drink from the same person every day."

She froze. "You have to drink blood every day?"

He shook his head and frowned. "You're meant to kill me because I'm a vampire—and therefore evil—but you don't know much about us, do you?"

"You're monsters!"

"Really? You don't eat beef or pork or chicken?"

"Pardon?"

"They were alive—they were 'murdered' so you can eat them."

"They're just animals!" Although it did pain her, to think of them dying for her dinner plate.

"And you're not?" He was leaning closer to her, and she could see the green of his eyes, the white of his smooth skin. She could *smell* him.

"I'm a person." He smelt *good*.

"Yes," he said, moving even closer. "The fact has not escaped me."

Leaning back, she asked, "What do you want with me?"

He paused. "I want to kiss you."

"But . . . why?"

"Because it's fun."

She shut her eyes. So that is it, Mina thought. *I'm a game to him, a toy.* She felt warm fingers cup her chin, smooth along her cheeks.

"Oh no, you aren't a toy." His voice was quiet; she could feel it vibrate within her.

Then his lips touched hers.

Ooooh.

It was the first time she'd ever been kissed. Warm breath mingled with hers and a funny feeling began to build in her belly. As his lips slanted over hers, and her hands dropped their blanket shield and wound themselves around his neck. Her breasts pushed against his chest and she felt shaky all over. His lips left hers and burned a trail down her jaw and onto her neck.

She froze.

He pulled away from her, moss eyes dark, his lips swollen. "What's wrong?"

Mina jerked away from him. "You were kissing my neck."

"Well, yes. People kiss necks all the time." He looked confused.

"You. Were. Kissing. My. Neck." She enunciated each word perfectly.

Realisation dawned and he growled. Actually growled like an animal. Thrusting a hand through his hair, he ruined his coiffeur.

She pulled the blankets up to her chin.

"Oh, there's no point hiding behind those," he said. He ripped them out of her grasp and sprawled across the bed, pinning her down. She could feel him along the whole length of her. He was hard where she was soft, and he smelt too good.

He groaned.

"Will you just stop *thinking* for a while?"

Startled, her eyes flew to his. His face was a mere inch above hers.

"I don't need your desire for me clouding my thoughts."

Her desire? Clouding *his* thoughts? Silly Mina, her mind whispered, as if he would want *you*. *You're just a snack for him, all wrapped up in an oversized package.*

His grip tightened on her hands, painfully. "Will you just *be quiet*? You are not a snack and I wasn't about to feed from you."

She tried to keep her mind blank. It was hard. She was too busy trying to think of nothing to be really thinking of nothing. And bits of something kept interfering in her nothing, like the fact that bits of thoughts were intruding. Thinking of nothing, Mina decided, was *hard*.

Another groan sounded. "God, you're giving me a headache."

"Vampires get headaches?" she asked.

"Only when they're around you."

"I—"

"Be quiet," he hissed. And kissed her, again.

He stole her breath, her desire to think, to move. She luxuriated in the feel of his mouth on hers, of his body pressing against her.

His hands let go of hers and slid along her arms, his fingers gliding up to her chin, tilting her face as he kissed her lips, the corner of her mouth, her jaw, her neck and lower. His fingers, moving so fast she barely felt them, undid the ties on her nightgown—she only realised he'd done it when she felt the fabric part, her breasts exposed to his gaze.

Gasping, she tried to pull the material together, but he took hold of her hands, stopping her.

"You are beautiful," he said.

"Don't lie," she whispered.

He flicked a glance at her before focusing his attention on her exposed breasts. The Earl lowered his mouth to one of them, breathing hot air over her nipple. Feeling it harden, she shut her eyes in embarrassment, wishing this wasn't happening, glad that it was. Warm, hot moisture suddenly bloomed on her skin and her eyes flew open. The Earl was suckling her breast. And it felt . . .

"Good?" He leaned away for a moment, smiling at her. When she didn't say anything he bent his head again. "Call me Ashton."

She said his name softly, "Ashton."

He kissed her breast again, and she lost track of thought, of time, of everything. Right up until he eased her nightgown upwards, when she felt cold air on her burning legs.

"W-what?"

"I'm going to make love to you," Ashton said. His face was flushed, his green eyes hazy with passion.

She snapped her legs together. "No."

He stopped moving and ran a hand through his hair. "No?" His shirt was unbuttoned, exposing a firm, lightly muscled white chest and his breeches were half-off.

"No."

"But, *why?*" He almost sounded like he wanted to cry.

"I'm a virgin," she said, as if to a simple child.

"I know," he groaned. He buried his face in her neck, in her unbound hair.

She stiffened.

"For God's sake, I am *not* going to bite you."

"Why are you doing this? I'm a virgin! I can't do—this—with you."

"I know you're a virgin."

Blood surged to her cheeks. "I am that inept?"

He locked his gaze with hers, "No. But you keep bloody thinking it."

"Then you can see why I can't."

He groaned. "No, I can only see why you can." Ashton ran his hand up her leg then, towards the apex at her thighs. Her skin tingled and she felt flushed all over.

"But—"

"Don't you love me?" he asked.

Startled, she stared at him. He knew?

"I've known for a while."

His fingers kept moving.

. . . . .

Philomena felt sore the next day. Sore in places she'd rather not think about, but happy. She wasn't really sure what would happen with Ashton, so she decided not to think about it. At least, not right this instant. There were three reasons why: one, it was over and done with and she *did* love the Earl, besides which; two, he was a vampire and she didn't think she could fall pregnant to him, which negated any risks; and, three, well, she was practically on the matrimonial shelf anyway, the way her Season had gone, so it wouldn't matter that she wasn't a virgin if she never married, which was likely.

Finger combing her hair, she stood and walked over to the mirror in her bedchamber. She wasn't going out tonight—she had convinced her uncle she was still unwell from her megrim the day prior—and had dismissed the servants for the night, as Uncle William was at White's. Part of her hoped that the Earl would come back, but another part wished he wouldn't. Mina didn't think she'd be capable of repeating their intimacy, and, even though she was happy about it, she knew what they'd done was *wrong*.

Turning her attention to her reflection she studied the woman there. Far too tall to be fashionable, the woman in the mirror was close to six feet in height. Her too curly hair was unbound and flowed to her hips—a boring brown, which thankfully, didn't show any hints of red in the candlelight. Her hips flared out and her breasts had 'unladylike proportions'. She was, she decided, simply too much. Too much height, too many curves, too much hair . . .

A knock sounded on her door and she spun around, clutching her nightrail at the collar.

"Philomena?" The voice was muffled through the wood of the door, but it was still identifiable as Edward's.

Frowning, she walked over and opened the door. Her brother stood on the threshold, dressed in riding clothes.

"Edward?"

His nostrils flared as he looked at her. "How could you?"

She took a step backwards, hand on the door. "Sorry?"

"You should be." Edward stepped forward and she could smell the liquor on his breath.

Mina went to shut the door on him. "You're foxed."

His foot wedged in the jamb. "No, I'm not." He pushed the door open with more strength than she thought he possessed. Mina stumbled back into the room.

"It's bad enough that you've been making doe-eyes at the Earl of Kent for weeks, but to have him visit you at night?" Edward's cheeks were a mottled red.

Mina stared down her nose at her brother. "I do *not* know what you are talking about."

"I saw him, Mina, climbing out your window this morning." He was turning purple.

"You imagined it," Mina said.

"I can smell him in here," Edward growled. And it was a growl, his voice rumbling and far deeper than anything she'd ever heard from him before.

"That's ridiculous."

"No," Edward said taking a step closer to her, "what is *ridiculous* is the fact that out of the entire *ton*, you picked a bloody vampire to moon over."

Mina backed away from her brother. "There's no such thing as vampires." She forced a chuckle.

"Don't feed me that horse shit." Mina made a sound at his curse, but he ignored her and continued speaking. "You think I don't know about our uncle's pathetic little Brotherhood of Wood? It's a joke, that's what it is!"

Mina made a strangled sound of protest.

"Do you know how many vampires they've killed in the last hundred years? Well, do you?" Edward was so close that she could see the wild look in his eye. Feel the spittle flying out of his mouth as he spoke.

Mina shook her head.

"None. Not a single, bloody one."

She opened her mouth to speak.

"And they didn't even *know* about the Earl of Kent until you opened your stupid mouth and told Uncle William."

Oh.

Mina felt a little like a fish, gasping for air.

"Then what do the fools do? Ask *you* to research the parasite. I bet they don't know that you canoodled with him, as well."

"How dare you!" Mina stamped her foot. On Edward's. He growled and backed a step away from her. He made it sound cheap, but she *loved* the Earl. She'd marry him, if she could. She didn't want to kill him, not when he'd made her feel so beautiful and . . . and womanly.

"Kent's stink is all over you." He was *sniffing* her.

"Get out!"

"You think you're so much better than me, don't you?" Edward's face had turned a dull crimson.

"No matter what you might think, I don't." She might not like her brother, but she didn't think she was better than him.

"Our uncle is so pathetic." Her brother threw his head back and laughed. "To not even recognise what he is related to."

"What is that supposed to mean?" Mina demanded.

"Oh, I'm not talking about you and your whoring ways. I'm talking about *me*." He started to unbutton his shirt.

Mina backed right to the window. "What are you doing?"

"I'm going to show you the family secret that our precious uncle doesn't know about." Buttons flew open, exposing a hairy chest.

"Keep away from me!" Mina flung her hand out, as if to ward him off.

"Oh, I have no intention of going *near* you." His shirt fell to the floor and he put his hands on his breeches.

"What are you *doing*?"

"Showing you what I really am."

Before Edward's pants dropped from his waist, hair started sprouting all over his body. Within seconds, a wolf stood in her bedroom. A *wolf.*

Mina was breathing fast, her hands like useless butterflies when a voice said, "Well, this is interesting."

Jerking around, Mina saw Ashton drop from the window seat and onto the floor, like a golden cat-god facing down a savage beast. Except this beast was her brother. A low growl permeated the room.

"I didn't think you knew," Ashton said.

"Knew?"

The wolf snarled and took a step closer to the Earl.

Ashton flicked a look at Mina. "That your brother was a werewolf."

"You *knew*?" she gasped.

"You didn't?" He raised an eyebrow and took a step towards her. She saw that his fangs were extended.

As soon as the Earl's hand touched her, Edward sprang. The two landed in a tangle of limbs and fur, snarls and hisses. Staring at the wolf and vampire as they rolled across her floor, she reached over and grabbed the nearest object—a silver candlestick. The stench of angry animal washed over the room and she could see that Edward had pinned Ashton beneath him, was about to use those jaws to rip at her lover's throat

Without thinking, she brought the candlestick down on her brother's back. He turned and snapped at her. She hit him again, this time on the head. Ashton moved, quicker than she could see, and pinned Edward, hands around his muzzle.

"It's rude to try and bite your sister." The Earl's voice was low, mean.

A deep snarl sounded.

"You deserved the conk on the head." Ashton said.

Mina wished that Ashton's reference of 'your sister' had been 'my lover' or 'betrothed'. She quickly smothered the thought and focused on feeling panic.

"I'm glad she didn't stake me. She wouldn't have done it, you know." Ashton said into the room. Mina realised that he was reading Edward's mind. Hopefully that meant he wasn't listening to *hers*. She thought fast, behind a smoke screen of worry.

"I would have," Mina said, but her heart wasn't in it. How could she stake him? How could she have ever thought she would?

And why had she needed to anyway? Why had her uncle even *asked* her to?

"Your uncle is too scared of me to do it himself." Ashton said to her. He was staring at her and he was so beautiful it hurt. Edward lunged at him, but Ashton was faster. He thumped her brother's head against the floor, hard.

Her uncle would try and murder her if he found out she'd slept with the Earl. Given herself to a vampire. She wasn't safe. Wouldn't be safe. Her brother was a werewolf, and she might be the spawn of one. She would never be safe. Would Mina turn into a wolf, too?

"No," Ashton said. He gave Edward another thump and her brother's head lolled as he sank into unconsciousness. Ashton stood and moved over to her. "If you were going to change, you would have already." The Earl started playing with her hair.

"How did he get like this?" she asked, ignoring Ashton's fingers and the tugs on her scalp.

"It was in your family. According to your brother, they thought the curse it had died out. Until your father, until your brother."

Oh. It all made sense, Mina thought, the loose ends tying together. Edward's hate, their father's lust for the hunt, the continual trips that Edward and their father had taken to the hunting lodge. The days when they would simply vanish.

"He hates me because I'm normal," Mina said.

Edward groaned, his eyelashes fluttering.

"You're not exactly *normal*," Ashton said. She wasn't sure if that was Ashton's opinion or her brother's. She decided she would prefer not to know.

Tears began to pool in her eyes, and she deliberately kept thinking about how much danger she was in. How she loved the Earl, how her heart was going to break, how she had failed on so many levels.

"Mina, you aren't in danger." He picked her hand up and held it close.

"No? My brother hates me because I'm not like him, and my uncle will kill me when my brother tells him what I did—and didn't do!"

Edward snarled. "I don't hate you." His gaze flicked to the Earl, "Get your hands off my sister."

"You won't tell your uncle," Ashton said to Edward, then swallowed. He looked Mina in the eye, "What can I do to fix it?"

Marry me. She didn't say it, but she thought it and stared at him. His eyes widened in shock.

"Marry you?"

Another snarl erupted.

"I'd be delighted," Mina said with a tight smile.

Ashton looked blank and then turned even whiter, which she hadn't thought possible. Edward's fur bristled. Her betrothed snapped a glare at him. "I don't care if you don't like it, but you're going to have to live with it." Mina thought she heard him mutter, "I'm certainly going to have to."

There was a short silence. "I'm *not* going to bite her and no, I'm not going to turn her into a vampire." Ashton flicked a glance at Mina. "Not unless she wants it."

Suddenly Edward was lying on his stomach on the floor, naked. Mina quickly grabbed his clothes, dumped them next to him and turned her back. Not a wise decision, but she thought that Ashton would look after her. He was going to marry her now, after all. She thought she heard a snort.

"You can't marry a *vampire*," Edward snarled. She could hear the sound of clothes being put on.

"Why not?" Ashton asked.

"You two are talking now?" Mina said.

"He was trying to bite you!" Edward said.

Mina froze. Edward had been trying to protect *her*?

"Why do people keep assuming that? I am *not* going to bite her."

Mina flicked a glance at the Earl. He barely looked rumpled, with his gold hair in place, his cravat a perfection of snowy lace and his dark jacket and breeches pristine, bar the occasional wolf hair. Her blond god.

Edward was staring at the Earl as if he had lost his mind. "You don't want to bite her?"

"No."

She all but wailed, "How am I going to explain this to Uncle?"

"Easy. I compromised you, you were found out by your noble brother, and he threatened me to a duel if the right thing was not done. After all, your brother doesn't know about vampires or the Brotherhood, right?" Ashton looked at Edward meaningfully.

Her brother nodded once, rubbing his head. "It *will* make Uncle really angry. Maybe it will give him an apoplexy," he said hopefully.

Mina frowned at him.

"What? The man asked *you* to do his killing for him. You. A girl. The man is a coward." Edward said.

Mina opened her mouth to argue.

"Since he swears he isn't going to bite you, I'm going to give him a second chance." Edward glared at them both. "I would have been happier if you had hadn't let the leech into your bed, but such is life. If this makes the old fool drop off early, then I'm all for this wedding."

"I'm glad to think you approve of our marriage," Ashton said dryly.

"We all would have been much happier if you'd just been staked and the whole thing over and done with," Edward said.

Ashton flicked a glance at her before saying, "You already said as much. And I wouldn't be. Happier, that is." The Earl grinned and waggled his eyebrows. "Your sister was very happy last night."

Mina took a step forward and slapped her blond god. "How dare you!"

He was thrown back a step. Rubbing his cheek he stared at her. "You're a big, *strong* girl."

Her brother laughed, his temper apparently back to normal. Whatever that was. "Time for me to leave. I expect you to formally call on our uncle tomorrow. I want to be there to see the old fool's face when you ask for Mina's hand. Maybe he'll die on the spot." Edward was rubbing his hands together.

Wolf and vampire grinned at each other.

"Uncle William will try and stake you," Mina said to Ashton, not liking—or understanding—her brother's glee.

"Not if I'm there to point out no other man is ever going to want to marry you, maypole." Edward looked at her, his face softening, "Kent's one of the few noblemen who can look you in the eye."

"What's that got to do with anything?" Mina asked.

Edward just shook his head and walked out of the room, shutting the door behind him.

"He means you're a little intimidating." Ashton's eyes ran up and down her figure. "You're a big girl." The Earl took a step towards her, but her look froze him on the spot.

"You've already said that."

The Earl rubbed his cheek again. "Men don't like to feel intimidated. I think it's a good idea to keep you human. As a vampire, you'd probably beat me black and blue."

Mina growled at him. It didn't sound as impressive as Edward's, but she was proud of it. "You'd deserve it."

He smiled then, wickedly. "I probably would."

Dances with Werewolves

Frank Summers

DAPHNE Parker nibbled my ear—a little hard for my taste. So hard, I checked to see if she had drawn blood. Even though for months we had seen each other once a week in dance class, tonight was our first real date. And I could scarcely believe we stood in her bedroom doorway.

I gazed into the most amazing eyes I had ever seen: azure with a fleck of brown in the right one. I marvelled at such a fine turn of luck. I trembled, knowing that I was in danger of blurting out that for our next date we could go to my apartment so she could see my life-size full-body Stormtrooper armour. That I still had the thing was a testament to my pathetic existence—and a soft *Star Wars* memorabilia market.

"Well," she said. "What do you think?"

"I think you are the most beautiful woman I have ever seen."

She blushed. "No, Roy. What do you think of my place?"

I looked around her spacious bedroom. I knew that investment bankers stood to earn a lot, but I doubted she made enough to pay for this mansion on several acres of wooded land. My mind boggled at how much cash must be tied up in her bedroom alone, with its four-post canopy bed, antique dresser, original oil paintings, and enough empty floor to park two pick-up trucks.

"All this is courtesy of my ex," she said.

Okay. Way more than I wanted to know.

"Shall we dance?" she asked.

I paused. I *really* needed to go to the bathroom, but I hated to ruin the moment. So I held my tongue.

Dancing was how we met. I'm not the best dancer in class, but I find it's a good way to meet people—especially the girl kind. My sole excursion outside Geekdom was starting to pay off.

She plunked her iPod into a docking station on her nightstand, lit several candles around the room and dimmed the lights. The passionate strains of *Por Una Cabeza* beckoned us to dance, and she struck a defiant angry tango dancer pose. I reciprocated and we circled, heads back, gazes locked.

Hands on our hips, we approached each other. And just as our bodies mingled, she stopped, kissed my cheek, paused the music and tossed the iPod's remote onto the bed.

"Tonight will be all about sharing secrets," she whispered. "I'll go first."

Secrets? I swallowed hard. *Oh, please* really *be a girl.*

"But first, I must . . . change." She slipped into the bathroom, and after a moment cracked open the door. "I left something for you on the dresser. A wooden box. Something for now and something for later."

For later? Was she into toys? This could get interesting. It could also get painful, depending on her choice of devices. I shuddered.

A loud crash came from the bathroom.

"Hey! You okay in there?" It was then that I noticed that almost the entire bottom half was one big pet flap.

Another crash sounded.

"Daphne?"

"I'm okay. My towel rack keeps falling. Maybe you can look at it later."

She didn't sound okay. Her voice cracked with pain. I crept toward the door.

"Did you look in the box?" Her voice sounded lower in pitch.

The box.

I turned to the dresser, then asked, "Sure you're okay?"

My fingers traced the intricate designs carved into fine rosewood. Something else from her "ex," no doubt. Inside, I found a small envelope addressed to me. Under the card, nestled in padded velvet rested a shiny silver Colt .45—the kind of pistol cowboys wielded in countless westerns.

"Uh . . . Daphne?"

"Did you read the card?" Her voice, lower again than before, was starting to scare me.

I opened the card.

"Dearest Roy, I hide a terrible secret. And I have mixed feelings about telling you. You're nice, and I like you. And more importantly, we've known each other for months now, and I've come to believe I can trust you.

"I want to take our relationship to the next level. But I feel that unless we really get to know each other, that cannot happen."

Next level. I liked the sound of that.

"Roy, I'm a werewolf. And even now, I am changing."

Right. Now . . . where did I put my car keys?

"I know you're scoffing . . ."

I looked around. Was the room bugged? Was I being "punked?"

"But please bear with me. I'm sure you've guessed by now the gun is loaded with silver bullets. I hope you don't use it. I am trusting you to use your creativity and charm to make this work.

"If you want to leave, now's the time. But if you choose to stay, three things can happen: You could kill me. I could kill you. I could bite you. If the latter happens, there are then two possibilities: if you kill me before you yourself turn, you will have only your wound to deal with. If, however, you turn, then it gets really interesting."

Behind the door, Daphne screamed, then snarled.

I dropped the letter. I hadn't finished, but pretty much had the gist. Again I crept toward the bathroom door. "Daph? You're kind of creeping me out," I said, a little too loudly in an effort to hide the quiver in my voice.

A loud bang and a couple of soft thumps came from the bathroom, followed by a sound like a dog's untrimmed nails clicking on tile.

The pet door rattled, opening and closing a fraction of an inch as some unseen animal's sniffing and snorts traced the edges of the swinging flap. My heart stopped as the pet door swung open wide, and through it emerged a fierce, feral beast.

In some ways, the animal looked like any wolf on TV, only bigger. Crouching low and inching closer, it stared me down with evil yellow eyes.

In true Deputy Barney Fife style, I dropped the wooden box twice before retrieving the gun. I fumbled with the revolver, lucky I hadn't yet shot off my foot, or something even more valuable.

No stranger to pistols, I cocked the hammer, readying it for action. My hands shook so badly, that I was sure I had little more than a twenty percent chance of actually hitting the damned creature. This kind of thing is *so* much easier when playing *Halo*. Only one thing kept me from trying: that stupid letter. Could this actually be a werewolf? By killing it, would I also be killing the only quality date I had managed in the last six months? Like an idiot, I pledged to wait until I could be sure.

With every step the werewolf took forward, I took one backwards or sideways, trying without success to reach the door. We circled like this for what seemed like hours. I wanted desperately to run. My heart sank as I realised that the bedroom door had the same kind of doggie flap that the bathroom had. Running would be futile.

My mind raced for other alternatives. What else could I do but shoot it?

Well . . . I could call for help, but Daphne lived in the boonies. Even if I knew who to call, I'd be ground beef before the cavalry arrived.

"Daphne!" I shouted. "This little joke has gone on long enough. Ha, ha! You really scared me! You can call off your doggie now!"

The werewolf inched closer, its evil gaze sizing me up with each step forward, baring its teeth through a fierce Elvis lip curl, its menacing fangs glinting in the candlelight. The snarl turned to a throaty growl.

The wolf crouched into attack position, seeming weary of our little pirouette and more confident that I posed no threat. My bladder, having tried in vain to secure my attention since I had arrived at Daphne's house, issued a frantic ultimatum.

In worrying about whether I was going to humiliate myself by peeing my pants, or worse—by dying, I must have let my guard down. The beast leapt.

Still unable to bring myself to pull the trigger, I dove for the bed, away from the attack. The beast brushed my leg as I hit the mattress. I flew across the bed and landed on the far side. The gun fired as I hit the floor.

The smell of burnt gunpowder hung in the air, and my ears rang from the shot. I rose to my feet, and as I did, I realised that the fingers of my left hand had closed around the remote to Daphne's iPod.

The wolf crept around the end of the bed now only four or five feet away. The gunshot seemed to have gained the beast's respect, but I knew it would attack again any second. The werewolf leaned back on its haunches.

Snarling, it locked me in its deadly gaze. A tiny brown fleck dotted the lower part of its sickly yellow right eye.

"Daphne . . ."

The werewolf growled and advanced, preparing for another attack.

I pressed play on the iPod's remote.

Shrill violins celebrated the passionate melody of *Por Una Cabeza*.

The beast stopped and perked up her ears. She stared deep into my eyes, most likely contemplating my place in the official werewolf nutrition pyramid.

I returned the gaze, looking for something familiar, some sign that she recognised the music, that she recognised . . . me. Then it came: the flicker. For a fleeting instant, I was certain she saw me. And I saw Daphne—beautiful Daphne, adventurous Daphne, two-legged Daphne. I cranked up the music. Her ears straightened and her head cocked.

In a complete act of faith and stupidity, I tossed the gun onto the bed.

In a perfect act of fierceness and grace, she leapt at me.

In a consummate act of cowardice and disgrace, I peed my pants.

Her massive paws pounded my chest, but she withheld the full force of her weight.

She stared into my eyes. I stared into hers.

Her muzzle nudged me, and she forced me back a step.

The message was clear: she wanted to dance.

And dance we did. As we swirled across the floor, fleet footed and graceful, our gazes locked. And in those glowing, yellow eyes smouldered a raw and feral beauty.

We danced song after song, long into the night, until the one song I dreaded came on: *La Cumparsita*.

La Cumparsita always signalled the end of the milonga—the last dance of the night. Would she recognise it for what it was? Had Daphne queued any more songs on her iPod after this one? As the music stopped, we stood cheek to cheek, her hot breath warming my face.

And in one fate-sealing act of passion she dropped to the floor, bared her teeth and sank them into my leg.

Not a light, playful nibbling, mind you. Not a little teasing, sexy nip. Nope, a full frontal, meat-shredding, chunk-taking gouge into the inside of my upper thigh.

I screamed and buckled in agony. "What did you do that for?"

With blood stained lips and teeth, she stepped back, sat on her haunches and waited.

I recalled the note. I glanced at the gun. No way. I had come this far with Daphne. I would go all the way.

Changing into a werewolf wasn't exactly *the* most miserable experience I've ever had. No, I reserve that distinction for sitting through *Gigli* . . . or maybe *Star Trek V*. Fire and ice raged like twin rivers through my veins. I agonised through a tortuous marriage of a bone-wrenching medieval rack and a steel-crushing modern day trash compactor.

But the end result was pretty cool.

I remember very little, actually—kind of like consuming just enough alcohol to kill millions of brain cells without extinguishing life entirely. I remember running, skulking, and stalking. And lots of sniffing. (While her butt didn't reveal her PIN number, I learned interesting facts about her health, her *real* age, and several amusing stories about her eccentric relatives. I can't *wait* to meet her Uncle Ned.) Together we howled at the moon and chased lots of things—lots of things that didn't fare too well. The rest is a blur.

We woke the next morning in the cool country air, arm in arm, both of us completely naked, my thigh miraculously healed.

All that was totally awesome until I realised we lay reeking in a pen of slaughtered pigs. We fled for the cover of nearby woods and collapsed again into each others' arms.

"Okay," I sighed. "Now I know *your* secret. I guess you'll want to hear mine."

"It's okay," she whispered in my ear. "I know all about your Stormtrooper suit."

Ah . . . the sniff fest. The nose knows. I blushed, wondering if she discovered my action figure collection as well.

"But please tell me," she said. "That you don't actually *wear* that thing."

I cleared my throat and looked away, desperate to find a way to change the subject. "How about let's shower, have coffee and go to my place. You can see it all first hand."

She gave me a knowing smile, nibbled my ear—hard—then whispered, "We'd better go. They'll be coming with the dogs soon."

We ran off into the cool crisp morning.

The Protector's Last Mission

Nicole R. Murphy

S Jazmine dried the last curl into place, the shiver that always came with the Queen breaking through the wards ran over her body. She pulled a face at her reflection—which returned it—and took a deep breath to counter the sudden burst of annoyance.

Damn it—it had only been a month since the last mission, she was supposed to get more of a rest than that.

Jazmine surveyed herself and wondered whether she'd have time to get fully dressed. No. She'd already taken long enough so, with just bra and undies on under the flimsy robe, she stomped into her loungeroom.

The Queen of the Fae was not the beautiful, statuesque woman that most fairytales spoke of. Actually, she looked remarkably like the real-world Queen—short, elderly, with tight white curls covering her scalp.

Except this queen wore long, whispery layers of translucent glowing cloth—not dowdy suits and florals—and she had wings.

Jazmine bowed, bending in half until she looked down at the floor before straightening. "Your Majesty, how may I serve you?"

"Jazmine, my dear." The Queen came forward and Jazmine lowered her head to receive the kiss on her cheek. A sweet scent stole away the remains of Jazmine's annoyance. "I'm sorry to ask this of you so soon, but you are the only one I can trust with my dear Gerbold." She swept her hand toward the end of the room.

Jazmine looked and silently swore. There, hovering by the window and checking out the stitching on her curtains, was a cherub.

The baby with wings turned, cocked an eyebrow and grinned. "Well, hello, gorgeous."

Jazmine swung back to the Queen. "You promised. No more cherubs."

"Just this one, dear. Gerbold's a good boy."

Jazmine felt the air around her stir as the fae flew toward her. "Tell it."

The Queen fluttered her eyelids. "I don't understand your prejudice, Jazmine. I can assure you that cherubim make superlative lovers."

Most people thought cute baby angels with wings were a sweet thing, a sign of love and innocence. What they forgot was that in being related to a newborn baby, they were also aligned with fertility, and what was the act of fertility? Sex.

In short, cherubs were randy little buggers. She may not have resisted some of the more human-looking fae she'd protected—she was only human—however, there was no way Jazmine was going to entertain the notion of sex with a winged baby.

"Tell it, or I will." She shifted her weight onto the front of her feet, ready to attack.

The Queen sighed and looked at Gerbold, who now fluttered by Jazmine's shoulder and was making sounds that wouldn't be out of place in a porno. "Not this one, my love. You will not seduce her."

Gerbold sighed. "But she's so tasty."

"And the rest," Jazmine said.

"Jazmine speaks with my voice. While you are here, you will obey her as you would me."

The first time Jazmine had heard those words, she hadn't been comforted. After all, if the fae obeyed everything their queen said, surely they wouldn't need a safe-house—a place outside the otherlands to while away the time until whatever trouble they'd caused was dealt with.

However, Jazmine had learnt that if you were thorough with your instructions, you could pretty much guarantee an obedient fae.

"Sit there," Jazmine said, pointing to her couch. The cherub pouted but did as he was told. Jaz flicked on the television and Gerbold gasped as the pictures appeared.

The fae loved television. They particularly loved soap operas, so Jazmine turned on her DVR and set up the several days worth of American favourites that she kept for just such an occasion.

With the cherub occupied, she turned back to the Queen. She had to wave her hands in the fairy's face to gain her attention.

The Queen pulled her eyes from the two actresses screaming at each other with a sigh.

"What do I need to look out for?"

"Gerbold cuckolded the Lord of Ashtaroth. He's a little annoyed at present but I'm sure it will all calm down soon."

Jazmine's heart sunk. The lord of the demon stronghold, a land most fae knew well to avoid, was not someone to be messed with. If Gerbold was bold enough to go into his realm and cuckold him, then how was she going to control him?

"You are the best of my protectors, Jazmine. I will be sorry to lose you."

Jazmine blinked. "I beg your pardon?"

"This is your last mission. Keep Gerbold safe until I return, and you will have repaid your debt and will be free of my service."

Jazmine pressed her hands together in an effort to maintain calm. "Free?" she whispered.

"Yes, dear." The Queen kissed her again. "Just keep him safe." She disappeared.

Jazmine stared at Gerbold, who hadn't moved a muscle since the television went on. Her last mission. The debt she'd accrued when she'd summoned and tried to steal success from a fae done with.

Freedom to live her life again.

She closed her eyes and took several deep breaths until her reasoning returned. Right now, she needed to focus on keeping the cherub alive.

She went to her bedroom and pulled on her black tracksuit, a True Blood t-shirt and sneakers. She tugged her carefully curled hair up into a ponytail and strapped her knife in its sheath to her right calf. Then she grabbed the pot of paint and brush and started to mark the apartment.

Her hand moved swiftly to paint her sigil of protection on her bedroom window, then on her bedroom door. It was the only internal door she'd paint—she didn't trust Gerbold to not find a way around the Queen's command.

Into the bathroom, then the spare room. Her apartment had wards at all times, but she liked to refresh them whenever a fae arrived. They could wear out over time.

Gerbold ignored her as she walked past him to paint the doors to the balcony. She took a quick look at the television. An actor was holding an actress's shoulders while she screamed her pain at his betrayal. Jazmine idly wondered who he'd slept with—her mother, perhaps.

Next was the kitchen window and then finally the front door. Jazmine was part way through the sigil when the door shook, as if something had hit it—hard. Her hand jerked away and she swore, then started to paint the sigil again. It would only work if complete.

Wood smashed, splinters flew and Jazmine ducked to avoid an ugly hand that blasted its way through the door. Sharp nails barely missed her cheek.

She whipped out her knife and sliced at the tender palm. There was a scream and the hand clenched.

Jazmine quickly painted a sigil near the bottom of the door— more bellowing from the creature attacking her. Another quick slice with the knife and the hand withdrew.

She painted a second sigil above the hole, then looked into it.

The face that looked back was dark and brooding and so handsome that her whole body tightened.

"Jazmine."

"Lord Ashtaroth.' She looked beyond him to where a tall, hairy creature was holding its hand to its chest, blood dripping onto the fur. "I hope you're going to fix my door."

"Hand over the cherub, and I will."

"You know I can't do that. You know you can't get him either."

The demon lord smiled. "Not with poor Ishteth here, that's true. He's injured. But I will return."

"Fix my door first."

"Of course." His face disappeared from sight and then the wood of the door flowed and filled the whole.

You had to hand it to the otherworlders, Jazmine thought as she painted a sigil on the new bit of door. They didn't stint on cleaning up after themselves.

So, Ashtaroth would return, but with the strengthened ward she had in place, Jazmine felt pretty confident they would be fine. She turned her mind to her next problem—taking a sick day.

Her stomach clenched as she picked up the phone. She hated having to take a day off—not just because she loved working at Bellisimo and finding the perfect dress for a woman, but she'd be leaving the other girls in the lurch.

Jazmine breathed a sigh of relief when her friend Li answered. "Hey. Can't come in today. Can you let the boss know?"

"Do I have to?"

"Please? You know I wouldn't do this if it wasn't important."

"Like it wasn't important last month? And several times last year."

"Please? I'll work an extra shift for you when I can."

"Sure, I'll—oh, crap."

"What, what is it?"

There was some muffled sounds on the other end of the phone, then an apple-tart voice. "Miss Kamapoori."

Oh, crap. "Good morning Mrs Henderson." Jazmine coughed a couple of times. "I'm sorry, but I'm not able to come in today."

"This has become a regular occurrence, Miss Kamapoori."

Cough, cough. "I know. I guess I'm not taking good—"

"I want a doctor's certificate."

"Of course, Mrs Henderson, I'll—"

"Today."

Jazmine stared at the phone. "Today?"

"I want it faxed or emailed through to me by five today or don't bother coming back in."

"But—" The phone was slammed down and Jazmine recoiled.

Shit. Usually, she was able to wait until the fae was gone before she sweet-talked a doctor into giving her a certificate. She didn't feel right about leaving Gerbold, particularly considering who she was protecting him from.

"I'm hungry," the little fae whined from his position on the couch.

Jazmine unlocked her store of fae food. It was to protect herself more than anything. She grabbed a bag of fairy floss and a party mix of lollies and took them to Gerbold.

Once he was happily moaning over the sugar, she started to call doctors. Sure enough, not one in the town had an appointment.

Great, she thought as she hung up the last one. If only she had a doctor that she knew, that she could ring and scab a certificate off.

Well, she did know one . . .

Jazmine winced. She couldn't call her ex-boyfriend, could she? She hadn't spoken to Rossiter since she'd ended their relationship, unwilling to put him at risk while she paid off her debt to the fae.

If she didn't at least try, she'd curse herself that she gave up her job so easily.

Her fingers shook as she jabbed at numbers still easily remembered.

. . . . .

*D*r Rossiter Lapinksi was driving down the main street when his phone rang. He looked at the cradle and the name displayed sent a shiver down his spine.

Jazmine.

Could she know?

With a trembling hand, he answered. "Hello?" He hoped his voice sounded firm.

"Ross? It's me. Jazmine."

As if he wouldn't know her voice. As if he didn't still hear it in his dreams. "What can I do for you?"

"Please, don't be angry. I know I shouldn't ask this of you, but I'll lose my job."

"What's wrong?" He turned from the main street into one of the older areas of town.

"I can't go into work today, I'm sick. The boss has said that if I can't have a certificate with her by five, she'll sack me. None of the surgeries are taking appointments. Please, can you help?"

Ross frowned. "She can't sack you because you're sick."

"I've been sick a lot lately."

No, you haven't, Ross thought. "Regardless—"

"Please, Ross, I can't argue the rights and wrongs with you. Can you help me?"

"Sure. I'm in your part of town. I can be there in ten minutes."

"Thank you, Ross. I really appreciate it."

Ross hung up, then turned into Jazmine's complex. He sat in the car, waiting the ten minutes before he grabbed his bag. He flipped it open, checked that he had everything he needed and went up.

Knocking at her door was a strange and invigorating experience. He hadn't been this close to her for nearly two years.

As his knuckles hit the wood, he frowned. He took a step back and tilted his head. Magic had been used on the wood, and recently to judge from the chill of it against his skin.

The cherub had only been dropped at her place an hour ago—was she already in trouble?

The door swung open and Ross caught his breath. He'd seen Jazmine like this before—in black sweats, with her hair pulled back, was her favourite uniform for her job as protector.

But damn, if she still wasn't the most beautiful woman he'd ever known.

"Ross, thank you." She stepped back to allow him into the apartment.

He felt her ward shimmer over his skin as he walked in. "You don't look that bad."

"I feel like shit." She coughed—a dry, obviously fake cough.

Ross put his bag on her dining table and spun around. "Let me feel your pulse." He held his hand out.

Jazmine winced. "Can't you just give me the certificate?"

"You know I'm not going to do that without a thorough examination. Hand, please."

Jazmine sighed, lifted her own and their skin was about to touch for the first time in years when a crash resounded through the apartment.

Jazmine jumped, then ran down the hall. Ross turned, opened his bag and pulled out a knife and blowtorch, then followed.

Jazmine was throwing open a door, somewhere having picked up a sword that glittered in her hand. She screeched and jumped into the room.

Ross stopped at the doorway and stared. A window had been blown in and the room was full of tentacles, writhing and grabbing. Jazmine was swinging with the sword, cutting tentacles in half even as a couple wrapped around her feet.

Ross threw his knife at the one around her right ankle and that tentacle released her. Then he started the blowtorch.

"Where the hell did you get that?"

He grinned at Jazmine. "Don't have time to talk, Jaz." He set about attacking the creature.

Eventually, they beat it back. As it disappeared out the window, Ross retrieved his knife. He grabbed the blind, pulled it down and jammed the knife in, pinning it to the windowsill. Then he pulled a texta from his pocket and drew his sigil on it.

"What the hell?"

He spun around. Jazmine stood in the middle of the room, her chest heaving, her sword arm hanging heavily by her side.

"Better get your client. I'll work on securing the room. You got hammer and nails?"

"Under the kitchen sink."

Ross went and got the carpentry. By the time he returned, Jazmine and a cherub stood in the middle of the room, the open cupboard door showing where the fae had hidden when the tentacled monster crashed into the room. The poor little guy was shivering.

"I only opened the window a crack. I just wanted a bit of air." The cherub wrapped his wings around his body.

"New command—you aren't allowed to open any windows or doors."

"I didn't think he'd bring Okra after me." The cherub stared at the blind.

"You must have really pissed him off," Jazmine said.

Ross set to work on the window. He started nailing the blind in place, to stop any gaps that magic could get through.

"It was his wife's idea. She wanted to get him back cause he's been cheating on her. She'll calm him down soon, you'll see."

"You'd better hope so. Now, back to the couch and stay there."

Ross heard the fae leave. He focussed on securing the blind.

"Would you like to explain what the hell you're doing carrying a blowtorch around? Or how you have a sigil? How the hell do you know the fae?"

The last nail was in. Ross turned and smiled.

"Did you really think I was going to let you dump me with that lame it's-not-you-it's-me speech?'

Jazmine's mouth gaped open and Ross almost laughed. He loved it when he got her.

"So what did you do?"

Ross shrugged. "Kept an eye on you to see what was really going on. Saw the first fairy come. Tracked down the Queen myself and did a deal with her—I'd help you, without you knowing. She was more than happy to have two for one. So ever since, after dumping a fae with you, she's told me and I've kept an eye on things."

"Oh my God, Ross. Oh my freakin' God." She rushed forward and pushed his chest. A strange heat ran through her body. "You knew, all this time? Why the hell didn't you say anything?"

"I couldn't. The Queen was quite clear that you had to do this yourself, to repay the debt. If you found out, I'd be stopped."

Jazmine spun around and back. "I can't believe this. I just can't."

There was something about her hands. Ross reached out and grabbed her wrists, stopping her. He twisted them so he could see her palms and stared at them. They were shimmering.

"Jaz, did you touch the cherub?"

"No." She frowned. "Did I? Oh, God."

Jazmine's eyes were wide with horror.

"His wings?" She nodded. Ross turned her hands so she could see the fairy dust on them. "And Jaz, you touched me as well."

She recoiled. He smiled, to hide the hurt.

. . . . .

*J*azmine sat on her couch, chewing the end of her ponytail. On the television, a character was revealing that she was another character's long-lost twin sister. Gerbold alternated between gasping and stuffing his mouth with candy.

Jazmine could hear Ross moving through the apartment, painting his sigil over hers to add strength to the wards.

There was so much for her to think about. That Ross had known all along. That now she'd found out, the Queen might cancel it all out and make her start again, this time without Ross's help. That she'd somehow let the cherub dust her, and had then put the dust on Ross and now their bodies were attuned and lust was building.

Jazmine figured by nightfall, it would be too much and she'd drag Ross to her bedroom and dust his brains out. And the worst of it all—she found the idea quite enticing.

She'd dumped Ross because she'd wanted to protect him, not because she'd stopped loving him or wanting to jump his delicious body.

She turned to Gerbold. "You disobeyed the Queen."

"No I didn't.' He popped a milkbottle into his mouth. "Hmmm, yummy."

"She told you not to seduce me."

Gerbold grinned. "Darling, if I'd seduced you, you'd be flat on your back and all sweaty by now."

Jazmine shuddered and pushed the disgusting image from her mind. "You dusted me."

"Sure did."

Jazmine growled. "She said not to seduce me."

"I didn't dust you to lust after me. Although, you wouldn't be disappointed, sweetcakes. I dusted you to lust after him. Maybe I should have gone for him myself. He's quite delicious."

"You little twerp." Jazmine leaned over and hissed, so Ross wouldn't hear. "You can't just interfere with people's lives like that."

The cherub just shrugged and stuffed his mouth full of lollies.

Ross came out. "All done," he said, wiping his hands on his thighs.

His long, strong thighs.

Oh, dear God.

"Great. Thanks." Jazmine reached over, grabbed a handful of fairy floss and shoved it in her mouth.

"You know that's just pure sugar."

"And she's sweet enough, right?" Gerbold glanced from one to the other, then sighed. "For the Light of Berneth, can you two please just get it on? And let me watch?"

"Jaz, a word, please?" Ross went into the kitchen.

Jazmine glared at Gerbold and followed.

"What's going on?"

"I don't know. Gerbold said he dusted me so we'd get together, but that's all I've got. I'm sorry. Perhaps if we both have a really good shower and get it all off, we'll be fine."

Ross looked at her—which wasn't helping her libido calm at all—and tapped his chin.

"I guess it's worth a shot," he said finally.

Jazmine went first and scrubbed her entire body until it was red and tingling. Then she pulled on the ugliest clothes she could find—an old pair of workpants from her days in fast food and a jumper with a stars all over it.

She walked out, took one look at Ross sitting next to Gerbold and silently swore. Not enough—she was still desperate for him.

"My turn." He stood and Jazmine scampered across the room to maximise the space between them as he left.

She turned around to tell Gerbold off and frowned. The cherub was sitting with his legs curled beneath him, his hands behind his back, a flush on his face.

"Watcha doing?" Jazmine walked towards him.

"Nothing." He quickly jammed both his hands into the bag of fairy floss. "Gotta any more of this, sweets?"

Jazmine looked him up and down—there didn't seem to be anything out of place, but she couldn't be sure. She turned toward the kitchen and shuddered when a bang echoed through the apartment. She spun around. "What the hell?"

"Crows." Gerbold had launched to his feet and was standing on the couch. He pointed at the balcony, his eyes wide.

As Jazmine watched, something black flashed forward and collided with the glass door with a horrible thud. The crow hovered for a moment then collapsed onto the tiled floor next to another pile of black feathers.

"They can't get in, can they?" Gerbold said.

Jazmine went over to put her hands on the glass and check the wards. She winced as another bird flew into it and fell.

"No, the wards are strong. The glass won't break. I dare say Ashtaroth is hoping this will be so distressing and annoying that I'll hand you over." She ducked down so she could look up past the balcony overhang. A massive flock of crows flew high in the sky, almost blocking out the sun. "We're in for an awful couple of hours."

"You won't give me to him, will you?"

Jazmine stood and smiled at Gerbold. "No. Just keep watching telly and eat your sugar. You'll be fine."

Ross came running out. "What the hell?" He flinched as another crow slammed into the door.

Jazmine looked at him and shook her head. "It's fine. Go put the rest of your clothes on."

Ross looked down at his bare chest—Lord, but the man was sexy—and blushed. "Right."

Jazmine went into the kitchen and put the kettle on. Ross came in as she was making the coffee. "White and one, right?"

"Right." He leant a hip against her counter and folded his arms across his chest. "So, I have a question for you."

"Can't guarantee I'll answer."

"Oh, you'll answer cause you owe me. What the hell did you do to put yourself in debt with the Queen of the Fae?"

Jazmine sighed. He was right—she owed him an explanation. She handed him his coffee and then cradled her own between her hands, staring down at the soft tendrils of steam rising from the black liquid.

"I summoned a fairy to give me my own store."

"You what?"

Jazmine winced, as much from the sound of another kamikaze crow as from Ross's screech. "I wanted my own store, so that I was a better partner for you."

Silence. She looked up. Ross was staring at her as though she were mad.

It did make her mad—angry mad. "Don't tell me that people weren't telling you that you could do better than a sales clerk. I know I was being told all the time how lucky I was to score a doctor. And I'd see those women you worked with and how smart they were and—"

"This was about your job?"

"I wanted to be worthy of you."

"Shit, Jazmine. I didn't have a fucking problem with your job. You loved it, you were bloody good at it and I was happy for you. I couldn't give a shit what you did, as long as you were happy."

"But others cared," Jazmine whispered. Why couldn't he understand how it had felt, to be the object of all the stares and the whispering.

"And how did you do it? Summon a fairy?"

"Well, one of the girls at work swore by magic and ritual for getting what you wanted, so I did some research and found an old ceremony. You were away at a conference and I could just picture you with all those smart, beautiful women so I got a little drunk and did it. I was stunned when it worked. I was more stunned when the Queen appeared a few moments later." Jazmine shuddered. The Queen had been so terrifying that Jazmine had ended up cowering under the dining table, babbling and begging and swearing to do whatever it took to make things right.

"So the Queen decreed that your punishment would be two years as a protector of the fae and took you to the otherworld for training and to find your sigil." Ross shook his head. "Then when I got back from the conference, you dumped me."

"I was so ashamed," Jazmine whispered. "So scared that you'd find out. So worried that somehow you'd get hurt."

"Nice work, Jaz."

"I'm sorry." She wanted to reach for him but was scared of the rejection. "I was stupid. I know what I did was wrong. I know the reasons I did it were wrong. The moment I let you go, I knew that it didn't matter. What was important was us, and how we felt about each other."

"Damn straight it was."

"I don't expect you can forgive me, but—"

"Oh, Jaz." Ross smiled and hope burst to life. "Would I have found the Queen, made her train me too and spent the past couple of years helping you if I didn't want us to be back together?"

Jazmine put down the coffee and was about to leap into his arms, but stopped when a rush of tingling power pushed through her body.

"What was that?" Ross said.

Jazmine went into the loungeroom and gasped. Gerbold was up against the glass and on the other side was a tall, extremely curvaceous, completely naked woman. With red skin. And bat-like wings.

"Oh my freakin' God," Jazmine whispered.

Gerbold spun around. "Just let her in. We'll convince her to talk to Ashtaroth and then it will all be over."

Jazmine stormed forward, pushed Gerbold behind her and put her hands on her hips. "Mrs Ashtaroth, I presume?"

The demoness sneered. "Speak to me with respect, human."

"When you deserve it, you get it. So, I hear this is all your fault."

The demoness ducked to one side and Jazmine tried not to flinch as a crow exploded against the glass. "This is none of your business."

"It shouldn't be, but it is. Now, you're going to go and tell your husband that this was all your idea and Gerbold isn't to blame."

A demon smile could be beautiful and malicious at the same time. Ashtaroth's wife was brilliant at it. "Or what?" she purred.

A flicker lit the corner of Jazmine's eye. She looked up and grinned. "Or I'll tell him myself."

Ashtaroth landed on the balcony with flames licking around his body. "Hexika, what are you doing here?"

Even under the red skin, Jazmine could see the demoness's face pale. Then she tossed her glorious black hair and smiled at her husband.

"I've come to help you destroy the one who defiled me."

To Jazmine's astonishment, Ashtaroth shook his head. "I felt the little one's summons."

Gerbold gasped. Jazmine glared over her shoulder. So that's what the little shit had been doing.

"Tell me why, if the tiny thing raped you as you claim, you'd answer those summons?"

"Raped her?" Gerbold slammed against the glass. "I did not rape her. She wanted me to do it, get back at you for cuckolding her. You tell him, Hexy."

A black tear squeezed out of Hexika's eye and trailed down her red cheek. "That's not true. I was defiled and humiliated."

Ashtaroth laughed. "Ah, you played me well, my love. When we get home, I'll punish you just the way you like."

Hexika gasped then pouted but Jazmine noted a gleam in her eye. It seemed things weren't going to work out too badly for the demon after all.

Ashtaroth nodded to Jazmine. "I think the cherub has suffered enough for the stupidity of taking my willing wife to bed."

A shiver—Jazmine glanced over her shoulder to see the Queen appear. She nodded, then turned back to Ashtaroth.

"I'm sure he won't do it again." Jazmine tapped Gerbold and he nodded vigorously.

Ashtaroth smiled. "When your service to the fae is up, contact me. I like you." He nodded to the Queen and disappeared. Jazmine turned and bowed.

"One cherub, safe and sound. Gerbold, you are once again the Queen's fae."

"Yippee." He flew up to Jazmine, wrapped his arms around her neck, kissed her cheek and whispered, "It was her idea to dust the two of you so you'd work things out."

Before Jazmine could react, Gerbold launched himself at the Queen. The carnal kiss was too stomach-turning for Jazmine to witness.

When she looked again, Gerbold was gone and the Queen was staring at her.

"Your punishment has been served, your debt fulfilled."

The whole world seemed brighter and more beautiful. "No more fairy summoning. I promise."

"I hope to never see you again, Jazmine." The Queen bowed her head and was gone.

Jazmine looked around the room, stunned. "Is that it?"

"I think you should count your blessings, Jaz."

Jazmine looked at Ross and realised how lucky she was. She'd paid her debt, learnt her lesson and had been loved enough not to lose the guy over it all.

"I love you," she whispered and reached for him.

"Uh-uh." He stepped away, wiggling his finger with a grin. "You asked me here for professional reasons. I need to give you a medical certificate."

Jazmine quirked an eyebrow, then grabbed the bottom of her jumper and pulled it off, flinging it on the couch. "Didn't you say something about needing to give me a thorough examination?"

She laughed as Ross pulled her close.

3am

Eric Ian Steele

THE town was quiet, even here at its core, where the hum of the traffic should have been at its greatest.

It lay slumbering, unaware of the drunks and nightly visitors that roamed its streets, so many fleas on a giant dog. Silver puddles wept. Red mingled with amber along the sidewalk. The crushed blooms of suffused streetlamps flooded the asphalt. Neon spilled from shop windows. Fallen rain seeped into every pore of its crooked alleyways, adding to the city's watery, sunken glow.

From doorways, cadaverous faces watched the pedestrians with hungry stares—hollow eyes undernourished by human kindness. Like sea anemones they reached out to beg for morsels from the passing human tide. Elsewhere, thigh-high boots tapped out a soulless chorus on the concrete, beating out a siren tune that called out to the twisted, diseased hearts.

Nobody saw this other city, the bizarre flipside of everyday reality—nobody but those desperate or foolhardy enough to venture out this late at night. Although this part of the town's reputation, like those of most cities, was exaggerated, it could still be hazardous if you pressed your luck. In reality, it was safe enough, if you let it be, and kept out of those darkened alleyways at night. Even a wild beast has to be shown some respect.

Lynne knew this all too well, as she tugged the girl along by the hand. They had to be quick, if they did not want to attract the wrong kind of attention.

Her footfalls caressed the sidewalk like passing clouds. Strong, purposeful, but so light there were almost intangible. The second set of footsteps belonged to the girl. They scuffled beside her, quickened and slowed as if lost—the timid footfalls of a startled deer.

Hidden colours danced under their feet, reflected in the aluminium pools from the recent downpour. A strange beauty existed amid this ugliness.

"So the party's around here?" the girl asked. Long, feathered hair framed a round face.

In the young girl's eyes, Lynne saw reflections of the store mannequins from a nearby window display. The dummies' plastic arms waved, stiff bodies draped with tawdry clothing. Fake things that mimicked being alive.

"It's around the corner," Lynne replied. "Think you can wait that long?" She forced herself to add, in a sing-song voice, "God, how much have you drunk?"

"More than you!" the girl giggled.

Lynne was older than her newfound companion, but how much older it was hard to say. She appeared to be in her late twenties, but her solemn expression and the shadows under her eyes spoke of many years of experiences. There was something measured in her voice that the younger woman missed.

"Trust me," she told the girl. "This is something you're never gonna forget."

The girl laughed, disbelieving.

"I told you," Lynne cooed. "It's a secret party. All the best people come here. Celebrities. Rich people."

The girl's smile widened as she anticipated her brush with fame. Her hand felt warm and sweaty in Lynne's grip. She could almost feel the girl's heart beating as nervous excitement throbbed through her veins. She had been promised glamour, excitement, entertainment—all the things any young woman craves. All the things that Lynne had craved. Once.

The two women passed through the red light district. The girl didn't appear to notice. In the afterglow of the rain, the only real giveaways were the difference in the gaudy neon signs. The girl staggered, slightly, then tried to cover up that she was truly drunk.

They turned a corner into a deserted alleyway.

"Do I have to pay? I haven't got much money," the girl said. Her voice was honey-sweet and out of place amid the grime.

They stepped down the alleyway. Wire mesh fences bordered it on either side. Shadows crisscrossed the ground like a checkerboard.

"Don't worry. You won't need anything," Lynne smiled. Her lips curved like a dark sickle. "I'll pay for us both. It's nice just to have some company."

"Is it really down here?" the girl asked. She seemed to be having second thoughts as she noticed the discarded heaps of refuse that littered the alley. "It's an awful long way. Maybe we should get a cab."

"We're nearly there," Lynne replied. "You know these places. They always have back entrances. It avoids publicity."

She watched the girl with intense interest. Even now, she felt acid churning her stomach. If the girl screamed now, or even struggled, they were too near the road. She would have to abandon her and flee rather than risk discovery. Then she would leave this town behind, like so many others. This city was merely the latest in a long succession of places she had forgotten, but it seemed a rich hunting ground and she was unwilling to run away just yet. It was big, anonymous—the kind of place where you could disappear.

She wondered whether she should have chosen a park or a deserted lot—but she was committed now. If something went wrong, the girl would almost certainly go to the police. She could not hesitate now. It was all or nothing. She convinced herself—as she had on countless other occasions—that she had no choice.

It all came down to looks. Nobody ever suspected her. She was just another young woman, out on the town. True, her hairstyle might only have been fashionable a decade or so ago. Her clothes were a little faded, her jeans a little worn. If you looked hard, you could see the tiny stains on them. But nobody ever did. She was charming, graceful, innocent even. In the streetlight, nobody ever noticed the pallor of her skin or the grey shadows under her eyes. In coloured neon, everybody looked strange.

A burly silhouette blocked out a red light above a dingy doorway. Her steps faltered. It was a cop. He didn't appear to be in a hurry. His movements were studiously lethargic. The officer swigged from a beer bottle, thinking he was out of sight—probably enjoying a free drink from one of the less respectable clubs on this side of town—most of the cops here could easily be bribed. It had cost a few of them their lives.

The cop uttered something to a heap of refuse on the ground—she realised he was talking to a hobo, indistinguishable from the trash.

She ushered the girl behind a dumpster. They both stayed there until the cop disappeared back into the building. The door closed. She breathed a sigh of relief. Not that she couldn't handle one cop. But the threat of discovery was a complication she didn't want.

However, the sight of him had unnerved the girl, who was now tensing in her grip. She had unconsciously exerted too much pressure on her companion's wrist.

"I didn't know it was that sort of party," the girl said, laughing with a hint of nervousness. "Maybe I should go."

Thankfully the vodka hadn't worn off yet, despite the long walk. But the girl was wary. She knew that something was amiss. If not with Lynne herself, then certainly about in the imaginary place to which they were headed.

She had to act fast.

"Come on, we can't stay here," Lynne said, mildly irritated. "The sooner we get there, the sooner you can see those people I told you about. The famous ones."

She pulled the girl along by the hand.

"Maybe we should go get my friends," the girl said. "They might want to come with us."

It was too late. She had been too eager in her mild panic on seeing the cop. Her hunger stank like a sewer.

"I didn't invite your friends," she said. "I invited you."

"I think I should go back," the girl insisted.

The girl stopped in her tracks. She was about to pull away. Then she would scream. They were probably far enough from the roadside, but not as far as she would have liked. And there was the drunk in the trash back there. But he hadn't moved in ages. Here would have to do.

"Don't go back," Lynne clamped her hand on the girl's shoulder. "There's no going back."

She clamped a hand over the girl's mouth to cover up the inevitable screams.

2:15AM

Luke paced the streets. His search had led him downtown, to where the suburban met the bizarre. Some sixth sense told him she would be here, where the poor and the curious milled about under the illusory bright lights that promised all manner of flesh and alcohol. The streets bustled with revellers. He allowed himself to be jostled about. A gang of shouting yobs passed him by, close to his ear. He let them continue on their way.

He had been searching so long now, it seemed like an eternity. He knew what to look for. It was not difficult. He imagined what she wanted, what she was looking for. He knew the places she liked, the places she haunted. He followed the signs.

He came across a pool of blood in the alleyway beside a movie-theatre, just far enough from the road to be obscured by the deep shadow from an air-conditioning unit. The theatre was showing a re-run of an old Eighties horror movie.

He was about to head homewards when he heard a distant scream before it was eclipsed by the mechanical screech of air brakes from a bus. He ran to the nearest back street, but it was empty. Had he imagined it?

The crowds thinned now as he left the fashionable party district behind and headed into the poorer areas, where drinking was a serious business and the pub doors were all closed. The faces he glimpsed no longer pretended to be happy.

Suddenly he halted. A strange scent drifted through the air. Somebody gasped. A bottle chinked. A newspaper flew past and hovered at the entrance to a darkened alleyway.

She was there.

Puddles of rain punctuated the cracked tarmac. Sounds of a scuffle echoed down the alley, then fell silent.

He knew he should never have let her out of his sight.

Luke stepped into the shadows. The cold, unclean smell of death was here. He saw Lynne bent over a body beside a dumpster. She looked up. Blood plastered her face. Her eyes reflected the streetlight like a deer's, only for a moment. Then they were normal.

"Lynne?" his voice cut through the stillness.

The body lay on the floor, no longer a young woman, now a pitifully ruined creature, its legs splayed over the concrete like a crushed spider.

"Jesus," he whispered.

"Don't look so shocked," she slumped against the dumpster. "It's nothing you haven't seen before."

She stood, coughed up a wad of blood, spat it out. It dripped from her chin onto her shirt.

She had looked beautiful once.

When he was a boy, he had gone to the movies with his parents and had fallen in love with an actress on the silver screen. Her impossibly large and perfect face had loomed over him, and he was smitten.

He had experienced the same feeling the first time he had ever seen her, waiting outside that bar in the sleepy town where he had grown up, bored beyond belief. Her alabaster skin aglow in the streetlight, she had turned those ice-water eyes upon him and smiled in his direction with lips as delicate as orchid petals. She was strange, exotic. She promised him everything. All he had to do was leave his life behind, and he had done so gladly. He was sure he would not miss it.

"You ran away," he said.

She ran her fingertips over his chin with a giggle. "Don't be mad," she said.

"I was worried."

Her smile dropped.

"She's too young. I thought we agreed. We take the old or the sick." His voice was flat with denial.

"What does it matter?" she replied.

"She had a life to live."

"So she's young," Lynne said. "Eighteen or eighty, what's the difference? In fifty years she'd be an old woman, in a hundred she'd be dead and buried. It's just a matter of time. What does it matter when it happens?"

He wanted to argue. Wasn't that what he had always been running from—the endless ticking clock that marked the seconds of his life? Wasn't that why he had chosen to be with her? Why he had sacrificed everything he had ever known?

But there it was again—the fear that he was losing her, that she didn't need him the way he needed her. It made him hesitate, so that he wouldn't sound like a possessive lover. But he did anyway. He couldn't help it.

"Don't ever run away again," he said. "If anything happened—"

Again, she touched his face. Her fingertips were wet and warm on his lips. He could not resist them. He kissed her mouth. On her teeth he again felt that molten, coppery sensation.

Anger turned to humiliation, then to guilt, then to disgust. And then to something else altogether. He tore away from her. Part of him wanted to taste that flesh, while another part of himself wanted to jump under a bus.

"Remember what you said?" she asked. "You said you would be happy if only we could last forever."

"I know, I just—wish there was something else, some meaning to it all."

"There is only us," she cupped his face in her hands. "Nothing else matters. Only us."

He hung his head, feeling the stench of warm blood fill his nostrils. He remembered one day in his youth after the death of a family pet—the desolate moment when he realised nothing lasts forever, that they were all mayflies buzzing on the rotten apple of the world. For years he had wandered in despair.

"If that's all, then what are we living for?" he asked.

"For this," she said, and kissed him back. Fiercely. The rush of adrenaline was within her.

He touched her forehead with his own. Both were cold as ice, dead as the earth and the stars.

The familiar rumble in his stomach drew his eyes toward the corpse. This was the part of his existence he had not been prepared for. The constant, gnawing hunger.

He stared past her to the lifeless body. His knees sagged. He sank to the earth. The corpse lay beneath him.

"Only to be with you," he murmured.

"I know," she said.

He embraced the clammy flesh. His body tensed, craving the raw taste he had denied himself so long, even back in their apartment where the empty fridge was stocked only with the anaemic dregs of slaughtered cattle stolen from the local abattoir and slopped into beer bottles.

He bit deeply, and drank.

As he took his fill, the sharp claw that gripped his stomach like a vice relaxed. The blood was bitter, but it satisfied him like nothing else ever could. A voice inside him whispered that she had taken everything from him—his life, his work, every shred of humanity—and left him with this.

He hated it and he loved it.

2:55AM

After he was done, he stood, unsteady on his feet.

Did she love him? He didn't know. Was he only a distraction to her, something to occupy herself with throughout the long, cold desolation of immortality? And what was wrong with that? She was as much an enigma to him as the moment they has first met. Perhaps it was the mystery that made her so alluring. He didn't care. As long as he could gaze at her face—the bright moon of her face that outshone the sun.

They cleaned themselves up in a puddle of rainwater. They could walk back home from here. The red neon glow that bathed the city would cover up the bloodstains. Maybe they would sleep rough again, or find a new city. A bigger city.

He stared up at the stars through a narrow gap between the buildings. Distant galaxies spiralled overhead. He saw them clearly now with his baptised eyes. A nebula swirled within Orion's belt, a million light years away. Beautiful, perfect. But all the more beautiful for their distance.

After what seemed a lifetime, she hugged his shoulder.

"Let's go," she said.

He nodded. A hobo lay dead at his feet, throat slashed. He didn't remember seeing her kill him. He glanced down at his blood-splattered wristwatch.

It seemed like an eternity had passed.

But it was only three AM.

Miss Luella's Magic Shop

Roxanne Dent

*J*ULIE Grant walked past the stores trying not to feel depressed. It was the day before Valentine's Day and every card store, Asian shop, nail and hair salon in downtown Haverhill, Massachusetts, celebrated the special day of love with big sales.

At twenty-five, slender, with shoulder length, straight, white blonde hair inherited from a Scandinavian ancestor and grey eyes, Julie had always been attractive to men. She was probably also the oldest person in the Western World who was still a virgin, she thought bitterly as she passed a restaurant that advertised a Valentine's Day special.

Physically allergic to men, Julie knew she was a freak. It wasn't men in general, just those who put the moves on her.

Once she almost killed a date when she read about aversion therapy and tried to have sex with Rudy Morales.

The evening progressed to the point where they were both partially naked but the moment he tried to slip off her bra, she started choking and coughing like someone in the throes of a TB attack.

Once the fit died down, her grey eyes with black flecks began to water, her sinuses throbbed and her nose ran like Niagara Falls. If that wasn't off putting enough, when he drew her to him, she sneezed so hard she knocked him down and when he tried to get up, he tripped over her discarded heels and hit his head on the bed frame.

Desperate, Julie helped him up and threw her arms about him. Another series of uncontrollable sneezes ensued, followed by Rudy lifting her up and depositing her on the bed none too gently.

When he tried to join her, he banged his knee on the end table, tangled his leg in the lamp cord and smashed his head again on the way down. Cursing, he rubbed it as he watched Julie wheeze and gasp for breath. He grabbed his scattered clothes and threw them on. In between coughing fits Julie tried to convince him to stay.

"What you need is a head shrinker," Rudy muttered as he limped out the door.

Julie had already spent three years with Dr Weiser without seeing any significant changes. She stopped the visits and saved her money to fulfill a dream of one day moving to the Southwest.

Most of the year, Julie was self-sufficient. She loved reading, watching romantic comedies, horror and mysteries. But she was physically active too, addicted to running, which always energised her. It was just the holidays, commercialised to the nth degree, that got to her.

It started to rain. As Julie crossed the street that led to her second floor apartment, she noticed a sign in the window of a store that must have opened overnight. Miss Luella's Magic Shop.

In the window were dozens of candles of every variety and colour, strange statues and icons of saints and the virgin. Fascinated, Julie peered in.

A tall woman in a turquoise and lime green turban, a long, flowing caftan to match, with shoulder length, auburn curls, and big hoop earrings stood behind the counter arranging bottles. Her skin was the colour of burnished copper. She appeared to be in her forties, possessing a voluptuous body that moved gracefully as she carried out a box of white candles from the back and set it down on the counter.

Julie walked in. A bell tinkled. The subtle smell of incense permeated the air. Julie loved incense. Strong aromas lifted her spirits. Even sautéing garlic and onions in olive oil restored her equilibrium and she was always surprised when other people didn't relate to smells the way she did.

"Good afternoon," Miss Luella said in a pleasantly husky voice with an attractive French patois.

"Good afternoon," Julie said shyly.

"Are you here to browse or do you need some assistance?"

Julie hesitated, glancing at the bottles behind the counter. "Do you sell love potions?" she blurted out, embarrassed.

Miss Luella's green eyes sparkled. Reaching behind her, she removed one of the brown bottles and placed it on the counter."

Julie stared at it and sighed. "Never mind, it won't work."

"All my potions work," Miss Luella assured her.

"But you don't understand. I repel men."

Miss Luella chuckled. "A pretty girl like you?"

"It's true," Julie insisted, her cheeks burning.

Her gaze wandered to three framed posters of wolves along one wall. Two were snarling, terrifying monsters. Their tense muscles, dripping fangs and blood red eyes made them seem alive, as though they were about to jump out of their frames and rip the customers to shreds.

The third was a moody depiction of a wolf in a snowstorm gazing at an isolated cottage. It was titled "Returning Home." Julie shivered and turned away. "Maybe I'm cursed."

"Nonsense! There is no curse. Your aura is a lovely, fiery red. Perhaps your gwo-bon-ange has angered one of the loa."

Julie stared.

"Allow me to introduce myself. I am Miss Luella Francois and you are?"

"Julie Grant."

"Julie, I am a mambo, or priestess, and you have come to the right place. I can help you find true love."

Julie doubted that. She glanced around the store at all the statues, charms and candles and suddenly realised what sort of shop it was.

"You're a priestess of Voodoo?" she murmured, taking a step away from the counter.

Miss Luella sighed. "Western people don't understand voodoo. It is a very old religion."

Julie wondered if she was expected to kill a chicken and drink its blood.

"We believe in one God like most people today," Miss Luella said with a sniff, "but we also believe the body has two forces, a universal soul and the gwo-bon-ange, or personal soul."

"Interesting!" Julie said brightly, preparing to leave.

"We become immortal through merging with the loa or spirits. You ignore the spirits and I tell you, bad things happen."

"I'm a Methodist," Julie mumbled.

Miss Luella laughed, exposing very white, even teeth any Hollywood actor would envy. "And I am a Catholic, but it doesn't stop me from serving the loa. I am also a mother and an excellent cook. Do you cook?"

Taken aback Julie nodded.

"One day you must taste my jambalaya. It is an old, family recipe. Every year I win a prize and that is not an easy thing to do in a place like New Orleans."

Miss Luella exuded charisma. Julie had never met anyone quite like her. "Why did you come to Haverhill?"

"Nothing has been the same since the floods," Miss Luella admitted sadly. "It was time to move and I have a niece here I haven't seen in a very long time. Do you have family in Haverhill?"

"No." Julie looked away. She felt the old sadness enter her heart. But Miss Luella didn't need to hear about her past.

"I'm sorry," Julie whispered. "I don't mean any disrespect but I don't think you can help me." She turned to go but her eyes were once gain drawn to the poster of the wolf returning home. There was something haunting about it.

"I knew you would like that picture," Miss Luella said softly. "It is my favourite too."

Julie smiled shyly and saw an answering smile on Miss Luella's copper face.

The older woman reached over and took Julie's hand. "I seldom boast, you understand, but I am a very powerful mambo. Why do you doubt me?"

Julie sighed. There was no one else in the shop to witness her pathetic desperation and she had tried everything else. "I'm allergic to men," she blurted out.

"Now that is serious indeed," Miss Luella agreed.

"I go into sneezing and coughing fits whenever a man gets close and the men become accident prone the minute they touch me. It's a nightmare," Julie admitted ashamed.

To her relief, Miss Luella didn't laugh. "Those other men were not for you. The loa drove them away. I have something that will fix everything so you can attract exactly what your heart desires."

Julie was skeptical.

"Listen to Miss Luella. A tall, dark and very handsome man will enter your life. He will bond with you on a deep level and he will stand by your side forever. Isn't that what you want?"

Julie flushed. "Yes, but . . ."

"You must be brave and have more faith." Miss Luella reached under the counter and brought out a red bottle."

"What's in it?" Julie asked uneasily, thinking of eye of newt and bat's wings.

"Nothing like that," Miss Luella chuckled.

Julie felt a chill. "Like what?" She hadn't spoken out loud.

"It's very funny but anyone who comes to me for the first time for a love potion thinks they will be drinking eye of newt and bat's wings." Miss Luella's green eyes sparkled. "Am I wrong?"

"No," Julie admitted, relieved, but still a bit spooked.

"The ingredients are quite pleasant but not to be swallowed. You splash it all over your body after you take a bath or shower.

"How much is it?"

"Twenty dollars." Miss Luella pushed the red bottle toward Julie along with a typewritten paper. "You must follow these instructions and expect the unexpected." She smiled.

Almost against her will, Julie removed a twenty dollar bill and laid it on the counter. Her desire for love and romance was stronger than her rational mind which laughed at her gullibility. Murmuring "thank you," she rushed out, missing the look of triumph in Miss Luella's green eyes.

Once Julie was in her apartment with the door locked, she read the instructions carefully and allowed herself to feel excited.

Setting up her CD player with a mix of continuous, romantic music, she took a shower and washed her hair, singing along with Pearl Jam's "Just Breathe." Stepping out of the shower, she towel dried her hair and opened the red bottle, sniffing it. It smelled clean, like fresh cut grass. Pleased, she rubbed it all over. It tingled and gave her body a warm glow. She felt sexy.

In her silky, blue Asian robe embroidered with red dragons, Julie pondered what to collect for the rest of the ingredients. She went through her apartment hunting for what she needed to make up the four elements essential for the spell.

Removing a pink crystal geode from her bookcase, she washed it before setting it aside to serve as earth, filled her favourite mug with purified water, lit a red candle left over from Christmas to act as fire and gardenia incense to represent air.

Satisfied, she painted her nails with her new Crimson Heart polish, changed into a sexy, off the shoulder, black lace dress she'd never worn, killer pumps and created a circle with sea salt on her clean, kitchen floor, then sat inside the circle.

Unravelling the paper she murmured, "I desire love and love comes to me." She repeated this three times. "I ask the spirits to act for me in this matter and beg forgiveness for ignoring them." She pricked her finger, winced and let the blood drip onto another piece of paper.

From somewhere upstairs, she heard the beat of drums and wondered if a musician had moved in. The sound didn't distract her or disturb her. In fact, her heart felt like it was answering the rhythm of the drums and she felt the excitement build within her.

"By my blood, I draw the chosen one to me." Julie held the papers to the flame and watched them catch, turning to ashes. Nothing happened.

Julie felt silly sitting in a circle in a black lace dress listening to romantic music. No man suddenly materialised. Nor was he likely to, she thought dryly, feeling like a fool.

Sighing, she stood, swept up the salt and dumped the water, leaving the burning candle on her kitchen table and the incense in her living room. The smell of fragrant, spicy food cooking drifted down from one of the apartments above and Julie realised she was hungry.

There was a knock on the door.

Startled, Julie went over and looked through the peephole. A man stood there holding a bottle of wine. A tall, olive skinned, handsome man. She stepped back from the peephole, her heart beating wildly. She told herself it was just a coincidence. Julie took another look. He had jet black hair and topaz eyes. He was totally gorgeous. She opened the door.

"Hi, my name is Kerrin," he said with a crooked smile that caused her heart to flutter. His eyes lit up appreciatively as he took in her dress and heels. "I just moved into 6B this afternoon. I thought I packed the bottle opener. It's pouring and I'd hate to go out again just for a bottle opener. No one else seems to be home so I wondered if you had one I could borrow."

Julie thought Kerrin's smile hypnotising, not to mention his tight jeans, black t-shirt, thick black hair and those incredible eyes.

"Actually, I have three bottle openers. You can keep one. Come in," Julie invited.

Kerrin followed, leaning against the entrance to the kitchen and watching as she opened the silverware drawer.

Julie could feel him staring at her and she fumbled nervously before locating the opener and holding it out to him.

Kerrin's topaz eyes glowed. "You look amazing by the way. I won't keep you. You're obviously going out. Lucky guy."

When Kerrin took the bottle opener his fingers brushed Julie's. She felt a spark of electricity. "I was experimenting with a new look. No date," she said lightly.

"The look totally works." He hesitated. "I was going to celebrate unpacking by opening this 1998 bottle of Cabernet Sauvignon. Would you join me?"

"I'd love to," Julie whispered. She took down two wine glasses from the cabinet. Her hands were trembling. So was the rest of her. But she wasn't sneezing, yet.

When she turned around, he was right behind her. She almost dropped the glasses but Kerrin carefully took them from her and placed them on the table. He opened the bottle of wine with a deft movement and poured the rich, dark, red liquid into the glass.

Julie watched him. His movements were graceful and sure.

They talked as if they'd known one another for years. "I went on vacation to New Mexico last year," Kerrin confided. "One day I'd like to live there."

"Me too,' Julie said flushing. "There's so much open space to explore and artist communities everywhere."

"I'm an outdoor enthusiast. I run, ski, rock climb, anything outdoors," Kerrin added.

"Every day I run by the lake for hours just breathing in the fresh air," Julie agreed. "It's so relaxing."

The one thing they didn't have in common was family.

"I have two brothers and a dozen cousins, aunts and uncles," Kerrin said as he emptied the last of the wine into her glass. "We're all close."

"I'm an orphan," Julie admitted. She felt the old shame wash over her. "I was left on the steps of 'Our Lady of Perpetual Sorrows,' as an infant and made the rounds of foster homes."

Kerrin frowned. He put the bottle down and took her hand, squeezing it. His voice was gentle but underneath there was anger. "That should never have happened. People are ignorant. They make mistakes." He looked as if he would say more but didn't.

Julie's throat felt tight with grief. She pulled her hand away and stood up. "It's late. I . . . I've had too much to drink. I'm not feeling well. I think you should go."

Kerrin didn't argue. "I'm sorry if I said anything to upset you. I didn't mean to. May I see you again?" he asked as she walked him to the door.

"Yes," Julie mumbled. He kissed her lightly on the cheek and it took all her self-control not to kiss him back.

As she shut the door, she felt mortified. She encouraged Kerrin, flirted with him and then demanded he leave. What was wrong with her? She wasn't a tease but she felt the evening had moved too fast.

Deep down, Julie was terrified Miss Luella's spell wouldn't work once things heated up. Tears came to her eyes as she changed into her red silk pyjamas and climbed into bed, wondering if she would ever see Kerrin again.

. . . . .

A recurring nightmare Julie had had as a child returned to haunt her. She was running naked through the woods. It was pitch black. The moon hid behind scuttling, black clouds. The smell of earth after rain filled her with exhilaration. Her feet pounded through puddles. Branches smacked her legs and arms as she passed and she heard the snap of twigs underfoot. The earth was alive with sounds. She was happy. Then she looked down. Her body was covered in blood.

She awoke screaming to find herself lying naked on the living room floor, her legs splattered with mud.

Trembling, she got up. Her heart was hammering in her chest. She took a hot shower and made herself a pot of coffee. There would be no more sleep that night.

. . . . .

*E*xhausted at work the next day, Julie stifled her yawns and counted the hours until five o'clock.

As she wearily turned down her block she recognised Miss Luella up ahead. Thinking she was returning to her shop, Julie waved but Miss Luella didn't see her. To Julie's surprise, she walked right past her shop to the corner and entered Julie's brick building.

Curious, Julie tried to catch up but by the time she reached her apartment complex, Miss Luella had vanished.

As Julie got off the elevator and put her key in the lock, a familiar voice inquired, "Would you join me for dinner?"

Julie whipped around, dropping the keys. Kerrin was standing so close she could feel the heat emanating from him in waves. He looked every bit as sexy as he had the night before, this time wearing jeans and a burnt orange t-shirt that made his skin glow.

Picking up the keys, Kerrin handed them to her with a smile. "The food at the Thai place around the corner is hot and spicy but it doesn't sear your throat. Do you like Thai food?"

"Yes," Julie admitted. "I love spicy food." The restaurant wasn't her favourite but Kerrin was new to Haverhill and it was less than a two minute walk.

Meeting up half an hour later, Julie discovered The Thai Palace must have changed chefs. The prawns and chicken in coconut and lemon grass broth was rich and fragrant. The small dumplings were sweet and spicy and the pork and beef with vegetables which they shared, was hot without burning their taste buds.

They took their time over the meal. The electricity between them was even more potent than Julie recalled and she discovered she hadn't exaggerated how much they had in common. It was as though her soul mate had entered her life and she felt she could tell him anything.

"You seem so friendly and outgoing. Growing up, I was mostly a loner," Julie admitted shyly. "I lived in books."

"With your background, it's not hard to understand why," Kerrin said sympathetically.

"I moved around a lot. It wasn't easy to trust people."

"You don't have to talk about it if you don't want to," Kerrin said gently.

For the first time, Julie realised she did want to talk about her loneliness, her feelings of rejection, the freaky dreams and her bizarre experiences with men to someone other than a therapist.

"The human race fears the unknown," Kerrin said suddenly. "I was born with an inherited gene that makes me different but I was lucky. My family supports me and I am valued and loved for who I am."

"You were lucky," Julie said wistfully.

"Your parents loved you too."

Julie frowned. "No they didn't. They left me on the steps of a church and never tried to contact me."

Kerrin leaned in, his gold eyes boring into hers. "Death may have taken one of them and the other could have been overwhelmed with fear, especially if the one left was not of the same race, so they gave you up. It only shows they lacked courage, not love."

Julie chuckled. "Interesting theory. You're suggesting I might be of mixed blood. Me, a white bread girl."

"There are a dozen other possibilities, all of which I'm sure you've thought of," Kerrin said sitting back and sipping his tea.

"Your version is more interesting," Julie admitted with a grin.

Kerrin studied her. "When did the dreams start?"

Julie looked away. "Shortly after I turned thirteen."

"What was the scariest thing about them, the blood?"

"That was definitely frightening but the fact that I woke up somewhere else was scarier. I wasn't in my bed or even in my room. Sometimes I woke up in the woods. And I had no memory of getting there." She shuddered.

The waiter came for the third time to check if they wanted anything else and they realised it was his subtle way of telling them it was time to leave.

"It's a beautiful, clear night," Kerrin said as they arrived at their building. Julie looked up. The sky was filled with stars and the moon was almost full.

"I used to think aliens lived on the moon," Julie said with a smile, "and that one day they would take me to live with them."

Kerrin laughed and kissed her and when nothing disastrous happened, Julie knew the spell had definitely worked. She opened to him, her tongue finding his.

As they kissed, she felt the night spin around her recklessly. Her body felt alive and she didn't care how many passing people stared at them. She didn't want the kiss to stop. She heard Kerrin groan and pull away. She stared into his topaz eyes and saw the reflection of desire.

He drew his fingers through hers as they took the elevator upstairs but at her door, he released her, a look of regret in his golden eyes.

"We're having a family reunion tonight," he said. "And my mother wants me home. Tomorrow?" he suggested hopefully.

"Yes," Julie whispered. "Tomorrow, dinner at my place at eight o'clock."

That night Julie dreamed the aliens came down from the moon and took her with them.

. . . . .

The next day turned out to be grey and gloomy. There were thunderstorms off and on but the weather didn't have the power to depress Julie. It was Saturday and she didn't have to go to work. She was relieved since she couldn't have concentrated anyway.

Julie knew Kerrin was a meat lover, so she carefully prepared the menu for the evening: steak pizzaiola, angel hair pasta with a spicy red sauce, broccoli cooked in oil and garlic, basil and red pepper flakes, with a sprinkling of Romano and a mixed green salad. She included a dry red wine from Portugal to wash it all down and lemon sherbet for dessert.

Kerrin showed up with another bottle of Cabernet Sauvignon at eight p.m. exactly, looking hot in jeans and a pale blue shirt, open at the neck to reveal a hairy chest.

Julie had chosen to wear jeans and a pink, silky top.

As she turned away from him, she felt his golden eyes on her derriere as she walked into the kitchen and smiled to herself. Oh yes, she thought, tonight's the night.

"I didn't mention it before, but you have a lovely home," Kerrin said looking around appreciatively at the posters on the walls, the Persian pillows on the couch, the colourful Asian rug and all the lit candles, flickering in the low lighting.

There was no awkwardness between them. As they ate, low, instrumental music played in the background and they conversed on a multitude of topics ranging from their own likes and dislikes to the latest crises in the news. He raved over the food.

"My family will love you," Kerrin predicted. "My mother is always scolding me, insisting I should become involved with a good cook. A woman's cooking reveals a lot about her," he said mimicking Miss Luella's accent.

Julie laughed. She understood now. When she spotted Miss Luella entering her building she must have been visiting her son.

"Do you believe in magic?" Julie asked wondering if he was also a follower of voodoo.

Kerrin smiled. "I do." He ran a finger down her arm and she shivered. "I found you," he whispered.

His touch was electric. Even the colour of his skin enflamed her. She wanted to kiss him everywhere, to run her hands over his muscled back and press her naked flesh against his. She could hardly breathe.

Kerrin stood up and crossed to Julie, pulling her up into his arms. "You're so beautiful," he muttered.

When his full, sensual lips touched hers Julie opened to him. Their tongues explored each other in a deep kiss. She could feel him press against her and knew he hungered for her.

Kerrin swept Julie up into his arms as if she weighed less than the bottle of wine he brought and carried her into the bedroom, his topaz eyes alight with gold fire.

When Kerrin put her down, Julie saw the window was open. It was late. The rain had stopped and there was an impossibly full, yellow moon.

Kerrin's strong arms encircled her waist, drawing her into him. He whispered, "La Bella Luna," in her ear. She smiled and turned in his arms. They were both hot and quickly divested themselves of their clothes. Kerrin laid her on the bed.

He was a passionate and considerate lover teasing her, arousing her body with his tongue and his hands. Kerrin drove her to the brink several times. Her body screamed for him to enter her. She fumbled in her drawer, withdrawing the condom she had purchased for that night long ago with Rudy Morales. Her hands were trembling as Kerrin took it from her and slipped it on.

"You should have experienced all this long ago," Kerrin whispered as his tongue flicked her ear, his breath coming fast. "Don't be afraid," he managed to say before passion swept all words away.

Kerrin groaned as she raked his back with her nails. The rhythm of their passion, combined with the wine she had drunk, created a strange sensation. Julie felt her skin stretching, her body elongating and she writhed in a mixture of pain and pleasure.

Kerrin growled and bit her. To her surprise, she snarled and bit back.

Suddenly Julie screamed as her bones cracked and bent. Her skin exploded with thick shafts of fur. Kerrin howled, his face no longer human as he too changed, exposing long, vicious fangs and claws. He leapt off the bed and through the window. Julie followed.

Two wolves, one black with topaz eyes, one white with grey eyes fled into the night. They ran through alleys, gardens and lawns, past parked cars and abandoned buildings until they reached the woods.

On a hill, a seven foot russet female wolf with jade eyes stood over the limp, torn carcass of a man. The beast held the head in her massive jaws and as she released it, the head rolled down the hill into a ravine, the eyes still open in terror.

The wolf's fangs dripped blood as she raised her head and howled into the night. The call was answered by a dozen other wolves that appeared out of the woods, circling Julie, sniffing her.

Julie looked back once, before the last remaining fragment of her human memory vanished and she joined her mate and the other members of the pack in the joy of the hunt.

The Sword of Darcy

Fraser Sherman

ITTING out her third dance in a row at Lady Lucas' ball, Elizabeth Bennett hid her face behind her dress fan when she saw her mother approaching. She lowered the fan once her expression was suitably composed.

"Elizabeth, Elizabeth." Mrs Bennett shook her head reproachfully. "You have not danced once tonight with Mr Bingley! He is a single wizard in possession of a large fortune—"

"—so he must be in want of a wife?" Elizabeth replied. "Unfortunately, since every mother in Meryton thinks as you do, we have more ladies here than men for partners. If Mr Wickham and the officers of his regiment were not absent . . . but Mr Bingley, in any case, seems determined to dance with every one of us. I'm sure my turn will come."

"And when it does, I trust you will have the sense to restrain that sharp tongue of yours, child? He's a most suitable match—"

"He's the most ineffectual wizard I've ever met, Mother. Nothing like Mr Wickham."

"I think all the better of Bingley because he can't summon demons or do anything to affright servants into giving notice; conjuring delightful illusions is more than enough magic for a gentleman. I do believe he cannot have more than single flaw."

— 123 —

"The company he keeps, yes." As one, the two women glanced at the punch bowl; to Elizabeth's surprise, the glowering Mr Darcy no longer stood there, hand on sword hilt, as he had all evening. "What can be said about a man who attends a ball so grievously short of men and refuses to dance even once?"

"I would personally say that he's a savage who—" Mrs Bennett's voice trailed off in a strangled gulp as she stared over Elizabeth's shoulder with a forced smile. "Clearly comes from one of the best barbarian families. Good evening Mr Darcy!"

Elizabeth, startled, turned and found herself staring into Robert Ervin Howard Darcy's scowling blue eyes, blazing beneath his raven hair with an intensity that made her breath, just for a moment, catch in her throat.

"Why, er, yes, Mama, it is Mr Darcy." Stuff and nonsense, she'd prove nothing was caught in her throat! "Sir, to move so silently you must have the grace of a jungle cat. All the more pity you refuse to employ that grace dancing."

"Dancing is civilised frippery." She would have thought it impossible, but Darcy's scowl grew even blacker. "Barbarism is the natural state of mankind, and it must ultimately triumph."

"We are English!" Elizabeth snapped. "We have nothing to do with the natural state of mankind."

"Ah, there you are, Darcy." Mr Bingley strode up, beaming, two cups of punch in his hands. "I take it you've met?"

"Be careful of this one," Darcy said, grinning at his friend. "I've been hearing how Mrs Bennett wants her daughter to snare you—as, of course, does every other mother here tonight."

"Darcy, please!"

"Mr Darcy, my mother—"

"So as your friend, I must intervene to save you." As a new reel started up, Darcy caught Elizabeth's wrist with tigerish speed, pulling her to her feet and towards the dance floor. "Have no fear, Mrs Bennett, your daughter will not sit out this dance!"

Before Elizabeth could protest, she and Darcy were out on the floor, to the clear astonishment of every other woman in the room. She should have protested at his arrogance, should have stalked off the ballroom floor, but—but it was her first dance in an hour, and she did enjoy dancing, even with such a partner as this.

Oh, true, he followed the figures of the dance well enough, but the arrogant northerner held no appeal for her. Her friends, her sisters might have been stealing glances at him throughout the evening, but she had not—well, once, perhaps twice, but—"You're unusually silent for a young lady, Miss Bennett."

"I'm numb with astonishment that you can not only dance, but do it well. After you sat out all the dances at the last two balls, I concluded you only came to our simple country gatherings because they provide so many people for you to glare at."

To her surprise he grinned again. "Do you know what I first thought of your simple country gatherings?"

"Do tell."

"The first ball Bingley dragged me to left me convinced a single harlot from the fleshpots of Zamora had more sense than all the eligible young women of Meryton put together."

Elizabeth forced herself not to gasp in indignation, since she rather suspected that would please him. "You, though, Miss Bennett, are the only girl in Meryton who isn't a ninnyhammer. All the more remarkable since your sisters are complete idiots."

"Do you normally insult a woman's family when you dance with her?"

"My father hurled me into a snowbank the day of my birth to see if I had the strength I'd need to live. I merely suggest that your sisters would have benefited from similar training."

"The very idea!" Not that he didn't have a point about Lydia and Kitty, but still! "I suppose I should expect such an attitude from a man who leaves his enemy's head outside his front gate on the point of a pike!"

"You mean the former owner of my estate? The high priest of Set for the entire county? Are you suggesting that instead of beheading him, I should have asked him over for tea and cucumber sandwiches?"

"I agree the late squire of Pemberley was a dreadful man, but surely some degree of courtesy, even dealing with black magicians . . ." The figure ended; Elizabeth's voice died away as Darcy's gaze caught her eyes once again. A gaze that spoke of gigantic melancholies, gigantic mirth, gigantic appetites . . . and gave her the appalling feeling her clothes had turned transparent as gossamer.

"We can discuss my lack of manners better during a moonlit stroll, don't you think?" Warm night air struck Elizabeth's face, and she realised that during the dance Darcy had somehow manoeuvred her over to the open French windows. In a trice, he slid his arm around her waist, and drew her out into the night.

"Sir, please!" She started to pull away, but his arm tightened around her, muscles rippling beneath his sleeve. "We are unchaperoned."

"What care I for your civilised conventions, I who have crushed the jewelled thrones of men under my sandaled feet?" They were already at the edge of the terrace, facing Lady Lucas' privet hedge. "Didn't your mother just harangue you about playing the wallflower?"

"This is not a solution she would favour, Mr Darcy. I must insist—"

"No, I must insist." He swung her around to face him, his smile mocking, and hinting at improper thoughts. "Or don't you think you'd enjoy—"

Before Elizabeth could even begin to speculate about what Mr Darcy thought she'd enjoy, a scaled horror thrust through the privet bushes and, with dreadful discourtesy, wrapped a slime-bedewed tentacle about their waists.

"Crom!" With a feral snarl, Darcy drew his longsword and cleaved the monstrous limb with a single blow. As it flopped quivering to the ground, Darcy shoved Elizabeth back, away from the grotesque, toadlike creature, only to have a dozen more writhing tentacles engulf him. His blade slashed through them as though they were but knitting wool, but Elizabeth saw with dread that for each arm he severed, another extended and ensnared him.

Without warning, one tentacle reached beyond Mr Darcy, caught Elizabeth and pulled her back towards the hell-spawn's monstrous, saliva-dripping jaws. Darcy cursed savagely and strained to reach her, but the horror's grip held him fast.

Elizabeth dug her heels into the lawn, but it availed her nothing. The fiend's foetid breath, a strange mixture of brimstone and sour wine, wafted over her as its mouth gaped to receive her. With a cry of fury, Darcy wrenched his arm free and hurled his sword past Elizabeth, into the abomination's maw.

The beast gave a bloodcurdling scream as the blade penetrated into its brain, then its death-throes hurled Elizabeth into the nearest topiary hedge. Darcy caught her as she fell, heedless of the slime and ichor that now splattered her dress.

"Wickham!" he snarled. "That his revenge should threaten you as well—Set take the man!"

"What?" Elizabeth stared up at him, her mind still befuddled with shock. "Mr Wickham? Why would you blame him for—"

"Enough of such things." He drew her to him, far closer than was polite. As the monster's body seethed and bubbled into a slough of vileness, her arms slid most improperly, and entirely against her will, around Darcy's neck. "After I save a woman from a monster, it's customary to—"

"Elizabeth?" Her mother stood in the doorway, quivering in outrage. "Mr Darcy, by what possible barbarian custom are you and my daughter—*embracing*?"

Elizabeth realised with dread that her near death beneath the fangs of a loathsome beast would in all probability not be the dominant topic of the coming week's gossip.

· · · · ·

"Get back, spawn of the pit!" Darcy snarled, thrusting Elizabeth behind him for what seemed to her to be the tenth time that fortnight.

The demonic ape-thing that had interrupted their rubber of whist capered madly atop the table, grappling futilely with the illusion of a mummer's mask Mr Bingley had skillfully cast across its fanged, leprous face. As it squealed in frustration, Darcy skewered it through the heart with a single, savage lunge. It fell to the floor, toppling the table and sending the cards flying, which Elizabeth found quite unfair since she and Miss Bingley had been three tricks ahead.

Like the other monstrosities Darcy had slain, it dissolved away almost at once, leaving behind only an appalling stain on the carpet.

"Damnation!" Darcy held out his sword, now a charred metal stump and strode across the room. "That's the third blade you've cost me, Wickham!"

"Oh, for heaven's sake." The tall, dignified sorcerer rolled his eyes as Darcy caught him by the collar. Elizabeth almost broke into a run, but Wickham held out his hand. "It's quite all right Miss Bennett. I know Mr Darcy quite well; if he were going to do more than scowl, the presence of a lady wouldn't stop him."

"Blast you, Wickham. Do you mean to tell me you still deny being behind these horrors?"

"Robert, please." Despite being dragged within an inch of Mr Darcy's scowling face, Wickham did his best to remain calm. "I know we are not the friends we once were—"

"Mr Darcy, let him go!" Elizabeth rapped the barbarian on the shoulder with her fan. "Whatever his differences with you, you can't possibly imagine he would put all of his friends and neighbours at risk as well?"

"Are you so blind to his evil?" Darcy shot her a glare that made her draw back a step, cursing herself at the same time for being missish. "Did he do anything to drive that beast back?"

"Now, Robert, you can't expect me to play whist with the preparations for exorcism on hand."

"Yet I admit," Darcy went on. "A man who's always aspired to social standing is unlikely to butcher the gentry—but I warn you, Elizabeth, no woman is safe in his clutches!"

"I would feel perfectly safe in his clutches!" Elizabeth snapped, then flushed. "That is to say—"

"I understand perfectly." Darcy released his grasp on Wickham, letting the mage fall to the floor. "He has *manners*. How could you think an Englishman with *manners* would traffick with the powers that lurk outside the world? I thought you had sense, Miss Bennett, yet no matter how many times I save your life, you—oh, for the fleshpots of Zamora, or even those of Brighton!"

Turning on his heel, he strode out the door, slamming it behind him.

"Dear me, Miss Bennett." Wickham rose from the floor, adjusting his clothes. "I am so sorry you had to see such a savage display, but my friend has always been prone to—well, as you see."

"Oh, Darcy's a fine fellow," Bingley said quickly. "It's simply that with so many unholy things assaulting you, Miss Bennett . . ."

"Me?" Elizabeth shook her head. "No it's Mr Darcy these dreadful demons have been pursuing. I'm simply at risk because, well—" A snicker erupted at one of the other tables, reflecting what all knew: she had been endangered because Darcy had contrived to be in her company constantly, these past two weeks. "I have never trod the thrones of men beneath *my* feet; why should any wizard unleash demons on me?

"Mr Wickham." She turned to him and put on her best smile. He had been so sweet, avoiding Darcy's company, and even hers the past two weeks, doubtless to prevent such scenes as this. "Please accept my apologies for this disagreeable turn of events."

"Miss Bennett, no-one could blame you."

"Nevertheless, the least I can do is ask you to join me tomorrow in the parlour for tea."

It was not, of course, done to invite men to tea, but it would certainly show Mr Darcy she had better things to do than wait for him to call.

Not, of course, that what he thought mattered to her in even the slightest degree.

. . . . .

I don't mean to pry," Elizabeth told Wickham with complete untruthfulness. "I realise there's not an atom of truth in his words. I know that you and Darcy were once friends. I merely wondered what could have happened that would make him so certain you are at fault. Mr Darcy, by his own admission, has been a thief, a reaver, a mercenary; he must have left many a bitter sorcerer in his wake."

"None who spend time in your company, Miss Bennett." Wickham set his empty cup down on the saucer, contemplating the tea leaves. "It is quite obvious his strong, savage passion is fixed upon you."

"Is it? I had noticed nothing of the sort."

"And that has inflamed an old bitter wound. Out of respect for his father, I had hoped not to bring this up. When I first joined the regiment, it was stationed far to the north, on the borders of Darcy's homelands. I met his father there, and assisted with a few trifling spells in protecting their village from marauding wolves and the like.

"For all Darcy's savage, unlearned ways, it seemed we were both kindred spirits, hungry for what life had to offer, eager to make our mark on the world, as young men so often are. I thought of us as brothers—though if I had been, I doubt I'd have survived being thrown into a snowdrift naked."

"Yes—I mean no, very fortunate for you." The thought of Darcy naked in the snow had distracted her momentarily. "Please, go on."

"The regiment's senior wizard was most impressed by the bonds I forged with Darcy's father, and the rest of the village. And there was a young girl in the village." For a long, sad second, Wickham said nothing. "More than lovely enough to make the chill northern winters bright as spring.

"Between my mentor's influence and Darcy's father, a man quite respected among his tribe, there was talk of my being stationed permanently at the small, abandoned vicarage of Mitra nearby. It would have been most delightful, and a more than adequate income—but Robert, like myself, had fallen for the young girl.

"As now, so he did then. With an insane, bitter jealousy, he accused me of practising the blackest sorceries, defiling the young lady, of binding his father to me with evil magic, spread rumours so scurrilous that my military career was almost destroyed. Finally, he led a mob of torch-wielding villagers against me, and I was forced to flee back to England."

"Ha! And he would have had *me* think I was prejudiced against him for being a barbarian!" She'd known he was a savage! The kind of savage who manhandled woman and put the most unseemly dreams into their heads at night. And yet—"If he were so enraged against you, I'm surprised he didn't gut you himself, rather than rousing his village to join him."

"He had a barbarian's fear of the dark arts, though he's clearly learned to overcome it since. But apparently his resentment of me is something he can't overcome."

"So it seems." Why, then, did she feel such pangs of regret at learning the truth about Darcy's black heart?

"Perhaps I should have spoken out sooner, but out of respect for Robert's father, I'd hoped it could be avoided." Wickham set the cup and saucer aside and with atypical boldness, he laid his hand gently on hers. "Now that I've spoken, I feel the burden of past tragedy has lightened somewhat. Telling the story to someone so understanding, someone I've always been very fond of—"

The door slammed open, and Darcy strode into the parlour, sword drawn. "Release her! Take your hands from Elizabeth, Wickham, or I'll gut you where you sit!"

"His hands were not on me, Mr Darcy!" Elizabeth sprang up indignantly.

"Not again, Wickham!" Darcy crossed the room, grabbed Elizabeth and thrust her behind him as he faced his former friend. "You defiled Yshara, but not Elizabeth!"

"Robert, please." Wickham looked at Darcy with utmost regret. "Can we not put aside the past—if not for her sake, then your father's."

"Speak of them again and I'll split your head like a melon!"

"There will be no splitting of melons—or heads—in the parlour," Elizabeth said firmly. Darcy turned his blazing gaze upon her but she stood her ground. "And by what right do you use my Christian name, *Mr* Darcy?"

"Any other woman would grant me considerably more privileges than that after I'd saved her life a half-dozen times!"

"None of which would be necessary if you weren't constantly in my presence."

"Elizabeth." Wickham coughed slightly. "I can see you would prefer to discuss this with Mr Darcy in private."

"No, not at all!"

"Yes you would!" Darcy snapped. "Begone, Wickham!"

"But I hope you will return soon," Elizabeth said.

"You do?" Darcy stared at her incredulously until Wickham departed. "You little fool! What the devil were you doing having that fiend over for tea?"

"Devil? A fine thing to say of the man whose life you sought to ruin!"

"Ruin him?" Darcy laughed mirthlessly. "If you only knew what that man is capable of!"

"No knowledge you can impart would change my feelings for that fine, respectable man, Mr Darcy!"

"The blackness in his heart would make the vilest wizards of ancient Acheron pale to confront it! If civilised law didn't make such an absurd fuss about proof of guilt, his head would have joined the squire of Pemberley the first time I saw him in your company! I was beginning to think you a woman of sense, Elizabeth, yet you take tea with a monster, you refuse my bed—"

"Peculiar behaviour, I'm sure, in those fleshpots you're so fond of—"

"—but I admit I've only made things worse. I let your refusal wound my pride and so avoided the obvious solution to bringing you into my arms *and* my bed!"

"How dare you!"

"As mistress of my estate." He smiled, and his look made her breath catch again. "As my wife."

He released her wrists, but only to catch her around the waist and pull her to him, hard. His lips, heedless of all decency, found hers—she must protest, she must!

Yet, after all, he had just proposed marriage. She would refuse, certainly, but surely it would be impolite not to wait a few minutes before saying so, just to show she had given him proper consideration . . .

After several minutes, she debated whether or not sufficient consideration had been given. The realisation the pelisse she wore over her dress now lay on the floor convinced her it had.

"Mr Darcy!" He smiled down at her, as a fox might smile at a particularly tricky rabbit. "Do you truly think this an appropriate match? You've more than once expressed your disdain for my family."

"I admit none of them but you would have any hope of surviving in the northern wilderness." His lips moved her neck, biting between kisses. "Tottyheaded, the lot of them. But what of it? You're English. As you say, you have nothing to do with life in its natural state. If they're the price for taking you as my wife—"

"I am not your wife yet, sir!" His lips pressed hers again, hot, demanding, impassioned, and she should have protested, but instead found her mouth responding in a most unladylike way.

Somehow her muslin gown had come unbuttoned and joined her pelisse . . . this was the parlour, he couldn't!

But if he did, she had a dreadful feeling she wouldn't really object.

The next second she found herself in her petticoats on the floor, on top of her clothes.

Darkness writhed and blossomed within the room: a formless obscenity that blotted the sun from the windows as it flowed towards them. Darcy had dropped her to reclaim his sword.

He uttered a guttural northern curse as the blade sliced through the slithering shadow without effect.

"Darcy, flee!" Elizabeth scrambled to her feet as the shadow engulfed him. "Stay back, whatever you are! You shall not have him!"

From inside the darkness she heard him curse. Then the shadow reached for her, with the cold touch of a nightmare born in nethermost hells. Darkness was all around her, Darcy called out her name, then Elizabeth knew no more.

.....

Awareness returned. For a second, Elizabeth knew only that she lay upon a cold, stony surface.

Then remembrance of the shadow flooded back into her mind; with a gasp of dread, she sat up and opened her eyes.

"Mr Wickham!" She sighed in relief to see Wickham standing in front of her in the dimly lit room, clad in an embroidered smoking jacket.

Elizabeth's relief vanished when she saw the embroidery depicted one of the more repugnant rituals of Set. She glanced down: she sat on a flat slab of blackest basalt, smeared with crimson stains, and what had felt like her corset round her waist was a heavy chain fastening her to the stone. And worse still. "Mr Wickham, I am unclothed!"

"I do beg your pardon, Miss Bennett," Wickham said, twisting his hands sheepishly. "Not for anything would I have had events take such a turn."

"You mean circumstances forced you to strip me of my clothes and shackle me to what I presume to be an altar?"

"As I was saying in the parlour before Robert interrupted—" He coughed awkwardly. "You must have noticed that I've grown very fond of you—may I call you Elizabeth?"

"You most certainly may not!"

"You let Robert call you Elizabeth, everyone says so!"

"I care not a fig what everyone says!" The sheer injustice of the charge provoked her to leap from the stone, only to be brought up short by the chain, several feet from Wickham. Even so, two black-clad acolytes emerged from the dimness protectively. "Bad enough you chain me here for your private amusement, sir, but to invite guests?"

"Heavens no, they're eunuchs! They have no interest in your lovely—er, no interest. And I truly meant what I said, I would much sooner have sacrificed one of your lackwit sisters than brought you here. In addition to your many charms, you're a sensible, practical woman, more than able to run an archpriest's household with all its many social obligations."

"You lied to me!" The truth was clear to her now. "Mr Darcy is not unfairly set against you, you deserved his enmity!"

"He's completely unfair!" Wickham sniffed. "Truthful, I admit, but completely unfair! I would have set him up as right hand in my empire, a sword against my enemies, if he hadn't proved so top-lofty about serving a 'foul spawn of the netherworld'. And had he not intervened, Yshara would have been sacrificed to Set, and the question of whether or not I defiled her would have become completely irrelevant.

"But enough of the past." He cleared his throat and drew closer. "My dear Miss Bennett, I truly do admire you, and I believe I could come to care for you greatly. This is not the ideal place for such discussions, but do you think you could find it in your heart to—"

"I consider it completely beyond the pale to entertain a proposal from one who speaks of sacrificing my sisters."

"Well my master must have some sort of sacrifice this night. Do consider, Miss Bennett, that if it's not to be Kitty, Lydia or Mary . . ."

"Myself?" Elizabeth drew herself up to her full height. "I most strenuously object to meeting your dark lord unclothed!"

"Oh, don't concern yourself on that account; Set isn't the least bit conventional in such matters." Wickham gave a deep, mournful sigh. "I rather feared it would come to this. Yshara, you, all the women in between, they all succumb to Darcy in the end. His virile muscles, his arrogant swagger. If only those horrors I summoned had finished him off, or—"

Elizabeth narrowed her eyes. "Mr Wickham, why did those creatures only attack when I was in his presence?"

"Yes, well." Wickham had the grace to look embarrassed. "After that night at the ball, it was obvious he had a tendre for you; I knew it would be cursed difficult to kill him—"

"So you thought you would pain him by slaying me while he watched? And yet you ask me for my hand?"

"Twenty years from now, I'd like to think we'd look back and laugh at such a trifle. No?" With another deep sigh, Wickham plucked a long sacrificial knife from a table. It glinted in the flickering light of the braziers as he and his acolytes drew closer "Of course, I wouldn't dream of defiling *you*, Miss Bennett, but I'm afraid much of what I will have to do, you will not find pleasant."

"Not as unpleasant as you'll find dying!" Darcy's voice rang out, then a scream came from the doorway. Elizabeth and Wickham both turned to see a guard collapse, his throat jetting blood, as Darcy plunged into the midst of the black-clad minions, cleaving heads from necks with every blow of his sword.

"Devil take you Robert, this is insufferable!" As his two acolytes joined the fray, Wickham spat words that curdled Elizabeth's blood, words that shook shadows free of the darkness, oozing towards Darcy. "I spared you in the parlour in hopes you'd see me wed Elizabeth, but there shall be no mercy now!"

As shadows and Set-worshippers swirled in a maelstrom around Mr Darcy, Elizabeth knew she would do anything to save him. She glanced around wildly for some tool, some talisman that could help, but saw nothing—and then her eyes fell on the knife in Wickham's hands.

Was he close enough?

A leap she feared displayed none of the grace of a jungle cat stretched the chain to its utmost extent. Wickham turned at the jangling of the taut links, but before he could act her fingers plucked the hilt from his grasp and thrust the blade into his stomach.

"Bother!" Wickham slid to the floor and expired with a last, despairing groan.

The shadows around Darcy dissipated, leaving the remaining acolytes barely time to cry for mercy before he dispatched them. As the last man fell, without warning or wind the lamps guttered and went out.

"Mr Darcy?" Elizabeth cried. "Robert?"

"Elizabeth!" He was at her side in an instant, crushing her to his chest, which felt remarkably different in her unclothed state. "You saved my life."

His lips found hers, and nothing was spoken for a very long time.

"Elizabeth," he said at last. "What I saw of you unclothed confirms you are more than the equal of any fleshpot strumpet."

"I'm delighted to hear it—Robert." Metal links clattered to the floor as he tore the chain from around her waist. "Of course it's the last such glimpse you'll have until we're man and wife."

"Tomorrow, if I have my way. I defeated the Veiled Prophet, I robbed the Tower of the Elephant, I can find a way to escape posting bans and all those witless English—"

"I'm sure you can, but you won't." She kissed him, gently this time. After a second he laughed, swept her up in his arms and made his way across the dark temple towards the door. "We'll make a civilised gentleman of you yet, Robert."

"There's more than a little barbarian in any woman who'd stab a sorcerer to death to save me. If you'd like his head on a pike—"

"My taste in wedding gifts runs more to porcelain and silverware, thank you." They entered the antechamber, where her garments lay neatly folded in one corner. "And I am truly, truly sorry that I allowed him to prejudice me against you."

"And I am sorry that my pride left me waiting for you to come to my bed, instead of asking your father for your hand the first day we met." Like a perfect gentleman, he turned his back as she donned her clothes. "It's just that no other woman has ever refused me for so long."

"Oh? And just how many other women have there been?"

He spun around, caught her up in his arms and kissed her breathless. "I think if I have just one more, it'll be enough."

"That's a very fine number."

He was, after all, a barbarian. Some allowances should be made.

Frostbitten

Kirstyn McDermott

LESS than three steps into his apartment before he's kissing her, hands reaching beneath her skirt, mauling at her bare arse like it can be moulded into something else if only he squeezes hard enough. Nina returns his kisses with equal ferocity, thankful that he's so eager.

Eager means quick, and quick is what she needs.

He doesn't bother with the bedroom, simply propels her into the living room, over to the modular lounge that lines two walls like a gigantic red L and throws her down on the shorter side. At least it's firm beneath her back.

"You're so cold, baby," he murmurs into her throat. She can smell the spice-sharp scent of his cologne, and the sweat beneath it. "Let's see what we can do to warm you up, hey?"

He's not awful—she's definitely had a lot worse—but he's young, and his repertoire isn't very extensive. Nina feels a slight twinge of remorse about that, but brushes it aside. She allows his fingers to chafe at her nipples for a bit before pushing them away, coaxing them further south. Misunderstanding, he unbuckles his belt instead, shuffles his pants down to his thighs.

"Fuck, you're a sexy thing."

He moans as he pushes himself into her, and Nina's glad she bothered to pre-lube back in the club's bathroom before they left. Foreplay obviously isn't his strong suit. She hooks her legs over his hips and echoes the noises he's making, clenching herself close around him, pulling him deeper. His fingers dig into her shoulders, and he moves like he's ploughing her, like he's trying to dig a trough right through the middle of her. She turns her head and bites his earlobe.

His spine flexes when he comes and he mewls like a frightened animal, teeth clenched and gleaming with saliva. "Oh," he says, twice, before collapsing onto her. Nina rubs his back, wriggles a little beneath him. He's no lightweight, and the muscles of her inner thighs are starting to ache.

After a minute or so, he pushes himself up. "Sorry, was I squashing you?"

Nina smiles. "I'm fine."

"Just fine?" He leans down and kisses her breast.

Nina keeps smiling. Beneath her hands, his skin is cooling. He rolls off and lies on the couch beside her, one hand over his eyes. "Man, that was intense. Give me a few and we'll go again, hey?"

"Sure." She sits up, swings her legs around. Her bag is at the end of the couch and she bends to retrieve it. "Where's your bathroom?" He waves his free hand towards the hallway, tells her to look for the second door on the right. Nina stands and straightens her skirt, fastens the three buttons on her blouse he managed to get around to undoing. She's still wearing her boots, knee-high black leather with heels high enough to lame a novice, and the apartment floors are polished wood. When she walks, it sounds like deliberation.

The bathroom is easy to find. Nina cleans herself up, then brushes her teeth with the help of an index finger and a smear of peppermint-plus-whitening. Her knickers went into her bag back at the club; she takes them out again now, pulls them up over her hips. Already she feels much better. Much warmer. The adjacent bedroom yields a quilt that smells stale and used, but there isn't time to hunt down a clean one.

Back in the living room, the young man has curled himself into a ball in the corner of the lounge. His hands are tucked into his armpits and his teeth are chattering as she covers him with the quilt. "It's so bloody cold," he says. "Aren't you cold?" His eyes are pale blue, the colour of frost on winter grass. She hadn't noticed before.

"I'm fine." Nina smiles at him. There's a reverse cycle air conditioner mounted on the opposite wall. She makes sure it's switched onto heat, then turns the thermostat up as high as it will go. Hot air begins to flood the room.

"I can't get warm," the man says. "Feels like I won't ever get warm again."

Nina's own face is flushed now, almost clammy. Between her thighs, a different heat is building. "I'm sorry," she tells him, fishing her car keys from her bag. "It won't always be this bad, I promise. Over time, it . . . lessens."

"Don't go," he pleads. "Stay with me. I need you to stay with me."

"I'm sorry," she says again, and wonders how long it's been since those words held any meaning.

. . . . .

*I*t's late, about to turn into early morning, and Simone still hasn't shown up. Nina's already showered and washed her hair. Washed her body as well with her favourite scented soap—coconut and lemongrass—that Simone says it makes her smell like a Thai curry, delicious and creamy and hot.

She paces the cramped confines of the motel room, biting her nails. Rubbing against the white silk of her negligee, her skin itches and burns.

What's taking that woman so damn long?

From the bed, her phone bleats the arrival of a new text message, and Nina lunges towards it. From Simone, the screen tells her. The text is short, and infuriating: *sry, couldnt find 1. 2morrow? stsp? sim xxx*

Nina throws the phone at the wall. It falls apart, the battery skidding a few metres across the carpet. Her hands are shaking. Does Simone think it's not just as hard for *her* to find them? To fuck them? Opting for men might speed things along a bit, but it doesn't make it any easier. Simone would see that if she ever deigned to sample from the other side of the menu. But she's too fussy, that's the problem, and too worried about possible consequences. Tonight, it's Nina's problem as well. But at least they won't have to wait another month.

stsp

Same time, same place. Nina takes a deep breath, then another, wills herself to calm the hell down. Trouble is, she's so damn hot. Tonight would have been amazing; who knows what tomorrow will bring?

She picks up the pieces of phone and puts them carefully back together, makes a silent wish as she presses the *on* button. The screen lights up white for a second before the annoying welcome tune kicks in and she's asked to input the current date and time. At least the bloody thing seems to be working. Nina takes the time from the clock on the bedside table, remembers the date from when she signed the motel registration. All her recent days have blurred together; they always do whenever she and Simone are about to meet.

She calls up the text again, types in a quick reply—*ok, tomorrow. stsp. miss you much. n xxx*—and presses send. Then she tosses the phone back to the bed and stalks into the ensuite.

Time for another shower. Cold this time, for as long as she can stand it.

. . . . .

Bent forwards over the man's dining room table, its hard-angled edge digging into her hips, Nina worries she's made a mistake, allowed impatience to get in the way of better judgement. He seemed harmless enough back at the bar, slightly shorter than herself with a body long since gone to seed, his round and ruddy face all but glowing with the sheen of desperation.

Now, she's not so sure.

He grunts with each thrust, his flabby gut slapping against her arse. He calls her a slut, a whore, a frigid fucking bitch. He tells her that he'll show her who's the boss, who's her fucking master. Clenching her teeth, Nina stretches out and grips the opposite edge of the tabletop. As though perceiving this as invitation, he fumbles at her right breast, pinches the nipple between his fingers and twists. Hard. Tears prick at the corners of her eyes but she doesn't make a sound; she won't give him that kind of satisfaction.

His hand tangles in her hair, pulling, lifting her head up and back as far as her neck will allow, and then just that little bit further. Nina realises what he's about to do and manages to turn her head slightly to the left as he slams her forehead down onto the table. Sparks burst behind her eyes and this time she does cry out. There'll be bruises to cover up later, but at least her nose isn't broken.

Behind her, above her, the man continues to grunt.

Nina pushes back against him, grinding her teeth against the pain that unfurls like razor wire in her skull. She needs him to finish, and she needs to be conscious when he does. Movement seems to excite him, so she begins to squirm, to writhe beneath the hands that now pin her to the table, although she can't quite convince herself that her struggles are entirely an act.

The man calls her a slut again, and asks her if she likes it. Then he tenses up and groans, his sweaty bulk squashed tight against her as he rocks backwards and forwards on his toes. Nina lifts her right leg beneath the table, braces herself with her hands, and kicks back as hard as she can. Not anywhere near as hard as she wants, but her spiked heel is enough to make him gasp and release his hold on her shoulders. He sways back a step, putting enough distance between them for her to deliver a second, infinitely more powerful, kick.

The man screams, a high-pitched, girlie wail that's music to Nina's ears.

She straightens and spins around, hands raised to fists in front of her face. He's hunched over, leaning against the wall with knees half-bent and wobbling, both hands at his groin. Blood leaks between his fingers. He lifts his head, glares at her with eyes red-veined and streaming.

"You fucking bitch," he shrieks. "Look what you fucking did!"

She doesn't want to look, is quite happy to live and let live from this point on, until the man takes a step towards her. More of a stagger really, but she doesn't even think before kicking him again. In the chest this time, the flat of her foot landing almost squarely between his nipples with the whole weight of her body behind it, sending him flailing to the ground where he slumps, badly winded. Nina is disappointed to see that all the blood is coming from a ragged hole punched near the top of his inner thigh, right in the crease where leg meets torso, and not from a more intimate wound. She moves in close, lowers her boot onto his neck. The heel sits neatly in the hollow where his clavicles meet.

"Don't . . ." he wheezes. "Please . . ."

Nina shakes her head. "I'm not going to kill you. There's no point." She lifts her foot and steps away. "This little hobby of yours, hurting women? You'll find it doesn't hold much interest for you anymore. There's not a lot that will."

He's trembling already. Whether from fear or the incipient cold, she neither knows nor cares.

. . . . .

This time, Simone has beaten her to the motel. As Nina opens the door, the other woman practically bounces from the bed where she's been sitting and rushes over with arms spread wide. Her grin falters as Nina steps into the room, into the light.

"What happened?" She reaches for Nina's forehead, stops just short of touching it. For one awful moment, Nina stops breathing. Then she sees the colour in Simone's cheeks, feels the heat emanating from her skin, and pulls the woman into her arms. Relaxing into the embrace, Simone runs her hands down Nina's spine, presses soft, warm lips to her throat.

"I'm off my game," Nina tells her. "Picked a bad one tonight."

"Oh, honey, you need to be more careful."

"I need *you*."

Their mouths meet, their tongues touch. Hesitant, light, sliding against each other with slow, teasing strokes. Then Simone is pulling her towards the bed, her hands firm on Nina's hips, her kisses more forceful. She's making those urgent, almost guttural moans that never fail to melt Nina right where it counts.

"Wait." Nina pushes herself away. "I have to shower first. I need to scrub this stink off me."

"I don't care about that."

"I do."

"Okay." Simone smiles, undoes the first three buttons on her pyjama top and parts the pale blue fabric. "I'll be waiting right here when you're done."

Nina bends to place a kiss first on Simone's left breast, and then on her right. She flicks the tip of her tongue over each nipple, coaxing them to dark and perky nubs. "I won't be long," she says. "I promise."

The first thing she does when she gets into the ensuite is swallow three rapid-action painkillers. Her head still hurts like blazes—not surprising, really, considering the face that reproaches her from the mirror. There's a swollen lump on the side of her forehead the size of a quail's egg; around it the flesh is already turning interesting shades of purple and blue. But no blood, no split skin, no need for stitches. Thank the goddess for minor mercies.

Nina lets the shower run until the ensuite is billowing with steam, then strips and steps beneath the water. Her skin flushes an instant, angry red but she makes no move to adjust the temperature. Tonight, with such fresh and bitter heat running through her body, not even boiling water could scald her. Eyes closed, she starts to sing as she lathers her hair with shampoo. That old Kate Bush song about Cathy and coming home and wanting to be let in; only in a bathroom could her splintered falsetto sound remotely bearable.

"Hey."

Nina jumps, opens her eyes to find Simone leaning through the shower curtain. She is naked, her long brown hair tied up behind in a messy knot, a smile lazing across her face. "Mind if I join the choir?" The question is moot; she's already stepping into the shower recess. Then they're kissing again, and Simone's tongue is in Nina's mouth, and Simone's hands are on Nina's breasts, and Simone's thigh is pressing into Nina's groin.

"How high can that voice of yours go?" Simone whispers, pushing her back against the tiles. Soap-slick fingers slide down where she burns most fiercely and Nina whimpers as they find their way between her folds. Her own hands grasp for Simone's shoulders as the woman kisses her hard, then soft, sawing Nina's lower lip gently between her teeth. Nina feels herself building, feels her whole body stretching thin and taut as violin string, and she moans, gives herself up to the play of expert hands.

Until brilliantly, blissfully, Nina breaks.

Still Simone holds her, supporting her weight until Nina's legs feel ready to work again. "I love you," Nina says, glad for the water that streams down her face and swallows her tears. "You're everything."

Simone squeezes her tight. "I love you too. So much." She reaches around and turns off the taps, pinches Nina lightly on the cheek. "How about we take this into the bedroom? Previews are over, my darling; time for the feature presentation."

. . . . .

Almost as soon as Nina drags herself into consciousness, she knows something is wrong. There's too much light in the room, the sun pushing its way through the cheap motel curtains as though they're made from mesh, and her stomach lurches. It's late, it's really fucking late. Simone's still sleeping, her head resting heavy on Nina's chest, one knee propped over Nina's thigh. Bare skin touching bare skin, in far too many places. As fast as she dares, Nina curls her arm around Simone's skull, taking care to keep her lover's thick swathe of hair between them.

"Simone," she says. "Wake up." Simone murmurs something unintelligible and starts to shift her position, but Nina holds her steady. "Don't move," she says. "We've slept in. I think we're cold."

Simone's fully awake now; Nina can feel her breathing start to speed.

"What do we do?" Simone whispers.

"We be quick."

And before the other woman can reply, Nina grabs a handful of hair and pulls Simone's head abruptly away. There's a too-brief tugging on her skin, like they're stuck together with superglue or worse, before something tears and Simone's shrieks in pain and surprise. Nina's feels burned—by frost, not fire—and when she risks a glance there's a raw, blistered patch of skin above her breast, glistening red in the sunlight. Simone's cheek looks even worse, torn and seeping like gravel rash, blood beading along her jawline.

"What about the rest of us?" Simone's voice breaks on the last word.

"It won't be as bad." Nina assures her, stuffing bits of sheet into the gaps between their bodies, assessing the places where there are none. "The way your head was resting on me, the weight of it, that made it worse. The rest is just touching, more or less. Not a lot of pressure."

"Are you saying I have a fat head?"

Simone's smile is so brave, so defiant, that Nina aches to hug her. Instead she offers a grin of her own—weak and falling down at the corners, but the best she can manage—then points down at their legs. "You need to move your knee now. Lift it up and off me, but quickly. Like with a Band-Aid, okay?"

"Or a wax strip."

— 144 —

"Only not as painful." They both know she is lying.

The second time seems worse than the first, maybe because they know what to expect, maybe because Simone is too cautious, too slow, and Nina has to pull her own leg away to finish the job. But the places where belly meets hip, where the back of an arm lies along the curve of a ribcage, hurt less to separate. Finally free, Simone rolls to the other side of the bed, shields herself with the blanket.

"I've got some antiseptic cream in my toiletries case." Cautiously, Nina pushes herself to her feet. "Some bandages, as well." A rudimentary first aid kit she's carried ever since their first careless touch—each of them cold as dry ice, forgetful as stone—that froze half of Nina's fingerprints away, and left marks like cigar burns on Simone's naked arm. They took weeks to heal.

Simone stares at Nina body, her gaze cataloguing the fresh red litany of wounds. "I can't believe we just fell asleep like that. If we'd woken up any later, if we'd gotten any colder—"

"Well, we didn't!" Her tone is too snappish; Simone bites her lip and looks away. "I'm sorry, Sim." Nina swallows. "I'll get the cream and stuff, okay?"

By the time she comes back, hands full of Savlon and gauze and cotton wool, Simone is up and packing her overnight bag. She's wearing the Chinese silk robe Nina bought her last month, turquoise blue with a phoenix rising on its back, but she's wearing it inside out.

"Come here," Nina says. "Let me fix you up."

Simone glares at her. "You can do that without touching me, can you?"

"As a matter of fact, I can."

The other woman shakes her head. "This has to end. Now."

Nina feels her stomach tumble for the second time that morning. "What are you talking about, Sim? What has to end?"

"Us." Her eyes are wet and pleading. "I can't do it anymore, Nina."

"But I love you." Right now, Nina would bear any amount of pain for the chance to touch Simone, the chance to hold her close and prove how much she loves her. She'd bear it gratefully—if she were the only one who would.

"I love you too," Simone says. "You know I do, but I can't live like this. Only being able to see you every few weeks, having to leave you again before the sweat's even dried on our skin—"

"So, we'll meet more often then. You're the one who wants to leave it so long each time; I'd be with you every night if you'd let me."

"You know that's impossible."

"Okay, maybe not *every* night, but three or four times a week if—"

"I'm not like you," Simone snaps. "I can't go out and pick people up the way you do, discard them like they're nothing. They're not nothing—they're people, they have lives of their own."

"Like the creep who did this, you mean?" Nina points to her forehead, which she knows looks even worse now than it did last night. "Bastards like him deserve what they get."

"Stop twisting everything I say. They're not all like that, not even most of them. You've said yourself, you feel sorry for them sometimes."

Nina narrows her eyes. "Do you know how many even bothered to ask my name? Trust me, all they cared about was how quick my panties could come off, and how soon they could boot me out the door afterwards."

"That doesn't make it right."

"It's not like they're dead, you know. It's not like we kill them."

"No, we just take what makes them human."

Nina laughs. She can't help it. "Their libido, Sim, their sex drive? You think *that's* what being human's all about?"

The other woman looks almost disappointed. "We take more than that and you know it. Warmth, heat, passion—whatever you choose to call it—that's what we take and that's what we squander every time we come to this horrible little room." She touches her cheek and winces. "I'm running out of justifications, Nina. Maybe I never had any to begin with."

"But last night . . ."

"Yes." Simone crosses the room and takes the medical supplies from Nina's hands, careful not to let their fingers touch. "I'm so sorry, Nina. I love you, I do, but everything else . . . it's too much. It's breaking me."

Nina sinks back down onto the bed, flinching at the pain that ripples along her flank. "You've been thinking about this a lot."

She doesn't really need an answer; the expression Simone wears is more than eloquent.

Closed, and contained. Final.

"Every day," Simone says. Hissing through clenched teeth, she smoothes cream over the raw patch of flesh on the inside of her knee.

"You can live like that?" Nina asks. "Being cold, all the time?"

"Yes."

"Being alone?"

Silently, Simone wraps gauze around her leg, around and around and around until there's nothing left to unroll. She tucks the end in tight and straightens, tests what little flex she has left in her knee. When she looks at Nina again, her eyes are red but dry. "Yes," she says. "I can live like that."

"Cold and alone, for the rest of your life?"

"You say it like we're the only ones." And there's nothing even remotely warm about the smile that hooks her mouth. "How hard can it be, Nina? After all, *it's not like we're dead.*"

Nina bows her head. There's a smear of blood on the carpet near her foot and it's this she stares at while listening to the other woman dress first her wounds and then herself. Because the way she's feeling right now—cold, yes; alone, oh a hundred times and forever, *yes*—she doesn't trust herself to look at Simone. Doesn't trust herself not to go to her and press their bodies together, to feel the freeze of skin between them and know that when they finally tear themselves asunder, it will be as bloody and messy and painful as her fractured, frostbitten heart.

. . . . .

Nina slides the room keys across the counter along with her credit card, pretends not to notice the receptionist pretending not to notice the bruises on her forehead.

"There's a late checkout fee," the woman says. "It's policy."

"Sure, whatever." She decides not to mention the bloodstained sheets; this kind of motel has probably seen worse. The woman processes her payment and puts the receipt on the counter for Nina to sign.

"I hope you enjoyed your stay."

There's an edge to her tone, a forced politeness only too familiar, but today Nina's skin is too thin to let it slide. "Is there a problem?"

The receptionist purses her prissy, middle-aged lips. "Generally, I don't give a rat's what you and your friend get up to when you come here, but there's some things I won't turn a blind eye to. Next time I call the police."

Nina blinks, confused. "I'm sorry?"

"That girl was the picture of health last night when she picked up her key. This afternoon I see her limp out of that room with her face all bandaged up like the Bride of Frankenstein." She points at Nina's head. "What happened, she decide to fight back?"

"You have no idea what you're talking about." Nina reaches out and snatches her credit card from the woman's hand. "Trust me, you have no fucking conception." She turns and slams through the reception door, trying to pretend she doesn't hear the bitch's reedy voice trailing after her—*I know someone who's been abused when I see them*—trying to pretend she doesn't care.

Less than two blocks from the motel, her hands are still shaking so badly she needs to pull over to the side of the road. Tears blur her vision, turn to ice on her cheeks. Nina tugs her mobile from her pocket, thumbs through to her most recent contacts and presses *call*. A recorded voice answers almost immediately—*the number you are calling is no longer in service*—and she gapes at the phone in disbelief. So soon?

Nina closes her eyes, tries to remember how Simone looked just before she left the motel room. Remorseful but resigned, shaking her head as Nina pleaded with her to stay.

There's no one else like us in the world, baby. We're all we have.

Then we have nothing. And we have to live with that too.

"Simone," she whispers, over and over and over again. Nina doesn't even know if that's her lover's real name; she never thought it important to ask.

Simone.

Solid as stone in her mouth, the word grows rapidly cold.

The Dark Night of Anton Weiss

D C White

AS the night wind wailed around the eaves of the old wooden house, Anton Weiss brooded. He did not brood over his lost love, though he had good cause. He did not brood because of the storm, though he could have. Rather, Anton Weiss brooded because he was in conflict.

Anton sat in the high-backed overstuffed chair, his black clothing melding into the night which surrounded him. Darkness was good for his soul, at least as he saw it, and he would need it. He shivered in the cold room. Tonight was Walpurgisnacht, and he was going to attempt something which would test his will and sanity to the utmost. For Anton the mania had begun over a year ago when the woman he loved, died. Lavinia had been his muse, his reason for living. Owing to the fortune left to him by his parents, Anton, having no job and fewer friends, slid into a morass of depression. He began to crave Lavinia's presence once more, to entertain thoughts of the afterlife. With a fervour he had not known he possessed, he returned first to Poe and Lovecraft, the books of his childhood, then to darker, more esoteric works. He had searched libraries the world over for them, books of black magic and forbidden lore. He secured an ancient copy of *De Vermiis Mysteriis* from a dealer in Prague, and even travelled to Arkham and the Miskatonic University to view their much-famed *Necronomicon*. He pored long over these dark, eldritch tomes, eventually reaching a conclusion which simultaneously thrilled and terrified him. He would speak to Lavinia again, though it would cost him dear. It had taken a year since then to amass the articles he needed: namely his beloved's belongings, all her clothes, and even the very house she had owned. It was in this house he now sat, his thoughts conflicted as he listened to the violence of the storm beyond the wooden walls. All was still within the room, the only noise save the shrieking of the wind, the heavy tick of the grandfather clock.

Anton sat, brooding. Behind him there came a rapping upon the door.

Quoth the raven, thought Anton, *nevermore*.

"Oi mate," yelled a voice from the hallway. "Are you going to be long in there?"

Anton sighed, the mood broken. He'd had his doubts about hiring the Australian occultist, but he was cheap and frankly, lost-love's-houses were not. Anton was, to his great embarrassment, not very good at black magic, which was why he had reluctantly called Terry Parkinson, Occultist and Roofer (Generous Rates for Pensioners).

"It's down the hall," Anton called back, his eyes rolling within his black mascara.

"I'm not after the dunny," Terry called back. "It's just that if you want to call up your sheila you'd better hurry; it's almost midnight."

Anton strode to the door, donning his black velvet cape on the way. "Ah yes," he told the occultist, "The witching hour. I do appreciate the occult significance, you know."

"Whatever. It's just that with this storm I expect the phone to start ringing any minute. Shingles aren't gonna hammer 'emselves back on y'know."

Anton sighed again, something which he didn't normally do but which had become quite frequent since the contractor had pulled up in his van this afternoon. Anton did not really know what an occultist would drive but he had been expecting something a little more stylish. As a mode of transport the 1982 Toyota Hiace had many things going for it, but panache was not one of them. What's more, the oaf had boxed Anton's hearse in.

In silence the pair walked downstairs to the drawing room. Here, Anton was pleased to see things looking more the part. A pentagram had been drawn on the floor in salt, and strange sigils had been inscribed on the walls. *This is more like it*, thought Anton as he rubbed his hands together.

"Righty-o Anty, you light the candles. I've got the kettle on." Terry moved off towards the kitchen.

Anton grimaced. He'd told the contractor early on he didn't want to be called 'Anty', but the Australian seemed to have a pathological hatred of any word not shortened with an '-o' or an 'ey'. Patience, he told himself, trying to calm down. *After tonight you never have to see him ever again.*

A thought occurred to Anton. "Why do you need the kettle on?" he called. "Is it to warm up the pig's blood?"

A laugh issued from the kitchen door, followed by Terry and a steaming mug. "No," he explained slowly. "It's to make tea with."

"Tea?"

"Yeah. I always get myself outside of a nice cup of tea before a summoning. Plus it's bloody freezing in here and those candles don't put out much heat."

Poe got Amontillado, but what do I get? A 'nice cup of tea'. Anton scowled as he bent over to light the first candle. Immediately he straightened up again. "Where are the candles?" he demanded.

"What, those pissweak little black ones you had? Useless as tits on a bull, they are."

Anton exploded. "I paid a lot of money for them at the Occult Fayre in Salem!"

Terry looked decidedly unimpressed and made a sort of 'phuff' noise with his lips. "And I bought these from Wal-Mart," he said, pulling a packet from the occasional table next to the doorway.

Anton stared in disbelief. "But they're just normal candles!" he shrieked.

"S'right," said Terry, opening the box and setting them at the points of the pentangle.

"Mine were black! And they had pentagrams inscribed on them!"

"And they were shit. One good occult blast and they'd be out. I've seen Force-five gales from the bowels of hell that couldn't knock these bastards out. Plus, they sell 'em in six-packs, which is handy if you drop one 'cause you've got a spare." Terry lit them with, Anton noted with disdain, a lighter in the shape of a naked lady whose nipples lit up.

There was a short pause as Terry slurped his tea noisily. "You right then?" he asked.

"Oh, you're going to start are you?" Anton muttered sulkily.

"Might as well." As the Australian put down his mug, KC And The Sunshine Band's "Shake Your Booty" began to emanate from him. "Shit. 'Scuse I," Terry muttered, and pulled out his mobile.

As he talked to someone who, it seemed likely, had just lost their roof, Anton inspected the pentagram and his former excitement began to surge back. He was finally going to see his beloved Lavinia again! Ever since her death he had yearned for her, and now, with the help of this pig of a man, he would communicate with her again. His heart soared and he clasped his hands to his breast.

"You right?" Terry asked again, depositing his mobile back in his pocket. "Have to get a wriggle on. That's two roofs up shit creek already tonight."

Anton's eyes gleamed in the candlelight. He was ready, at last. "What do you want me to do?" he asked.

"Stand in the corner and shut up," was not the response he had expected. Piqued, he did as he was told.

Terry stepped towards the pentagram, pulling a book from the pocket of his overalls as he did so. Anton strained to see in the dim light. What was that inscribed on the cover? Mystic runes? More eldritch sigils? His spirits sank as he glimpsed the word 'Spirax'. Outside the wind had risen until the walls began to creak. *As if,* Anton thought, *the very building were quaking!*

"Astul niggrauth chu'thon," Terry said, his nasal strine rather ruining the feel of the thing, "Bastu'rath ul unct'gro Hashopeth zarupeth Horeb!" He reached around to the side table and picked up a Tupperware container from which he drew a dead mouse. He threw the mouse into the pentagram. As soon as it landed, the floor, previously quite solid, disappeared, to be replaced by a hole from which a foetid wind spewed, oily and full of decay.

From the pit there came a growling which could be heard even over the shriek of the wind outside. Anton reeled, throwing his arm up over his face to counter the unexpected stench. He glanced over at Terry, to see him slurping his tea.

"Righty-o," Terry said. "What's your sheila's name again?"

"Lavinia. What is . . . is . . . is that?" Anton pointed to the spewing pit around which, he noted with distaste, the candles were still shining.

"Bloody hell." Terry rolled his eyes. "Haven't you ever seen the gates of hell before?" As Anton watched the Australian reached behind to the side table again and drew out another Tupperware container.

"What's in there?" Anton yelled over the roar of the wind.

"Mettwurst sandwich," Terry replied with a wink. "Important not to get the two containers mixed up." He took a bite. "Well," he said to Anton, nodding towards the gates of hell. "Get on with it then."

Anton steeled himself. "Lavinia!" he cried in anguish, "Lavinia my love! Come to me, Anton. I await you, my darling!" He placed his and to his brow theatrically.

Nothing happened.

"Shit a brick," said Terry. "You call that a yell? Let's have a go." He stepped to the edge of the pentagram. "Oi, Lavinia!" he yelled, making Anton flinch. "Y'in there?"

The room got suddenly very cold despite the heat which had been roiling from the pit. Anton could see the frost forming on the black velvet curtains. He felt rather than saw the presence enter the room.

"WHO SUMMONS THE SPIRITS OF THE DEAD?"

"G'day, it's me, Terry. Is Lavinia there?"

"LAVINIA WHO?"

Terry turned to Anton, stage whispering, "Lavinia who?"

Anton thought quickly. "Grokslant."

Terry laughed. "Really? Shit, eh? Oh well, none of my business." He turned back to the pit. "Lavinia Grokslant, apparently," he told whomever he was speaking to. Anton didn't like to ask.

"SHE IS HERE."

"Beautie. Could you get her for us? Sorry; I've got a lot on and it's a rush job."

"I'LL SEE WHAT I CAN DO."

The room returned to normal temperature. For a moment nothing happened save for Terry eating his sandwich. Then the flames of the five candles leapt up in the air, stretching from the wick to the ceiling. They bowed inward, each flame doing a complicated dance like the ribbons of a maypole until the weave they formed became the image of a human head.

Lavinia's head! Anton thought. He also thought about swooning, but decided against it.

"You have summoned me," the apparition said. "I am here."

Terry nudged Anton on the shoulder. "That her?" he asked around a mouthful of sandwich.

"Er, yes," Anton told him. He wasn't sure what to do. Truth be told he'd thought so much about getting to this point he hadn't given thought to what he was going to say. There was also the small matter that his love for Lavinia, whilst she was alive, had been less in the 'actual and realised' and more in the 'unrequited' category. Anton realised that he should have thought this through a bit harder.

"I'm waiting," said the ghostly flaming head of Lavinia.

"G'day," said Terry, pointing to Anton with his mug of tea. "This bloke here wanted to talk to you."

The apparition's gaze shifted to Anton. "Who are you?" it said. "Why have you summoned me?"

"Lavinia, it's me, Anton."

The apparition peered at him. Anton began to feel embarrassed.

"Oh, that's right. You were that odd one in English Lit."

"Er, yes," Anton forged onwards. "I have summoned you here, my love, because I wanted to tell you . . ."

"Tell me what?"

Anton swallowed. This was it, the moment he'd been waiting for. "Tell you in death what I could not tell you in life! Tell you that I . . . I love you, Lavinia, that I love you with all my heart!"

He stood before the flaming head in the pentagram, his soul stripped bare.

"What, you?" The apparition laughed. "Mr Black-Clothes-That-Always-Smelled-Like-Mothballs?"

While this was not quite what he had been expecting, Anton wasn't prepared to stop there. *In for a penny, in for a pound*, he thought as he struck a tragic pose, going down on one knee. "My dear, my love, if you only knew what efforts I have taken to contact you!"

The apparition rolled its eyes. "Alright," it conceded. "I'll give you that. As far as proving your love goes, raising the spirits of the dead gets you on the table."

"Good," said Anton.

There was a pause.

"Well?" said the apparition.

"Well what?" replied Anton.

"You've told me you love me. Is there anything else you wanted to get off your chest?"

As far as Anton was concerned spirit summoning had not been all it was cracked up to be. "I don't know, but you're here now and we should make the most of it, I think."

"You can't come inside the pentagram and I can't come out. In any case I'm composed entirely of the flames of Hell right now so a kiss is probably out of the question."

Anton decided to show off. "Look around, my love," he told her with a smirk. "Recognise anything? This is your house. I bought it just to summon you in!"

The apparition's eyes narrowed. "You bought my old house?"

"Yes," replied Anton. "And all of your things. As many as I could get hold of."

The flames surged suddenly and the apparition seemed to grow. "If you have indeed bought my old house," it cried. "Then three things must you know . . ."

Aha! thought Anton, *this is more like it*!

"Yes?" he asked, "And what are these three things?"

The apparition fixed him firmly in its fiery gaze. "First," it intoned. "If you want to stop the tap in the laundry from banging you must turn it on then off again quickly, then on slowly."

"Oh," said Anton, crestfallen but still hopeful. "Alright, um . . . I'll make sure I do that. What else?"

"Beware the tree at the bottom of the garden."

"What of it? Is it haunted?"

"No. It's a Dutch elm. It needs mulching once every six months and spraying to prevent fungus on the leaves."

Anton scowled, stood up and dusted his knees off.

"Well, this has been a complete waste of time," he said to no-one in particular. "I'm about ready to wrap things up."

"Hold!" the apparition shrieked, its image swelling until it filled the confines of the pentagram. "One last thing must you know."

"Oh, really?"

"Its importance cannot be understated."

Despite himself, Anton was interested. "Yes?"

The apparition frowned. "Beware Fridays," it intoned gravely. "Neglect them at your peril!"

"Oh my god! Why? Why? What will happen?" Anton cried, his mind awhirl at the possibilities.

"It's bin night."

Phantom Lover

Donna Maree Hanson

IT was midnight and swirls of light mist curled around Kayla's boots as she strode down Mort Street. The frost bit at her nose and ears so she pulled the collar of her black leather coat higher, hoping to trap the warmth between her chin and neck. Her gaze ranged around the street, checking for signs of disturbances as she headed for her patrol at the bus interchange.

Beneath a flickering streetlight on the other side of the road, an unkempt man lay slumped to one side. The man's complexion appeared grey in the bluish glow, indicating he might be fading fast. Jogging across the road, she lowered her visor and began scanning for signs. She saw faint traces of movement and a pale green radiance. Honing in on the apparition, her visor revealed a small demon sucking on the man's life source. If she didn't do something the man would be dead by morning, showing nothing but signs of hypothermia.

Kayla pulled out her laser pointer and zapped the nebulous creature with a burst of concentrated light. It gave a surprised squeak before dematerialising. Checking over her shoulder, she made sure that there were no more minor demons around, or worse a major or two. Then she retracted the visor and knelt down. Her foot dislodged an empty wine bottle and it rolled away to clang and clink into the gutter. Thankfully, he didn't smell bad. Maybe he wasn't a habitual street bum, she thought. Possibly, he got drunk and felt the need to sleep it off. It wasn't a long step from that to falling prey to one of the mean beasties that lurk on Canberra streets.

She shook the man on the shoulder and he roused, burping loudly in her face. He opened his eyes and gaped at her.

Nodding once, she said, "Keep moving. Head home, okay? It's not safe out here."

The man rolled onto all fours and groggily climbed to his feet. He mumbled something as he lurched toward Cooyong Street and a taxi rank.

Kayla brushed off her hands and turned down the street, crossing Bunda Street toward the nearly deserted interchange. A bus engine idled. In the distance, youths called to each other, intermingled with a girl's laughter. The clubs hadn't closed yet. She worried for the young: drink, drugs and vulnerability made them easy prey. The little demons were easily dealt with if you knew how, if you acknowledged that they existed, which most people didn't. A laser pointer usually shooed them away, a charm warded against them, but the larger ones? No laser pointer was going to shift them. Best not let them attach in the first place. Big, juicy and mean, they gained an edge when humans indulged their darker sides.

Kayla continued her lonely patrol up Alinga Street, past the piss smelling bus shelters and stepping over patches of dried vomit. A street vendor was still open selling greasy slices of pizza, dripping with pepperoni and congealed cheese. There was a short queue there—an older man and a skinny teen in a raggy t-shirt and few swaying older drunks. The bus revved its engine and the teen peeled away from the queue and jumped through the door of the bus as it snapped shut.

Kayla turned back at the corner of Northbourne Avenue and traversed the interchange again. She felt movement to the side of her and swung around, jumping back slightly in surprise. There was a face hovering there, a handsome, smiling face. Then as she looked, an image of a man took shape. He was tall, thin, wearing a long dark coat, similar to hers. Immediately, she dropped the visor over her eyes to scan him. Nothing. She flicked it up away from her eyes and stared. The man was gone. There was no trace of what she had seen and no evidence whether he was some kind of spirit or major demon.

Kayla chanted a spell, hoping to find traces of the apparition's passage. The space was empty, devoid of any vibrations or afterglow. She stood gaping, rattled by the appearance. She shuddered before moving off to continue her patrol, tempted to call in the sighting. Yet what could she say? There was no evidence of anything except an active imagination.

On autopilot, she checked for demons in the dark doorways and smelly drains, as she pondered the strange apparition. It had not appeared aggressive or unfriendly, but that could be deceiving. As she neared the corner of Mort Street on completing the circuit, she saw a tall man in a bright green hoodie. She recognised the stance and the hunch of the shoulders. It was Henry Buchanan, a wannabe patroller. He had never quite made the grade—not enough 'psi' for him to register for duty, not enough courage to brave the elements, or so the rumour mill had it. Sometimes he came to keep watch anyway, not accepting the academy's decision. He always seemed to do it when she was on duty.

"Hi, Henry."

"Are you okay? I saw you start a minute ago."

Kayla shrugged and felt herself blushing. "I thought I saw something. You didn't see anything unusual did you?"

Henry's mouth gaped and he pointed to his chest. "Me? No. Didn't see a thing. You want me to keep you company?"

Kayla narrowed her gaze, annoyed that he implied she was afraid. "No, no I'm fine. See you around."

She turned away and tried not to shrug. Something about that encounter made her cranky. Freaking out unnecessarily was one thing, being seen doing it was another thing all together. It hadn't always been like this in Canberra. Five years previously, some dark cult opened a portal on top of Mount Ainslie and next thing anyone knew the occasional instances of drunken violence had turned more serious and frequent. Street people turned up dead, cold as ice and slumped in gutters with increasing regularity.

It took a while for the connection between the cult's activities and the strange occurrences to be established. A huge manifestation above Parliament House made most people realise that the capital was infested with demonkind. Now there were patrollers, and 'psi' ability and guts were prerequisites for enlisting. Kayla liked to think she had more than a bit of both.

. . . . .

She headed up London Circuit and stood in front of Club Y, her gaze sweeping the car park opposite and then the deserted doorways on her right. A screech of brakes at the intersection distracted her. She turned her head, catching sight of a car avoiding a pedestrian. Before she could react, the club doors flew open with a loud commotion and a heavy body knocked her over. It was the best she could do to stop herself from hitting her head on the pavement as she came down. A large man rolled off her, shook his head and screamed. Then he lumbered to his feet, bellowing as if his hair was on fire.

Kayla tried to climb to her feet. She was shaken and felt dizzy. The burly man tried to stamp on her, thumping the ground near her with his big work boots. She shuffled backwards to get away. She pulled out her laser if only to distract him, but fumbled. It rolled into the gutter and she followed close behind, using her momentum to get up. Lunging to her feet, she swung around at the last minute to block a hit. The guy was enraged, unnaturally so, as if she had run him down and not the other way round. He was strong too. Blocking him had bruised her arm.

Dropping her visor, Kayla swore, when she saw the large stream of green power flaring above the man's head. Latched onto him was a major, a real nasty beast who was trying to take the man over and create as much havoc as possible. To give the guy credit, he was fighting it off. Kayla backpedalled to the traffic island, while rummaging in her coat pocket for her phone. She pressed the emergency number. In two rings, it answered. "Major incursion in progress at London Circuit and Northbourne. A rather large man way out of control and coming for me, driven by a very nasty major."

"You hurt?"

"Slightly injured, but I'm well out of my league. I've not seen one this strong before."

"On it. Help will be there in five. Stall and stay out of danger."

Kayla clicked off the phone with a grunt. Over the sound of the man's howls of rage, she heard another voice. It was coming around the corner. Another man came into view, flailing his arms and hollering loudly. His green hoodie glowed eerily. The visor revealed nothing to her sight. Must have been electric or some kind of radioactive paint creating the visual effect, she thought. Bystanders gathered, some yelling at the show.

"Henry?" She stepped forward, her hand outstretched. "Stay back. It's too dangerous." She was too far away to intercept him.

Henry ignored her and kept running at the man fighting demon possession.

"Bugger." Kayla shut her eyes at the moment of impact. Henry had been screaming some kind of chant and, then when he hit the man, there was a loud detonation. Kayla opened her eyes to see two bodies on the pavement, bathed in the flashing lights of an approaching police car. Through her visor, she checked the man, who lay still but breathing on the pavement. From the angle of his arm, she'd say he'd broken it when he fell. There was no sign of the major, except for a faint aftertaste of burnt tar in the air.

Henry lay still and dazed on his back. "Stupid dork," she whispered under her breath. She felt his head to check for a wound. Nothing. Then she ran her hands down his arms and legs checking for breaks. He sucked in a breath and then another, as if he had died and come back to life.

Kayla felt tears prick her eyes. The stupid man was always trying to look out for her, and now was in trouble himself.

An ambulance pulled up with a whirr of siren. First, the paramedics checked the demon target and then one came over to Henry. As soon as the paramedic touched his arm, Henry sat up. He gaped stupidly at the prone man, now free of his major demon, and blinked.

"You okay sir?" asked the paramedic.

Henry gaped some more and then spoke. "I'm fine. I must have slipped. Will he be all right do you think?"

"I think so. You're sure you didn't hit your head or something?"

"No, I'm fine. Really." He pushed Kayla's hands away and stood up. "See?"

He turned away from her and took a few steps. "Hey wait," Kayla called out, unable to hide her annoyance. "You can't walk away. We have to talk about what happened."

Henry turned back and lifted his hood to cover his head. "Cold out isn't it? Nothing happened. I slipped, that's all."

"Aw bullshit. If you don't tell me what is going on with you, I'm never speaking to you again. So spill."

He kept walking. Kayla stood there, hands on her hips and foot tapping. When he turned the corner, she felt like screaming. Grinding her teeth, she turned away and bumped into her boss Great timing. Mike Taylor: cute but cold. She tried not to react to him, tried not to let her attraction to him show.

"You reported an injury. Show me."

"I've got nothing but a few scrapes. He caught me off guard. I'm fine now."

Mike shook his head. "Not fine. You were hurt and could have been killed. Be more careful next time. I'm taking you off duty for two days."

"What?"

"You will take a short course in major demons, the signs and treatments before you return to duty. The course starts in," he checked his watch. "Seven hours. Suggest you go home and get ready for it."

Kayla dropped her gaze. "Yes, sir." She turned on her heel and headed back to her city apartment in Mort Street. She was bitching angry but let it go. Negative emotions were a real draw card for demons and she was in no mood to deal with them right then. Her boss was right, she needed to have remedial sessions for that botch up.

When she returned home, she saw someone loitering at the entrance to her apartment building. As she drew closer, she recognised Henry. She walked right past him, too angry to talk.

On seeing her, he raced over. "I'm sorry. I couldn't talk to you with Taylor standing there. I had to get away. He's already warned me off patrol a few times already."

She paused and looked over her shoulder at him. "Taylor's warned you off? Do you mean you track other patrols besides mine?"

He looked down. "No. Well sometimes. I think his real beef lately is that I enrolled in an online 'psi' development course and he found out about it."

Kayla felt some unease. Not that she thought he was lying, exactly, more that there was a niggling sense of truth in his words. Taylor had been keeping an eye on him, for sure.

"I see. Well I'd better go up now. I've been stood down for two days."

Henry moved forward, a shy smile on his face. "Want to have a coffee or something and I'll tell you about what happened?"

Kayla nodded and opened the door for them. "I'll make coffee while you talk. And no funny business."

Henry followed her into her apartment—a Spartan one bedroom with modern touches. She ground coffee and put on the cafetera.

Her guest checked out the room and the view to the street from the large window. "Sit down and tell me what is going on."

He sunk into one of the sofas as Kayla pulled down two mugs from the cupboard. "I've been studying the art of demon fighting and doing 'psi' strengthening exercises."

"But I . . . well, I thought you didn't have 'psi' abilities. The test, it . . ."

"Mmm . . . Taylor tell you that, did he? Interesting, because I had myself tested independently and the results were different to what the academy told me."

The cafetera bubbled coffee into the server and she poured it out into the mugs, chewing her lower lip.

What Henry revealed warred with her sense of justice. She believed him but found it hard to credit her boss having been involved with something underhand. The patrol needed people with 'psi' abilities. The academy couldn't afford to lock people out for no good reason. It didn't add up.

She passed him his coffee and sat on the opposite sofa. "Tell me, is there a history with you and Mike?"

"Not much of one. We went to Grammar together. Not really friendly or anything."

Kayla sipped her coffee and hugged the mug with her hands. There was something Henry wasn't saying.

"Tonight then. What was that chant you were spouting when you hit the major?"

"A standard warding, sung in Latin."

"But it had so much power behind it. I don't get how you could do that without—"

Her phone rang and she answered it. "Hello. Oh, yes, boss. I will set my alarm. No, I'm all alone." She looked at the phone and avoided meeting Henry's gaze. "Night."

Kayla felt herself blush. Why did Mike Taylor suddenly take an interest in who she was keeping company with? Her gaze met

Henry's and then he shrugged. After downing his coffee hurriedly, he stood up. "Better go and let you rest."

She put out a hand to pat him on the shoulder and accidentally touched his cheek. A bolt of power rocked her. "What in heaven's name is that?"

Henry paused and shrugged again, blushing very red. "Sexual attraction?" Then he laughed.

Perturbed, she studied his face. Avoiding meeting her gaze, he hurried out. She held the door open and watched him descend the stairs quickly. He had to be joking, she thought.

Kayla felt the tingles in her fingertips from where she had touched the dweeby Henry. Something strange was definitely going on.

After a long shower, which helped to soothe her aches and clean her scrapes, she crawled into bed around 2.30am. Immediately, dreams engulfed her. The phantom came to her, more fully realised than the previous glimpse of him at the interchange. The way he moved and smiled teased her senses, she felt herself respond to him.

In the dream, they were in her bed. He caressed her, kissed her and touched her hot, naked skin. Her nipples hardened and her sex moistened. She wanted him hard and fast inside her. Part of her mind wanted to break free, scared that this was some kind of demon, an incubus, sent to prey on her. The phantom talked to her softly but she could not understand him. They were sing-song words of a chant.

The piercing tone of the alarm rapidly dispelled the dream and the phantom from her mind. Gasping in her bed, she felt an intense arousal still. Cracking open her eyelids, she practically ran into the shower and used the hand held nozzle to bring on the pending orgasm. Leaning on the wall of the cubicle, she panted as the ecstasy washed over her in shuddering waves. Her knees buckled and she slid to the floor, letting the water wash over her until it went cold.

. . . . .

Later, in the training room, she found it hard to focus. Even chocolate and coffee did not improve her energy or concentration levels. At the lunch break, she shut herself up in the research library, trying to diagnose what was preying on her without success. She wasn't suffering the right symptoms for possession or even a demon sending.

At the afternoon break, the lecturer, Mr Lealand, asked her to go to administration and select some case files for the class to go through in the afternoon session. Pushing open the office door, she saw that Taylor was out and only the young receptionist, Jodie, was around. "Lealand sent me to collect some files from the cabinet. Can you show me which ones?"

Jodie waved at a bank of six filing cabinets and dived for the ringing phone. With a shrug, Kayla headed to the back of the office and opened a drawer. In the third, she found the files she wanted. She pulled out eight and put them on a nearby desk. As she was pushing it closed, she saw a familiar name written on one of the files in the drawer—Henry Buchanan. Why was it sitting with the other case files, not the confidential personnel files?

Checking that Jodie was otherwise occupied and that Taylor had not returned, she slid the drawer back open and pulled the file. Her heart beat hard in her chest. She was breaching Henry's privacy and who knew how many academy rules. Curiosity won out. A quick flick and it opened on his entry test scores. She slammed the folder shut and shoved it back in the drawer. Sweat beaded on her upper lip as she grabbed the other files and headed back to the training room.

.....

*H*enry had an incredible 'psi' rating and his test overall said he was highly suited to patrol. Why then was he not recruited? On the surface of it, Henry had been unfairly treated, but what could she do about it? If she spoke up, they would know that she had looked in a file she had no business with. Lying about it was out of the question.

"Kayla?" Taylor spoke from down the hall, as she was about to go in. She started and jerked her hand back from the door handle. She turned, tried not to blush and failed dismally.

"Hey boss. In a rush, I have to get these files to Mr Lealand."

"I won't keep you. Come see me after class and we'll have a chat at Gus' Cafè."

"Sure." Kayla escaped into the classroom and sat there brooding. Taylor had never been chummy before. A one-on-one with Mike Taylor would have been a dream when she first started at the academy. Now it made her edgy. She was no wiser about what was plaguing her. If it was an incubus, she'd have to be quarantined and she hated the idea of that. There would be an investigation too, into how she had attracted one and what behaviour she had been engaging in. Not that she had been doing anything dangerous or even risky. It was the investigation itself and all the rumour and innuendo the process brought with it.

There was no official way to investigate her circumstances, not without alerting her boss or the board of the academy.

When she arrived at the cafè, Taylor already sat in a cosy corner table. As she sat down, a coffee arrived for her, exactly how she normally had it. She blinked away her surprise and thanked the waiter. Next, a plate of warm apple crumble appeared with a huge lashing of whipped cream and ice cream.

"Oh? Is that for me?"

"Yes, unless you want to share."

Kayla felt uncomfortable. The shift from handsome, aloof boss to friendly man, ready to share a dessert, unnerved her. She shoved a spoonful of crumble into her mouth and then gulped some cafè lattè.

"So how are things going with you? No ill effects from last night?"

Kayla swallowed another mouthful of food before answering. She wondered if he meant the strange apparition or the demon. "I'm fine, really. Is there a problem?"

"No problem. Just want to make sure my star girl is doing okay."

She looked at her plate, suddenly not hungry at all. A movement at the door caught her eye. She spotted Henry standing there, looking right back at her and then his gaze travelled to Mike Taylor.

"What the fuck is he doing here?" said Taylor from next to her.

Looking from Henry to Taylor, she said. "It's a public place and a popular cafè. No grand plan there."

Taylor checked himself. He'd half risen out of his chair and let himself sit back down again. Henry changed his mind about coming in and went further down Garema Place. She didn't like the look of betrayal in his face. She didn't owe Henry anything. They had no understanding, no relationship other than friends, but she was certain now there was something, some history between these two men.

While she finished off her snack, Taylor talked to her about the academy. He didn't particularly seem interested in a response so she got away with muttering 'uh huh' in the right places and finished off her food. Then she checked her watch and dug out her purse.

"You need to be somewhere?"

"Well I thought I shouldn't take up too much of your time. Besides, I have some homework to do. Tomorrow is the second day of training."

He nodded. "Don't be ridiculous. Put your purse away. I ordered the food and drink and I'll pay for it."

"Well . . . er thank you. And thanks for the chat too. Bye."

Kayla did her best not to dive for the door and run up the street to her apartment. She saw no sign of Henry, so she quickly headed home. Something was very odd. Was she being silly being on edge because her boss was giving her friendly overtones?

A blood-orange sunset lit the sky, sending peachy hues overhead. Was it too late to go visiting? Without giving herself a chance to change her mind, she flagged a cab. "Mawson please. Wilkins Street." She let out a huge breath and thought about what she was going to ask her grandmother. Kayla had inherited her 'psi' ability from her maternal grandmother. Gran was a soothsayer, a clairvoyant and the only hope she had of finding out about the apparition without making it official.

Using her spare key, she pushed open the door.

"Gran? Are you home? Are you decent?" Her grandmother liked to wear wraps, which at times left little to the imagination, much to Kayla's embarrassment when she'd been a teenager.

"Kayla, baby. So good to see you." Her grandmother walked in from the garden room in track pants and matching top. Kayla relaxed when she saw the conventional attire. After hugging her grandmother, she said, "Gran, I need your help and on the quiet like. Is tonight a bad time to do some scrying?"

Her grandmother frowned. "Are you okay, baby? Tonight is fine, but we can start now while the night and day are in flux. I'm worried about you. You don't often seek my gifts to help you out."

"I know but this is kind of delicate." While her grandmother made herbal tea, Kayla told her about the apparition.

"Mmm . . . we'll I have to do a bit of a ritual and you too. I'll need to make sure the lines around you are quite clear."

It took over an hour for her grandmother to prepare, while Kayla meditated and inhaled purifying incense.

They started and, within a few minutes, her grandmother spoke.

"It's not an incubus or a demon sending."

Kayla nodded and didn't speak, afraid to break her grandmother's concentration. Relief flooded through her.

"Ah I see something. Strong emotion. Love. Someone loves you quite strongly. There are traces of protection; a sigil of warding has been drawn around you. Whoever did this wants to keep you safe." The old woman lifted an eyebrow. "Strong willed and powerful too, but not well trained."

Kayla blinked. Was it her boss? Was that creepy or really quite touching? "Who is it? Can you tell?"

"I cannot say who, only that I sense he is prevented from speaking his heart to you. The phantom lover is his true self, the image of what he wants you to see in him as well as the desire in him.

"When you find him, you will find this love he has for you and the phantom lover will merge back with he who created it."

"So he made it to follow and torment me?"

Her grandmother opened her eyes and flicked incense smoke around the room to clear the energy. "I do not think he knows he has created this phantom. I cannot be sure but it could be unconsciously done. He may dream of you, think of you perhaps, and the phantom appears beside you. He is very strong in 'psi'."

. . . . .

The phantom arrived sometime near morning. She wasn't sure of the exact time, just that sense she had been asleep for hours. Again his soft voice caressed her along with his mouth and hands. The phantom's presence was gaining in strength. She could almost feel the muscles moving under his skin as he lay on her, rubbing his hard cock against her.

How did it feel so intense? She wanted to bite and scratch him and she wanted to pull his hair and make him kiss her. She wanted to taste the hunger she suspected he had for her. She wanted a declaration, a clue as to who he was.

Again in the shower, she trembled as the orgasm seized and slowly released her. Every nerve ending felt alive. She dressed and headed to Garema Place, hoping to grab breakfast from Cafè Essen. She'd just sat down when Mike Taylor walked in and plonked himself down next to her. Her gasp of surprise was quickly converted to a "Good morning".

Freshly shaved, she could detect a slight whiff of aftershave. It didn't tease her senses. She didn't warm to him. Her mind and heart was captivated by the phantom. Did the phantom come from him? She shuddered.

"Sleep well, Kayla?" he asked before ordering a long black coffee.

She hesitated. Had her own idle lust for him snagged his attention, washed over him so that he desired her? Was it because of her that this phantom had been born? Great, she thought. The only way to be rid of the phantom was to meet its conjurer.

"Well, thanks," she said and took a sip of her coffee. When she had first started at the academy, she hadn't failed to notice that he was on friendly terms with at least one female patroller. That must have fizzled out because she had seen him with Macie a few months later. She'd stopped noticing after that as he always ignored her and barely spoke to her, except to criticise.

The more she knew him the less she liked him. Playing favourites was his game and she'd never been the one to catch his notice. He touched her hand lightly then squeezed it. "Good to hear. We have to look after you don't we?"

Kayla stilled as his other hand slid up her knee along her inner thigh. Without thinking, she leaped up, spilling her coffee all over the table. The milky brown puddle gushed into his lap.

"Oh God, I'm so sorry."

He mopped at his lap with a serviette, cursing loudly. Kayla checked her watch. "Gee look at the time. Got to run or I'll be late for class." She ducked out of the cafè, forgetting to pay her bill. Rather than go back, she rang the cafè on her mobile and left a message to say she would pop back in and left them her details. Her heart beat frantically. What once might have been a dream come true filled her with revulsion. How could he touch her up like that?

Could she go to class at the academy knowing that he might accost her again? She didn't know what to do. What if that bloody phantom was him? She felt so ill she didn't think she could face training. Changing directions, she headed back to her apartment.

A voice calling her name prompted her to increase her pace and she tried not to break into a jog.

The voice sounded closer, she was tempted to turn around when the phantom appeared. He chanted softly at her. "Stop it!" she screamed and then broke into a run. The phantom kept pace with her, his gaze ranging around them. He frowned and looked worried. She slowed her steps and looked behind her. Henry jogged along behind her and slowed when she stopped running.

"Are you okay? You seem upset," he said as he came up heaving breaths.

Tears fell then, stupid hot tears that made her feel terribly embarrassed. Henry stepped forward, trying not to touch her but she threw herself on his shoulder and sobbed. The tingling sensation on touching him added to her confusion. She blurted out what had happened, her words muffled by his shirt. As she let the story tumble out, he spoke soothingly to her. "It's all right. You'll be fine. We'll sort it out. It's okay baby. Okay."

Eventually she quietened and, flushing, tried to look away. A shadow loomed behind them. It was her boss, his fists balled tight, angry snarl on his lips.

"Kayla? Is this guy bothering you?"

Henry turned around, putting himself between Kayla and Mike Taylor.

"I might ask you that same question. I saw what happened in the cafè, you pervert."

Taylor blustered with his fists. "You nosy little fucker. I'll fix it so you will be run out of town, telling your little tales. Don't think I've forgotten what you did. Snitch."

Kayla found anger had replaced shame and fear. "Leave off, Mike. Henry is my friend and he can touch me anytime I want him to. You, on the other hand, have no right to come on to me. None."

"Come on, don't be like that. I know you have the hots for me. Don't you think I don't smell your arousal when you're near. You want me, want me right now in fact."

He made to grab her arm but Henry was there. Power shot out of his palm, knocking Taylor backwards into the gutter. "Leave her alone. I'm going to report you. The academy will be investigating this little incident."

From the ground, Taylor continued to hurl insults. "What? You don't think they'd listen to a crank like you, do you? You're nothing. Just a gutless little snitch. Pathetic and weak. You couldn't bed a woman if you tried."

He climbed to his feet, ready to lunge at Henry, when a car pulled up. Kayla blinked. Two board members from the academy were inside. They stepped out. "Mr Taylor?"

Mike turned and gaped. "Mr Snodgrass, er . . . and James?"

"Would you be so kind as to come with us please? We have some things we'd like to discuss."

With a shallow dip of his head, Mr Snodgrass nodded to her and then to Henry. Taylor climbed into the car with them and they could hear what he was saying. "I don't know what you've heard, but that geek is a snivelling little twerp. He's always had it in for me since school. And that little tart, well she tried to touch me up. Imagine that . . ."

The car pulled away from the curb. His voice died away as they drove off. Kayla clenched her teeth. She felt like punching her boss. Hopefully, her former boss.

When she drew her gaze away from the receding car, Henry smiled at her and held up his phone. "I was watching from the other side of the cafè and called it in. I hope you don't mind."

Kayla started to shake. Henry frowned. "Come on. I'd better get you upstairs. You look like you could do with a good long bath and a nice cup of tea."

Kayla nodded and pulled out her key.

. . . . .

*I*n her apartment, she sat in a daze, with her legs curled up underneath her. Her mug of hot tea cooled in her hand. Henry sat opposite her.

"So tell me what happened just then? I know something did but it is not making much sense. Taylor called you a snitch and you called him a pervert. I thought you said there was no history between you two."

Henry blushed. "What could I say? He had been accused of sexual harassment at the academy and also prior to that, maybe worse. He raped a girl I knew when we were in college and he got away with it. It never showed on his record. The girl killed herself rather than face him in court."

Kayla took a sip of tea, feeling warm and glad that she had escaped. "Funny how someone can appear so nice, but hide such coldness, such heartlessness. How did he get to be head of the academy with a history like that?"

Henry frowned. "That is still being looked into. I've been told that he forged his test results. He has some 'psi' ability of course, enough to fudge his way through."

"Test results. Oh, God. I'm so sorry. I saw yours. I didn't go looking for them, but I saw them in a filing cabinet. Not in the confidential files mind you."

He sat forward. "You found them? Where?"

She described the cabinet, position of the file in the drawer. Henry dialled a number and relayed the location to someone on the other end.

"Thank you," he said and hung up. "We've been looking for those. We think Taylor switched the results."

"So you do have strong 'psi' ability?"

"Like I said, I had myself independently tested. I wrote to the board of the academy and asked them to investigate. They could find no record of my test, only the score recorded on my computer file. They've been investigating Taylor for a few weeks now."

"And inadvertently stumbled on him trying to feel me up?"

Henry put his head in his hands. "I'm so sorry. I wanted to protect you, wanted to keep you safe. I'm such a failure. Did he hurt you much?"

"You wanted to protect me? Why?"

Henry looked up, his face stricken. "Well, you're a good patroller and I, er . . . admire you, I guess."

Kayla nodded. "I see. Henry Buchanan, you don't happen to be in love with me do you?"

His dark gaze met hers. She saw his Adam's apple bob as he swallowed. He didn't speak. She edged herself onto the carpet and moved over to him. Taking his unresisting hand in hers, she lifted it, kissing it gently.

"Kayla?"

"Yes, Henry? You were saying?"

"I . . . er . . . um . . ."

She reached up and cupped his chin. His eyes widened then she kissed his lips. At first his mouth was unresponsive and then he engulfed her in a hug and a searing kiss, a kiss she recognised.

His phone rang. She sighed. "Answer it. Go on."

With a nod, he pressed the receive button. "Hello, Buchanan speaking. Yes, mmm. Yes. I'll be there first thing tomorrow. Thank you."

"So . . . ?"

A big smile lit his face. "I start accelerated training tomorrow morning." Still kneeling in front of him, she hugged him tight. He pulled back suddenly wary. Reaching out, she held his face between her hands and gazed into his face. Her lips brushed his softly and she revelled in the tingling his touch aroused. The heat in her surged. She wanted him.

"Henry?" she asked as she pulled back.

His eyes were shut and his face was relaxed. "Have you ever dreamed of making love with me?"

"Oh God, yes."

"I thought so." She undid her shirt. "Take your clothes off."

His eyes flew open and his gaze was fixed on her as she stripped. Then she reached over and helped him tug his shirt off. She ran her hands over his naked body while he ran his hands over hers, pausing to admire her breasts. Their eyes met. She saw the burning passion in his gaze. She knew then for certain, knew that Henry was her phantom lover.

It was in his eyes, in his smile and in his kiss. Her grandmother said that once she found his love, her phantom would disappear. She thought not. There would always be part of the phantom in her Henry. Should she tell him about it? Tell him about the creature he had conjured with his love and desire? She thought not. It would be her little secret.

Hunting Rabbits

Annette Backshall

SILVA was caught during the moon's third quarter. They sniffed her out of her hiding place in the burnt out hollow of an oak. And with her own silly dog no less. Damned animal was all tail and tongue when he found her. Silva growled her disapproval at him for leaving the cabin. His ears dropped for a moment, though his tail didn't falter dusting everything around it.

"Kuche," she whispered, wrapping her arms around his huge neck. He licked her face. "Did you ever hear the saying, 'I had a dog, he helped the wolf'?" The men weren't so pleased with the finding game. Silva smelt their sour anger under the pungent ripeness of days-old sweat. Two separate bands had tramped through the maze of elm, oak and ash with about as much subtly as bears amongst garbage bins for a day and a night. She'd been as quiet as the red deer, as cunning as the grey wolf, only to curse their blind luck under anxious breaths.

A squat, hairy Turk and his skinny fair-haired companion used the light of the waning moon to pick their way down through a tangle of roots towards her. A vicious looking gun swung this way and that on the Turk's hip. He stumbled and skinned a shin on a root spitting curses at her in at least four different languages. She took a step back.

"Stay there," he said in Bulgarian.

She licked her lips and glanced at his gun. *I can't outrun bullets*, she thought. Kuche whined and bumped against her thigh as the Turk came close. She glanced down and put a hand on Kuche's head to calm him. As she looked back, a knuckled ball of anger smashed her face.

Her head snapped back, constellations wheeled. Silva heard Kuche snarl, felt his fur brush past her. There was an explosion of light and sound, a thud against her side, pressure, warmth, fur and moisture. She and Kuche fell back into her hiding hole, her dog landing half on top as she hit the leaf-littered floor. The ringing in her ears receded and she heard Kuche panting hard and whining, felt his weak legs kicking out, trying to rise. Silva smelt the metallic signature of blood. Was it hers or her hound's? She looked down. A hole gaped in her pet's chest. She got a hand beneath herself and tried to rise. Her head spun. She had to think. How could she save her dog? Was the vet in the village today? What day was it?

She heard a rustle of clothes, boots on leaves. Her arm was in a vice and her body yanked up, out from under her struggling companion.

"Kuch'! Kuche!"

Kuche tried to rise, his feet pawing the air. He made soft wheezing noises between quick shallow breaths and whimpered.

Silva pulled back towards her friend. "My dog! Let me go. I'll kill you, you bastard!" She snarled, turned and clawed at the thing that held her.

"You couldn't kill a flea, bitch! Stop it!"

"I'm coming, Kuch—"

. . . . .

The smell of fear, brine and diesel filled Silva's nose as she awoke, almost smothering the subtle feminine tones that drifted under the harshness. A petite round face framed by a waterfall of blonde hair swayed above her through the dim light. A hesitant smile smoothed the girl's brow. She touched Silva's hair with long soft strokes, brushing back the veil of dull pain that fogged her thoughts. The room surged and pitched.

Silva started up. They were on the floor of a small, bunked cabin. An array of wide-eyed young women stared down at her. Some huddled together in clumps of arms and legs, others sat apart, appendages folded in on themselves.

"No," she whispered. "No, no, no, no, no."

Silva's head spun. Gentle hands guided her back to the soft lap. *Oh my poor Kuche.* Tears leaked, running into her ears, making the throb of a nearby engine sound tinny and far away.

"Suss, suss, suss. It is alright," the girl above her whispered in Bulgarian, though her accent suggested she was Russian. She dabbed the corners of Silva's eyes with the edge of her skirt. Silva took a shuddering breath, reached up and squeezed the little hand in thanks. Sitting up was a series of stiff, ungraceful movements.

"How are you feeling?" one of the older girls said.

"Like I drank a bottle of Mastika," Silva replied, swallowing her rising nausea.

The young woman nodded.

"I'm Violeta," she said.

"My name is Silva."

Names flowed back from the others; Oana, Crina, Dorina, two Anas, Mirela, Sorina, Rada. Next to her in her soft Russian lilt came, "Diana."

Silva pulled herself up between the bunks. The cabin rocked and swayed, amplifying her dizziness. Hands extended, stabilising her while she got hold of the rust framed porthole. Grey water scudded past, vertical rain across a dusk-smeared sky.

"Do we know where we are?" She asked.

"The Black Sea," Violeta said.

"Heading for Trabzon's my guess," added Diana. "High demand there, it's whispered."

Silva shuddered. She'd known the fate of these girls as soon as she'd discovered them that first morning as the tent flap opened. She'd thought the men illegal campers and had wandered down to warn them; the Rangers' fines were hefty. But young women chained to one another in two neat rows was no camping holiday.

If only she'd gone deeper into the forest instead of doubling back to her cottage to use the phone. She shook her head. There were a hundred 'if onlys'.

"I am a child of the forest. I must not be caged," Silva said to the sea. Her eyes stared into a black future, a vast hall of darkness that echoed with the screams of her companions. Her legs became sticks of jelly. She turned and fell against the wall, allowing gravity to guide her to the floor.

If only the rangers had found them first.

. . . . .

Silva caught sight of a waning crescent moon, set just above the midnight horizon when they were lumbered off the ferry.

Silva held Rada's hand ahead and Diana's, who was last in the line, behind. She turned as Diana's weight dragged. The girl was looking back toward the boat. She turned to the moon, then to Silva and smiled. It was a mirthless smile and Silva shivered.

The group was delivered and unloaded swiftly to a warehouse that sat amongst a lattice of narrow lanes and other nondescript industrial buildings. They were stored in a small room. Two stained mattresses and an broken swivel chair were all that furnished it.

"What is this place?" Crina asked, her face screwed up.

"The dispatch office." Diana said flatly.

A grime-covered window blocked any view to the outside; bars blocked any exit. There was a small, connected room with a shower and toilet. One by one their keepers let them off the chain to relieve themselves and freshen up as best they could without soap or towels.

"Will we split up here?" Silva asked as she sat on the edge of a mattress next to Violeta.

"I don't know. But if we do," Violeta said, "I am counting on you girls not to forget my aunt's recipe." Violeta nudged Silva.

"I will remember," she said, solemn.

In the three nights Silva had been with the women, most were spent in quiet conversation. A patchwork of lives stitched together by words in the dark, each sharing what was dear to them.

There was not only Violeta's lozova surma recipe. Ana had her great grandmother's surmale recipe. Crina shared her prize winning Easter egg design, lovingly drawn on a salt-crusted porthole window. Catalin gave the name and address of her parents, with an 'I love you' message. Sorina had a poem for a lover, Oana a present idea for her brother's twenty-first birthday, next year. And so it went, each memorised by the others.

"And what about you?" Crina had asked Silva on one such night.

"Oh, me? No, I'm pretty boring. I study mushrooms. Macrolepiota procera mainly, an edible parasol variety. Some of you might have seen them: the large ones with the tops that look like the face of the moon."

"I have, they grow through the woodlands near Svode," Rada said. "They are beautiful."

"But, mushrooms only? What about your family?" asked Mirela.

"The only family I had was Kuche." Silva dipped her head, and took a deep breath.

"They murdered him when he tried to protect me."

"I'm sorry," Mirela said.

Silva nodded and the conversation broke up into smaller groups.

Diana shuffled across the floor to sit closer to Silva.

"Are you alright?" she asked, taking her hand.

"I'll be alright when those monsters pay."

Diana glanced around at the other girls, bending forward she whispered, "I am planning on escaping and getting back to the family. And that means *all* of us getting out. There will be justice, my friend. I promise you that."

She fumbled for Silva's other hand in the gloom and looked at her, intent.

"There is a saying, 'You call a wolf, you invite the pack'."

Silva sat up straighter, tilting her head to one side.

"The pack will come, and it will bring a wrath so cold it would make the gates of hell freeze."

"How?"

"That I can't tell you. Believe me my friend, it is safer that you don't know."

She paused, as though thinking then added, "I will tell you this though. But you *must* keep it secret."

She waited for Silva to nod her assent.

"We will be free no later than the full moon."

Silva looked at Violeta, then around the room at the other girls perched on the edges of the filthy mattresses. They were her friends, she realised. She'd had so few friends throughout the years. Their faces were drawn, eyes tired, lips thin with fear. The best she could hope for was that she was split from the rest. She didn't want to see them hurt. If not, before full moon they would be free, she reassured herself. Diana had promised.

. . . . .

The moon tracked briefly across the high slit window of Silva and Diana's room. Its first quarter face reflected a deep cerise hue from the dawn sun. The dark half was a chalky pink reflection against a paling blue sky.

Diana was sleeping. Her head rested on Silva's shoulder, an arm across her belly, their legs entwined. A wave of hair covered her face and spilled out over Silva's breast. She whimpered in her sleep. Silva pushed back her hair, and stroked her face, bending to kiss her brow.

"Suss, suss, suss."

Silva could not sleep. She lay listening to the murmur of the waking city increase to a drone, though it did not drown out Rada's weeping noises from the room next door. The girl had cried most of the night.

Poor Rada. At least the fucker who had beaten her had gotten his. Girls with broken faces did not make money. You mark the girls, Mehmet marks you. Except for the ones with enough filthy money, Silva thought, remembering poor Violeta. The man, they told her, had paid big lira for the privilege. *Privilege?* Silva turned her head from side to side. The vision of Violeta's blue and purple face, swollen like a pumpkin, was branded onto Silva's memory as permanently as the cigarette burns that scarred Violeta's cheeks. Silva let out a ragged sigh, turning her head towards the wall and listened. Rada was quiet now, thank goodness.

Her finger absently traced a bite mark on Diana's shoulder, given amidst the groping, thrusting and grunting of the night before. Dried scabs and skin brushed away with her touch. Strange, the welt was almost healed. Silva frowned. She raised her own arm and looked along its length, examining the brown and yellowing pinch marks that dotted the surface. Do not mark the girls—much.

Silva rubbed her eyes with the back of her hand and released a breath. *Best not to think. Act only to endure.* The phrase was Diana's, one of her many lessons in survival.

Silva's education had started on the first day at the brothel. She remembered the greasy fat fucker that stood in the middle of the lounge rubbing the stubble on one of his two chins, looking at

Diana, then at Silva and then back to Diana. He was the friend of the owner, given first pick of the blondes. Silva couldn't help but sneer as she watched his indecision. *Will seeing our teeth help, you ugly fat fucker*, she'd thought. Her eyes flicked across to Diana, who seemed intent on his dilemma. She had looked then at Silva and smiled. And with a sudden up and over movement Diana slipped into Silva's lap.

"Have both of us," she'd said to fat fucker as she draped an arm around Silva's shoulders.

She leant into Silva's neck, kissing and nibbling. Silva stiffened but Diana's lips moved quickly to her ear and whispered, "It is permitted to walk with the devil, until you have crossed the bridge, my friend. Let us not just walk with him, let us dance."

She pulled away, looked back at the fucker while slipping a hand down the front of Silva's nightie. She stroked her breast and pulled at her nipple. Silva looked at Diana then looked at the fucker. Decision made, she pouted and released a shaky groan.

Silva had tugged at Diana's arm as they followed the fat fucker to the room. "This dance with the devil," she'd muttered. "I have limited experience . . ."

Diana squeezed her hand. "Don't worry; I will lead, you follow."

Diana had stood in front of her when they arrived all too quickly to the bedroom, but Silva could not look at her friend. Instead, she flicked a glance at the fat fucker sitting on the bed. He'd pulled his penis out through the zip of his pants and the thing lay there like a pet slug on his lap. He started to stroke it. Bile burned the back of her throat. She fought against gravity, as the floor began to sag.

Diana reached up and cupped Silva's chin, moving to face her. She saw Diana's eyes, wide but steadfast. Diana's tongue darted quickly over her lips. She held Silva's gaze a moment then moved in to kiss her.

Yes, that first week was a strange time, thought Silva. They had fucked each other, but were not lovers, not until the night of the crescent moon, after one of Diana's rants.

"Suck me, lick her, pull this, finger that. Why do the fuckers always want to talk? Can't they just sit and fiddle with themselves?"

They had been washing themselves for the last time that day. Silva yawned and pulled a nightshirt on.

"It's the same dance. Well mostly. Just a different order to the steps," she'd said.

Diana smiled. "Da, they do not have a lot of imagination, do they?"

Diana patted her face with the flannel then dropped it back into the soapy water and looked at Silva. Her voice dropped.

"One thing we must remember, Silva is that what we do is exactly that, a set of physical movements that change in order. That is all. It cannot be connected with us in any other way - in here." She stabbed violently at her chest, her look glassy. Her mouth drooped at the corners, her chin quivered, and then the damn of emotion broke, and the tears flowed.

Silva had stepped forward encircling her with her arms. She stroked Diana's heaving back, kneaded along her shoulder blades and upper arms. She lightly kissed the top of her head, her closed wet eyes and her pale cheeks. Diana's lips were bruised, so she avoided them, avoided all the places the fuckers had ravaged. Diana's breathing slowed, her body relaxed and she moved closer into Silva's embrace, their breasts touching. Finger tips and lips, soft as butterfly wings, danced over skin, the first steps to a new dance.

No, Silva would never forget that night. It was the same night that Violeta had tied her lingerie around the bars of her window, then around her throat and stepped from her bed. Violeta tried to hang herself, but her neck did not break. She had died in pain and alone as the weight of her body strangled her slowly to death.

A week and a day had passed since Violeta had gone. *So much in such a short time.* Silva let out another long sigh and disentangled herself from Diana, careful not to wake her. She rose and started pacing the room. She ran Violeta's lozova surma recipe through her mind. *Two dozen grape leaves, two large onions, two pounds of ground beef . . .*

"Anxious again?" Diana said, blinking up at her through half opened eyes.

Silva stopped, her voice pitched just below hysterical.

"You have to get them out of here, Diana." Her body started to tremble, blossoming into a shake. Her hands rubbed together in a violent washing motion. "You promised—before full moon."

"Da." Diana said, sitting up. "We have nearly a week, Silva." Her head tilted slightly, her brows knitting.

"Do you not trust me?" She slid to the edge of the bed, and swung her legs down, looking at Silva, her face flushed.

Silva lunged at her, grabbing the girl's arms. Diana gasped, but Silva did not let go. Her face was close to Diana's, but her eyes stared past her. She spoke in a low slow whisper close to her ear.

"No more of my friends must be hurt, Diana. Do you understand that? *You* must not be hurt."

"Da, da, I understand, love," she said, her voice soft but unsteady.

Silva looked at Diana then and nodded with the slightest movement of her head. Her fingers were digging into Diana's thin arms. She released her grip and tried to rub away the marks she'd left.

"I'm sorry," she said as she looked Diana in the eyes. "I just can't stand the thought of . . ." Her face contorted into a frozen mask of pain and she let out a strangled cry.

"Suss, suss, suss. It's alright." Diana leant into Silva, and eased her lover's head onto her shoulder.

"Almost there, my love. Almost there."

. . . . .

It was almost six of Silva's steps from wall to wall. Silva turned and paced back. She tried to keep her attention on her feet, counting the steps. Yet she could still see in her periphery the walls bend into her, as though listening for the next whimper. She tried to take a deep breath, but the bed rose up to smother her with the smell of old sex.

She glanced up at the window, at a slice of the vast world beyond. The darkening sky was a deep red, fading to orange and slate. *Diana, where are you?* The window shrunk. The room tilted and turned. She lurched across the room, her pace increasing. She panted steps. One, two, three . . .

The familiar slide and clap of the door bolt halted her. The tide of walls, ceiling and floor ebbed. She disentangled her fingers from her hair, rubbed her face and shook her head. The steel lined door opened.

Mehmet walked in and locked the exit behind him, dropping the key into his front pocket. Hope drained out of her body through her feet as his stench entered her nose and filled her mind. Scenes of the forest, the moon, her dying dog. His breath was thick with fresh raki; his day off.

"What is this? My little rabbit does not look pleased to see me," He slurred in Bulgarian. "And here I was thinking that you would be looking forward to nibbling the nice juicy carrot I brought for you."

He barked a hollow laugh.

"Ah! I see, you were expecting your little girlfriend. I didn't think you liked it when I made her sit and watch me bend you over like a dog."

Silva bent her head and spoke to the floor. "I was waiting for my check—after Diana."

Mehmet was silent for a moment. In a flat voice he said, "You won't be seeing the doctor today. He left with your whore. I don't know what she took, but when I saw her she was delirious, frothing at the mouth and making strange noises."

A roaring flooded Silva's ears. She looked at the keeper, looked to see the lie in his face.

"It can't be," she stammered.

"It is," he snapped.

She tried to order her mind, grab a logical thought to hold on to, stay afloat. But each slipped from her mental fingers as she was pulled along on the quickening current of animal panic. *Oh, Diana, no!*

Silva heard a voice. It sounded like her own.

"Please," said the husky echo. "Not now, I, I beg you."

Mehmet's mouth tightened, as though he had stood in dog shit. He slapped her open-handed, hard across the face. The bitter, hard light of reality struck.

And so this is how it was to be, she thought. There was no escape from losing those she loved. What she feared most had come. Best not think on that, she would act only to endure.

She rubbed her cheek, and studied the creature that stood before her. The light in the room had changed. The diffused glow of the sun's last rays had been replaced by the cold silver-blue of the rising full moon. It gave his body a dull steely hue, made him look metallic, she thought, a tin man.

"I'm not going anywhere until you eat me, bitch."

Her hand dropped from her face.

"You know," she snarled. "I just had the exact same thought."

The moon's beams reached down to her, touching her blonde hair and turning it silver. Her face glowed, as pale and emotionless as the moon itself. She stripped off her clothes, her gaze never leaving Mehment, who leered and played with his groin.

She stepped out of her panties and slunk towards him. Her body throbbed with vitality, the power of the moon giving her a surge of primal energy, and with one fluid movement she punched him in the mouth, mangling his lips and teeth. He fell back, slamming into the wall. He exhaled in a violent rush, labouring for breath. Slack-jawed shock subjugated his bloody face.

"Go hunting for rabbits, get eaten by wolves," she growled down at him.

Silva stretched almost luxuriantly in the moonshine. Her body glowed in its hoary light. The rays infused her with potency; she tingled with growth. It took no more than a minute for her to reach her full seven feet of height, her head brushing the mould stained ceiling. Hair sprung from every pore, tickling her skin as it grew. Her fingers flexed as nails lengthened and hardened into claws. She let out a long, slow howl of pleasure when the change was complete.

A report of distant gunfire punctuated the silence that followed. She swung toward the door, ears up, twitching left and right. More shots, downstairs.

She turned her attention back to her quarry. He sat rigid, eyes large with horror. *What would this thing know of horror?* He was about to find out, she thought. A low guttural rumble escaped her muzzle as she bent closer.

Her wet snout left a slimy trail on his face as she snuffled him. Fear and blood, yes this was what this thing should smell like. Drool dripped in long viscous tendrils from her maw and into his lap. Urine spread out around him. She watched her reflection in his staring eyes as she licked his blood-smeared face.

"P-please . . ."

She opened her jaws and tore out his throat before he could say another word.

The noise from downstairs moved now to Silva's floor. Her head came up, she shook it, gore splattering around her. Sound rolled down the hallway, footfall, doors banging open and slamming closed, urgent voices, crying, and then just as quickly died away. She moved on all fours, away from the pile of intestine, bone and flesh to sniff the gap at the base of the door. Footsteps again. She backed into shadows, crouched on her haunches and waited.

The doorknob jiggled. Silva growled. Violent hammering followed and the door burst inward, light behind it. The silhouette of a large man with an axe was framed in the doorway. From behind a small shadowy figure appeared. She stepped into the room, arms outstretched pointing a gun up, down, side to side. Silva's nose came up, sniffing the air. Images of soft blue eyes, plump cupid lips, golden hair, gentle hands—Diana.

Diana inched her way into the room, the man with the axe stayed on guard at the door. She did not see Silva sitting there in the gloom, her attention was fixed on the half-lit remains by the bed.

"Silva?" she whispered, taking a step closer. "No, no, Silva. What have they done?"

"Dar-an-a," Silva spoke around her teeth, standing.

Diana turned and in one smooth movement her arms swung up. She fired three blasts straight into Silva chest.

Silva's body jolted with each hit. Wounds opened and closed like lazy yawns. She howled, sounding out a long and mournful "No!"

Diana fired again. But Silva was upon her. She grabbed the girl by the throat, pushing her hard against the cupboard. She could feel Diana's flesh break as her claws dug into the back of her neck. Smelt her blood run. Diana brought up her arm, attempting another shot. Silva snapped Diana's wrist and the gun fell from her limp hand. Diana screamed. Silva snarled.

"Diana!" came a voice from behind.

Pain peppered Silva's side. She dropped her prey and turned to the second attacker, ripping the pug faced head from the man's shoulders in one tear. Blood sprayed fountains of red high into the air. His body thudded to the hallway floor, red painting the wall and carpet. Silva threw the head out after it.

Silva swung back toward Diana. The girl had fallen forward onto her knees, holding her wrist against her chest, taking in rasping breaths.

Diana. Silva backed away, pawing the floor, swinging her head from side to side.

"Run," she growled.

Diana got her shaky legs beneath her. Her eyes glassy balls in her pinched face as she looked from the head and body back to

Silva. Silva lunged at her snapping at her face and snarling. Diana didn't move, whispering, "Silva."

Silva howled and swung away, throwing herself against the wall, cracking and denting the plaster. She dug at the cracks with her paws, ripping pieces away with her jaws and shaking her head as the cladding shattered between her teeth. A squeal erupted from the other side of the wall. Silva shoved her muzzle into the gap and sniffed. *Rada.* She took a step back and threw herself at the hole once more.

Heavy steps thudded down the hall. Diana's name was called. All movement ceased except for the swing of their heads toward the sound. The two looked each other in the eyes then, holding the connection for just a moment. Then Diana staggered sideways to the door and slammed it shut behind her.

Silva heard the bolt slide home, heard Diana yell in Russian, "Stop! Stop I said, Ivan!"

Silva paced the walls, whining and gnashing.

She could hear Diana's voice in the room next door then further away yelling, "I said fucking stay there! Back up."

Silva stopped, her ears pricked. There were questions, mutterings.

A shot was fired.

"Next time I won't fucking miss! Clear the building, *now!*"

Silva launched herself as the door bent and groaned.

"Move!" yelled Diana.

. . . . .

A squadron of dragonflies danced above the water of Silva's pond as she sat waiting for the car to appear. From a distance it looked like a huge black beetle as it crept along the track, stopping at last by her cabin. Four black-clad figures emerged, three hulking men in black suits, one a slight, fair-haired female in a blue fitted skirt and jacket.

Silva stood and brushed sand and twigs from her backside, waiting as the woman approached. Silva's heart knocked urgently against her ribs. Her stomach did flips. She swallowed.

Diana smiled at her as she drew close.

"I'm glad to see you made it, Silva. You look well, my friend," she said as she stopped an arm's length away.

"Better than the last time you saw me, you mean?" Silva asked.

The smile gone, Diana said, "That's not what I meant."

"No. You didn't deserve that."

"Actually, I probably did." Diana's gaze dropped to the ground. "I shot you."

Silva shrugged and looked back out over the pond.

"I thought it was you there, on the ground. I thought you were dead," Diana said, squatting down, hugging her knees. She blinked back tears.

Silva bent down beside her and rubbed her back.

"How do you tell someone you are a monster?"

Diana rose and wiped her eyes with the back of her hand giving a shuddering sigh. She looked back up towards her car.

"You don't," she said.

Silva nodded, and reached for Diana's hand. "Why are you here?"

Diana looked at Silva, raised her free arm and moved her hand around in circles.

"This should be in a cast."

Silva's narrowed her eyes.

"Don't worry. My saliva has to enter the blood stream directly for you to change. The healing thing is an interesting side effect of kissing, no more." She dropped Diana's hand, turned away and made toward her cabin.

"So is love," Diana said to her back. "An interesting side affect of kissing, I mean."

Silva's steps faltered, her pace slowed. Diana caught up, interlacing her fingers with Silva's.

"Come, walk me to my car, my friend."

As they approached, Diana nodded to one of her bodyguards. He turned and opened the back door. Diana reached in, re-emerging with a big ball of fur in her hands. She petted a sleeping pup then looked up at Silva.

"It's for you."

The pup woke as it was transferred between hands. Silva brought it up to her face and breathed in its scent. It licked her cheek. Silva smiled.

"Thank you."

Diana stepped forward and kissed her gently on the lips, turned and slid into the back seat. Silva could see only her own and the pup's reflection in dark windows as the door closed, then the car rolled away.

"What is your name, little—she pulled the pup's tail up and looked—girl? What shall we call you, hum?"

The car stopped, the window slid down. Diana called back to her.

"I forgot to tell you, she's half wolf!"

Marriage of Convenience

Liz Coley

IS eyes smouldering with barely contained passion, Altan drew the scarcely breathing Hanlea into his arms and buried his lips—

A discreet knock at the door interrupted both the fictional Altan and the young woman who sprawled across an enormous four-poster canopied bed, absorbed in his gripping, romantic tale. She hastily stuffed the book under a feather pillow.

"Yes, Madra. Come in," she called, rising to her feet as the door swung. She tucked a wayward dark curl behind her right ear and slowed her breathing.

However, it wasn't the maid who entered, but the king, and Princess Althea was doubly glad she'd hidden her reading matter. It wouldn't do for her father to know her fantasies—unfulfilled and now, in light of her impending marriage, unfulfillable.

She schooled her expression to enthusiastic surprise. "Oh, Daddy! He's here? Already?"

"I came to tell you myself, Althea, my dear." The king smiled at his daughter, but she caught the tightness in his voice. "We're just making arrangements to move in the Prince's environmental support tank from the transport."

Princess Althea tried to keep the bright look on her face from fading at the mental image. No strolling the bustling markets of the capital with a support tank. No galloping across fields on twin horses with a support tank. No long, leisurely suppers by candlelight, holding hands across a white silk tablecloth—with a support tank.

The king plucked at a loose thread on his vest. "My dear, it's not entirely too late. If this is just too hard, you know. You did . . . you did agree willingly, did you not? You don't feel that the ministers and I forced you . . . ?"

Althea grabbed her father's hands. "Daddy, please. Stop. I understand that a strategic alliance with the Deleauxians is vital to Frinland's independence. True?"

"Of course," he said with a sigh. "You know, when I was a lad, we were just an insignificant planet in an obscure sector." His eyes stared past her to a long ago time. "I could even wish it were still that way, but the diquontium changed all that. Now our mines are the envy of many a stronger world."

"And so, my marriage will link us with the most powerful species of all."

"And the succession . . ." he began, a hesitant catch to his voice.

"Cousin Eban is delighted to take on that mantle. You know I never aspired to rule."

The king inclined his head. "But children . . ."

Althea stopped his mouth with her hand. "Shush, Daddy. My cousin's numerous offspring will suffice for my entertainment." Her tone was light, but acknowledging the impossibility of cradling a babe of her own tugged at her core.

He pressed her tiny hands between his. "You are still so young, my dear. I only wish . . . well, you know how dearly I loved your mother."

Althea knew that a lock of her mother's auburn hair still hung in a locket about his neck, beneath his mantle of office. Their wedding portrait in the national gallery displayed such devotion in their eyes that passing lovers made a tradition of kissing in front of it. Althea had never been in love, excepting a childhood crush on the junior stable boy. Hopelessly admiring him mucking out the stalls from afar held just the right tinge of star-crossed romance to fill her diary for two or three months.

"I am sure the Prince and I will become . . . good friends. In time." Althea spoke the words with certainty, but nothing was less certain in her heart. Across the species barrier, who knew where they might find common thoughts or interests? They couldn't even do something as simple as take a walk together, speak aloud, or share a meal.

Still, a properly raised princess knew her duty to planet and people. Now was not the moment to indulge in misgivings.

"You're a good girl." The king dropped a kiss on her cheek. "I'm very proud of you."

"Well, I've had a good role model," Althea said. "And now, Madra's here to dress me."

The king retreated in haste.

The maid bowed low as she entered, then raised her wrinkled eyes to her mistress. "Princess Althea, the foreign wedding party has arrived. I have seen them."

Althea caught the look of revulsion that swept across the fond, familiar face before Madra hid it behind professional, subservient blandness. She must be deeply upset.

The maid smoothed the brocade coverlet and straightened the pillow. Her expression under control, she added, "The Prince has asked to pay his respects to you before the ceremony."

Madra's self-restraint spoke volumes to the Princess, who had known her for a lifetime. Madra's hands had been the first to rock her cradle and cuddle her back to sleep sixteen years since. Now their trembling caused a matching flutter in Althea's heart.

Althea said lightly, to calm them both, "That used to be considered bad luck, but I suppose since we have never laid eyes on each other, it's not an unreasonable request."

So. Her future consort was as curious as she, or perhaps as unconventional. She let her lavender satin robe slither to the floor.

"Well then, Madra. Dress me for inspection."

Madra hurried across the warmed stone floor to the gilt wardrobe and selected Althea's most formal wine-red leather vestments. The white leather bridal suit hung stiffly beside. As Madra's hand brushed across it, her shudder was obvious.

"Oh, dearest Princess," she moaned. "Why must it be this way? Why must you marry that sea slug? That octopus?"

Sixteen years of royal training permitted Althea to push away the might-have-beens. She had always known her marriage would be dictated by political expediency, not the softer emotions, and she had almost convinced herself that she welcomed the simplicity of such an arrangement. Almost.

"Oh, Madra. Hush. Please."

"But Princess," Madra protested. "How is an alliance with a water world to answer?"

"The psionic powers of the Deleauxians are renowned, dear Madra." Althea reached for the skin-hugging leggings. "I've heard that a single Deleauxian can send the bravest warrior running in terror for his life with the merest touch. Ten massed minds can turn an army." She forced her foot through the narrow opening. "A hundred can scatter an orbiting fleet, the captains gibbering in fear."

"And one of these, you would marry?" Madra's eyes filled with tears.

"At peace, they are a kind and gentle race, so I've been told. Once the Deleauxian prince and his retinue adopt Frinland as their home world, we shall be safe from attack. Marriages of convenience between royal houses are traditionally the best insurance for a lasting pact, far more than signatures on treaties. And I am truly honoured—"

Althea caught her breath in a gasp as Madra tugged the laces of her vest, squeezing her body into conformity with standards of beauty. Her eyes caught the corner of the romance novel peeping out from under her pillow. Only the heroine's face showed, tilted back with an expression of impassioned abandon. Well, such a love was never to have been her fate. She swallowed against the tightness in her throat. "I am truly honoured if I can serve as the—"

"Sacrifice to the beast?" Madra interrupted.

"Enough!" Althea said with unusual severity. "I'll not have you speaking that way about my future husband."

Madra dropped her eyes to the floor, but stood silent, the tension in her shoulders shouting her disapproval.

Althea strode from her chamber as quickly as the too-snug leather leggings would permit. Pray her courage would carry her through the upcoming ordeal. Marriage of convenience, indeed! How inconvenient for a human-stock land dweller like herself to marry someone who had to transport his warm, salty, wet environment with him wherever he went.

She slowed at the entrance to the welcoming room and glanced about as she composed herself. A huge, wheeled tank stood in the middle of the room. A splash of water dotted the centuries-old thick plank floor. Her father, ever a practical man, was standing on a ladder-stair with rolled up sleeves, reaching deep into the tank to shake tentacles with the visitors.

Althea stepped to the foot of the ladder. "Daddy . . . ?"

"Ah, that was quick my dear," he called down in a hearty voice. His eyes were encouraging. "Come up and meet your betrothed. Charming family." His tone of approval made it certain. There was no backing out now.

Althea tugged at the vest, which was chafing the back of her neck, and pushed up her own sleeves. She climbed up to the riser just below her father's feet. "Daddy, what does it feel like?" she asked.

He chuckled. "Oh, a bit warm and squishy . . ."

Althea's stomach flipped. "No, I mean the talking part. What does that feel like?"

"Ah!" He lifted a wet hand from the tank and dried it absently on his leg. "It feels like the answers to your questions pile into your mind even as you ask them. Almost as though they have known you forever. You can't keep any secrets from them, my dear heart."

Althea inhaled as she realised the extent of her father's trust, his dependence on her to establish and maintain this planetary alliance. Daddy had proudly called her "my only hope." Now that she understood what he meant, she was determined to prove worthy.

Filling her mind with pleasant thoughts, she extended a hand into the water. A warm and squishy tentacle brushed against her, and she wobbled in surprise. "Ma'am! You're not the Prince. You're to be my mother-in-law."

A wave of reassurance flowed through her as a thought burst into her head.

"My dear, you are a very brave young woman. I hope you'll soon treasure my son as I do. Yes, I do understand. You are truly a princess worthy of her people. I assure you he is likewise a prince worthy of his."

As another tentacle reached her hand, Althea "heard" a new voice.

"Mother, please leave us alone for a moment."

The Prince's mother slipped away.

Instantly, Althea felt her heart, her fears, her losses laid bare for the Prince's inspection. She trembled at this sudden unveiling of all she preferred to hide. Then with shock she realised her perspective was flipped—it was the Prince who had opened his heart and mind to her. As in a mirror, she saw revealed in the Prince's mind a tidy drawer of carefully folded and put-aside dreams, the might-have-beens for him with a beloved wife of his own species.

Her inner vision filled with an underwater vista of towering corals, brilliant flickering fishlike creatures, fronded sea plants swaying in the currents. The benthic beauty remembered from his perspective touched her heart. Then the scene dissolved, and the barren tank stood prisonlike before her. Whose loss is the greater, she chided herself.

"I'll try to be a good wife/husband to you," they thought at precisely the same moment. Althea smiled, the small pain in her heart meeting its twin.

"Please accept my wedding gift," the Prince offered.

A member of her father's guard stepped forward with a large box, which Madra accepted on her behalf.

"Peace until tomorrow," they bade each other.

. . . . .

*B*ack in her chamber, Althea motioned Madra to put the package on the bed. She untied the ribbons with nimble fingers, and lifted out a gown that shimmered and flowed like sunlight on water in her hands. She rubbed the silkiness against her cheek in delight.

"What is it, Princess?" Madra asked.

"A wedding gown. A proper wedding gown." Althea sighed.

"But what about your white leathers?" Madra urged.

"Traditional leather be damned," Althea said. "This is perfect."

. . . . .

*P*erfect it was, as Madra agreed the next day when her mistress stood radiantly before her. The gown clung where it should cling, draped where it should drape, and caressed her skin deliciously. And, very conveniently, it was sleeveless. Althea awarded her groom points for both style and thoughtfulness.

She noted the way the virginal white silk flattered her sun-kissed skin. Perhaps I'll always wear white, Althea considered.

It would certainly be appropriate for the long life of chastity that stretched before her. She pinched herself and dismissed that wistful thought.

The wedding itself was an odd ceremony. The humans gathered around the tank, touching the clustered and linked Deleauxians. Celebrants of both species were present to ensure that the traditional rites were observed. Finally, the nervous couple were pronounced Deleauxian and wife, and the Prince was decanted into his own shallow aquarium.

Several guards helped wheel him down the wide corridors to the Princess's chamber. They parked the tank against a tall window and set the safety brake. Then, with a discreet cough from Madra, the guards left. With a final, tearful parting glance at Althea, Madra followed them out. The door clicked closed.

Now what?

Althea dragged an embroidered bench to the edge of the tank and sat down.

The Prince floated against the glass and beckoned her with a tentacle.

She cursed the tremor in her hand as she reached into the tank. The end of a tentacle brushed against her fingertips, but the Prince was quiet.

She looked away from the tank, from the strange, faceted eyes fixed on hers through the glass. Her gaze rested on the rose bushes in the knot garden below. "My husband," she began, testing the unfamiliar phrase. "Can you see the view at all?"

"Oh yes," was the immediate reply. "I see it in your mind. Your gardens are delightful. What a shame the flowers don't grow underwater. Is that a salt-pond in the distance?"

"Why, yes," she said. "I could get you some hybrid sea lilies for your tank. Let me just send for . . ."

Her rush to rise was checked by a firm tug on her wrist.

"Don't mind about that now. Please, come in." The Prince patted the bench in the tank with another tentacle. "I saved you a seat." The joke had a tentative feel to it.

Althea's hesitation was too obvious.

"Oh dear. You weren't expecting a romantic wedding night, were you? In fact, that never even entered your mind, did it?"

Althea shook her head. Her pulse thudded in her ears.

"Oh, yes. I see. Well." The Prince's surface colour brightened from its deep olive-grey to a jade green. "It is actually possible, more or less, in a way, that is, if you are willing."

Althea stared at the tank in front of her with trepidation. Nothing in her upbringing had quite prepared her for . . . whatever he was suggesting.

"How will it work?" Althea asked bravely.

"Mentally and physically," the Prince answered. "Please. Trust me?"

Althea unbuttoned and slid out of her gown and underclothes. A hot blush from head to toe battled with the chill air. Don't be stupid, she chided herself. His idea of a beautiful female has four more limbs and soft grey skin.

She climbed into the water, a welcoming warmth, and sat down on the bench. It was just the right depth for her to recline comfortably with her head above water.

"Now . . ." A tentacle probed along the inside of her thigh, parting her legs.

"Oh my . . ." she scrunched her eyes closed and tried to think of Frinland.

As she yielded to the Prince's touch, Althea felt herself drawn into a pair of brawny arms. Her hands twisted through thick, coarse curling hair. She felt a lover's hot breath on her neck, heard his murmured words, "My angel of paradise, how long I have waited for this moment!" She was pressed into silken sheets as his lips found hers, and his hands . . .

She moaned aloud as the pulsing warmth flooded her senses.

. . . . .

When Althea came to herself again, she found she was clinging tightly to a warm, soft tentacle with both hands. It was shaded a pale violet hue.

"Your mind is fabulously passionate, beyond my wildest dreams," the Prince said with awe in his mental voice.

"And . . . you, too?" Althea managed. "But I don't understand exactly. Was that really you?"

"Yes, in a sense," he replied. "My desires, my . . . new feelings for you, dear wife. I will always strive to give you in mind what I cannot in body. Will you forgive my peeking into your hidden hopes for the husband you might have had?"

Two tentacles caressed her lower back, and she had no desire to flinch away. In fact . . .

"Forgive? Of course I do." Althea smiled and knew the Prince could read her intent. "Indeed, I believe I can grow accustomed to it. But how can I ever make up for the hopes you also sacrificed?"

"There is a way, my sweetest, if you'll allow me."

"Yes. Yes, I will." Althea closed her eyes and reached her arms around his head.

As the Prince's tentacle gently traced a line from her breasts down to her slender waist and beyond, Althea abandoned herself to a strange dissolution. Her limbs softened, flowed, multiplied. She reached out her warm, gently throbbing tentacles to twine with his, sensing a crimson, incandescent heat where they met. As their bodies glided with excruciating pleasure against each other, she offered him her last coherent thought for some time. *This is going to be a wonderful marriage.*

Resurrection in Red

Jason Nahrung

CYNTHIA sits motionless, a fly suspended in the amber of doubt. The taxi's cracked vinyl reeks of smokes and booze and sweat. Mardi Gras beads and a Bacchus coin hang from the rearview mirror. On the other side of Royal, a man stands ready to usher her into the gallery. What awaits her there? A part of her still can't believe she's here, dressed like a screen goddess, her skin still sizzling from unexpected sex, an aura of which wraps around her like a boa. She feels Papa Legba, a day old but still with his hooks in her groin, chuckling at the surprise twist her mundane life has taken. She thinks of Tania, waiting at home for her with wine and questions; of Alexander Rakoczy and his unfathomable desire to meet her; of the strange path that has led her here. The drums beat loudly in her ears as her heartbeat accelerates. She has reached a crossroads.

. . . . .

Last night—only last night, when her life had been simple, bland but simple—she had met Tania off the Greyhound and they'd chatted on the walk-bus-walk to her cramped, water-stained condo on Barracks. The name Alexander Rakoczy hadn't been mentioned, not even in passing, no more in their consciousness than Louis Armstrong or Anne Rice or any other local made good.

Their thoughts had been focused on the weekend, special in and of itself, made more so by their being together once more.

They'd eaten, showered, dressed in their traditional black, and then Cynthia led Tania out into the Quarter. The babble from Bourbon Street was a constant background noise, like surf, but she'd promised her friend something better than the drunken antics of frat boys for her visit. It was, after all, Halloween.

They arrived in time to join the crowd, maybe fifty strong, maybe a hundred, choking Dumaine outside one of the voodoo shops. Cynthia was from an old New Orleans family, not moneyed, but old. Voodoo wasn't something she considered suitable tourist fare; it was a religion, after all: a way of life. She found the Spanish moss and chicken-feather dolls palmed off onto visitors looking for love and fortune to be ridiculous, a bit like selling effigies of the Pope or Christ in the Vatican. But that was New Orleans, too. Nothing was too sacred to make a buck from. Tonight, however, with the narrow streets of the Quarter choked by Goths and Goths-for-the-night and tragics in masks and risqué costumes, this ceremony felt apt.

The crowd was gathered in a rough semi-circle around the shop's entrance where a half dozen practitioners had lit their smoking torches and were, even now, starting to dance to the tribal beat belting out from a stereo bigger than a milk crate. A black man wearing shorts and sweat kept rhythm on a tom-tom as the dancers jerked their feet up and down in time. The houngan had introduced the rite to the crowd: a collection of middle class tourists with their silly hats and plastic cups of booze in hand; a small flock of Goths; some hippie types.

"This is one of the most authentic shops in the Quarter," Cynthia whispered to Tania, who nodded. Her wide blue eyes were fixed on the houngan's muscular chest, where a necklace of alligator teeth and God-knew-what else rattled and bounced with every purposeful move.

Tania's eyes grew even wider as the man blew alcohol across a brand, causing a flare of flame and a blast of heat, and Cynthia took her hand in hers. It had been too long since her old friend had visited; it felt better than good to share this with her.

A dancer brought out a pale snake, as thick as her thigh and longer than her body. She struggled with it, but managed to present it to the crowd. It lay still, as though it knew the attention was simply its due, and that the fuss would soon pass and it would be allowed to resume its slumber.

The crowd broke into awed smiles. Some of the hippies danced in time, bobbing from foot to foot. The Goths nodded, keeping beat with the minimum of energy, as though afraid of upsetting their hair or shaking loose their piercings.

Cynthia swapped smiles with Tania as the beat intensified. She faced the houngan, who smiled at her, his teeth white in a dark face, his chest shining with sweat and oil. He blew another flaming breath.

Papa Legba invaded Cynthia with a suddenness that left her breathless. The loa flung her forward, limbs jerking on invisible strings attached to the drum beat. The houngan laughed and opened his arms to her in welcome. She danced with legs spread wide; she hitched her sundress up her thighs to give herself freedom of movement. Her breasts bobbed and she resented the confinement of her underwire bra. She slipped the straps off her shoulders and let the dress care for itself as she waved her arms high. The houngan leaned close and sprayed her face with alcohol. She delighted in the taste of it on her lips, the feel of it running down her throat and chest. Legba laughed, deep and resonant, in her mind, and she couldn't help but laugh along with him. She hadn't felt this free since the divorce, since before the divorce. Those dark days, in the aftermath of the storm when both her city and her marriage seemed barren and hopeless, faded far, far away under the merciless, unrelenting beat. Her heart hammered as her sweat flowed and her feet pounded the pavement. Heat filled her, roiling out in ever-strengthening waves from her groin. Her mouth grew dry, her lips parched, her face flushed; her nipples ached, seemingly straining against the constraint of her clothes.

The houngan sprayed her again and she greedily licked up the alcohol. She felt her dress sliding down, sticking to her stomach and hips. The Cynthia who cared was buried far away, under the beat. The air was thick with rum and incense, sweat and arousal. The drums reached a crescendo and a flood of energy washed over her. The woman held the boa high, the snake's cough triggering a gush of heat through Cynthia's body. Her breasts felt as though they were on fire; a phantom cock rammed deep inside and she cried out in explosive release.

The drums stopped. The world fell silent.

Cynthia collapsed into the arms of the grinning houngan as the city vanished into a cloud of night. Tania's flushed, concerned expression followed her down.

. . . . .

*L*ate the next morning she was woken, exhausted and aching and barely able to remember the late-night stumble home, by a pale Creole girl with a flat chest and no bra who brought her a scarlet dress and an invitation she couldn't refuse.

"Would you please stop saying 'damn'?" Cynthia begged. Standing on a crate in her living room, she felt as if she was one of the human statues in Jackson Square as Tania took yet another circle around her, hands on hips, eyes bulging with mock amazement.

"Damn," Tania said. "You are one glorious hooker."

"This is a mistake, isn't it? What in the hell am I thinking?"

"No, that's not what I meant," Tania said. "It's really great, Cyn. I haven't seen this side of you since college. First you do the wild thing on the street, and now this."

A blush warmed Cynthia from toe to cheek. She and Tania had shed quite a few inhibitions when they'd hooked up at university, both studying fine arts. She'd only recently sold the last of her paintings from those carefree days, having had to pay the rent; they'd made the piece together by rolling around naked, covered in paint, on a very large canvas. Washing the paint off each other had also been fun . . . But they hadn't been lovers since they'd graduated. It was, they'd agreed, a phase of their development. Both of them had failed marriages to show for their newfound maturity.

Cynthia ran her hands over the dress. It cupped her curves, the front pulled tight across her breasts by the knotted ties around her neck. The back was cut so low it revealed the black swirls of the tribal tattoo hanging over her butt cheeks.

"You have a beautiful back," Tania said, and poured them each another glass of cheap champagne.

Cynthia bit her lip as her cheeks flared. She wasn't used to compliments; wasn't used to feeling this good, for that matter. Something about a dead child and a broken marriage and a devastated city, she guessed, and then glugged down a big swallow of bubbles before the familiar sorrow could destroy the moment.

Tania held out the black leather clutch purse they'd found at the French Market. It had been a good buy, but still dearer than the red heels they'd lucked upon at the thrift store. "Come on, give us the full show, then."

Cynthia took the bag and gave a curtsy. Juggling her glass, she piled her long, black tresses lazily on top of her head so tendrils hung down across her cheeks and bare shoulders.

"Damn, girl," Tania said, and Cynthia was proud of the fact that she didn't spill any champagne as she thwacked her friend with the purse.

"So what is Madam going to wear underneath? The garter? The fishnet stockings? The saucy g-string or crotchless panties? After all, one will be attending high society."

"Shush, you," Cynthia said with a giggle as she handed the purse back to Tania. "The split is so high . . ."

She plucked at the place where the satiny material fell open to reveal the length of her right leg, the cool folds caressing her hip and pelvis. A bra she could happily do without; the dress offered ample support and cover for her breasts, an empowering feeling she hadn't exercised since college. She could just get away with it, and Tania agreed with a look on her face that was one part jealous, one part lust. Tania wasn't so well endowed; in fact, she had trouble finding bras small enough. She felt compelled to wear one in her native Georgia, but here in the Big Easy, she was happy to let her puppies off the leash, as she liked to say.

"The G?" Cynthia hoped her friend had a better option. She'd never been comfortable in g-strings—they made her feel too vulnerable, somehow.

"Do you suppose your host is trying to tell you something?"

"God, Tania, he's never even met me. I can't even guess how he knows I exist."

"Maybe he saw you doing the sweaty mamba in Dumaine last night and wants an encore."

The invitation had come written on a thick, white card in stylish gold script, a bold splash against the neatly folded dress inside the box. "M Alexander Rakoczy requests the pleasure of Ms Cynthia deLille for a private art showing." The address, an exclusive gallery on Royal, was at the other end of the Quarter from her rickety condo. He had used her maiden name.

"Monsieur Alexander Rakoczy is in serious trouble," Tania said. "I hope he knows what he's in for, because my girl is definitely one hot fox."

"Enough, Tania, or you'll put me off."

"Not likely. You've been running hot ever since last night's little outing. You nervous?"

"Of course I'm nervous. Rakoczy's one of the most sought-after portrait painters in the city. He's famous."

"Infamous, more like, from a long line of infamous. And he knows women. That dress is the perfect colour for you; it's sure brought out the best of you."

A tear burned in Cynthia's eye and she hastily wiped it away. Her native ancestry had given her lustrous hair and deep brown eyes and olive skin in a combination that her husband—ex-husband—had found irresistible, at least for a few years. But she hadn't dared wear anything this bold and bright since . . . in years.

Tania's hand swept over Cynthia's shoulders, tousled the dangling locks. "I haven't seen you this—confident?—since college. Haven't seen you this beautiful since your wedding day."

Another tear tracked Cynthia's cheek as the memories surfaced. From those free and easy university days at LSU, to the joy of marriage, and then the nightmare fall of the storm, a stillbirth and a divorce in quick order. And her art career, dead on the floor before it had even taken off, submerged in her sorrow and a constant conga line of waitressing jobs as she tried to pay the skyrocketing rents post-Katrina. But she'd stuck it out, determined to stay in her city where her parents and her grandparents and their ancestors, way back before the Spanish and the French had ever worked their way up the Mississippi, had made a life for themselves.

"I do look all right?" she asked, chin trembling with suppressed emotion.

"Honey, you look good enough to eat." Tania kissed her, a peck on the cheek, and then a wet kiss on the lips. Her voice was low and gravelled when she said, "If you're going to go commando tonight, you'll need to shave."

Cynthia almost fell off her perch.

"Commando?"

Papa Legba laughed, a seismic ripple that flowed from her head to her groin. The scent of rum and incense wafted around Cynthia as her pulse thudded in her ears.

"Are you mad?"

"Completely." Tania filled their glasses, then tilted hers towards Cynthia's until they clinked. She strode to the bathroom door, then turned and asked over her shoulder: "Coming?"

Cynthia gulped champagne to drown a flutter of nerves, then reached to release the knot holding her dress up. "Maybe."

She heard—felt—Papa Legba chuckle again, and she found herself walking towards Tania, a hesitant smile tweaking her lips as she wondered just how far she'd go this night.

. . . . .

*I*n the taxi, Cynthia lets her fingers lightly brush her lips. She presses her thighs together to suppress a sudden rush of moist heat as she remembers Tania taking great pains to shave her, and love her, then bathe her, and dry her, and prepare her make-up. "No more tears," Tania told her with a squeeze of the cheek. "You'll wreck your eyeliner."

Cynthia wonders if Papa Legba had been exerting some influence over them both, stoking their lust, removing their barriers, allowing them to be themselves for the first time since graduation. If so, she owes him, even if it has left her feeling confused.

Or maybe they are both healing now, finally accepting a true part of themselves that had been buried under the expectation of family and society. Tania is actively bi, Cynthia knows that. It's part of the reason Tania makes her annual pilgrimages to New Orleans, where she can explore her sexuality without reproach. But Cynthia is surprised at how easily she succumbed; her flesh so sensitive from the razor, Tania's tongue and fingers leaving Cynthia panting on the bathroom floor. Maybe any touch is a good touch at this stage of her life, and who better than from her dearest, closest friend? How is Tania feeling, after sharing such an intimate moment as they did barely two hours ago, and then packing off her lover to perhaps be seduced by one of the most infamous lotharios in New Orleans?

"Maybe I shouldn't go," she'd said, wrapped in Tania's arms.

"You have to," Tania had answered. "He's an institution, a patron of the arts. You can't look this gift horse in the mouth."

And then added lustily, "But y'all come back now." It had taken an effort of will to not sink into that cheeky, sexy smile; to finish dressing and head out into the night.

Cynthia retrieves her makeup mirror from her clutch purse and studies her lipstick. Her lips look a little swollen under the scarlet paint, a reaction to the recent passion. They look good, she decides, even as she feels again Tania's lips on hers, her thrusting tongue and nibbling teeth, working down her throat and breasts, down between her legs.

"We're there, lady," the cab driver says. "You gettin' out or what?" He gives her a curious look in the rearview mirror. Cynthia uncrosses her legs, aware of the pulsing heat her memory has re-ignited.

No backing out now, Cynthia thinks. She pays the driver and stands on the street, aware of her excitement, certain she can smell her own musky scent rising up underneath her subtle, floral perfume. The smell of stale beer and stagnant water floats about her. Somewhere, maybe on nearby Canal, someone laughs extra loud, a real mule bray, and she hears the unmistakable rumble of the street car. They are sounds from another world.

Her attention is focused on the building opposite, where a man in a black suit stands at the top of a short set of stairs leading into a gallery.

She takes a deep breath and clutches her purse. "Papa Legba, if you're still riding with me, please don't let me down now." She lets out her breath, willing her heart to stop trying to leap out of her chest, and walks with what she hopes is confidence and grace across the uneven street to meet her host, the charming and enigmatic Monsieur Alexander Rakoczy.

Her heels strike the cobbles. The sound rings of confidence she doesn't feel. The night air is chilled by a breeze coming off the Mississippi; finally an autumn night with a touch of winter. The cool drifts around her naked legs, steals through the slit in her dress. Every step is a reminder of recent pleasure, of a fire relit from ashes.

Now, with a loa in tow and the love of a good friend still burning on her skin, she announces herself to the man at the door and can't help but smile as his eyes flick from his clipboard to her breasts to the pale expanse of leg. He clears his throat and swallows his interest to tick off her name, greet her, and direct her to a circular iron staircase at the far corner of the room. Cynthia takes her time, making a show of considering the paintings of nudes that adorn the walls—variations of age and style but all exude a sense of confident sexuality she finds reassuring. She enjoys the echo of her heels on the timber floor, the weight of the man's eyes on her butt. The tattoo that arches in swirls and circles across her lower back warms under his hungry gaze until she reaches the stairs and starts to climb. A part of her is reluctant to leave those portraits; she was like those women once, or so she felt. She wonders if she can be again. Down deep, past the thumping of her heart and the gentle pulse in her groin, she can hear last night's voodoo beat and Papa Legba's gravelled chuckle.

A woman in slacks and suit-coat opens a door at the top of the landing and Cynthia almost recoils from the blast of heat and noise that greets her. The thundering, wailing cacophony of metal she has rarely listened to since university makes her ears ache. Nightclub lights blind her with flashing primary colours splashing against dark, brick walls.

With a nervous glance at the woman at the door, Cynthia forces herself to enter, her curiosity aroused even as her nervousness blossoms.

There is art on the walls, but it's almost invisible in this lightshow. She senses rather than sees the forms: women and men, some with animal heads, in various acts of congress. An animorphic bacchanalia with all the style and grace of Ancient Rome, possibly drawing from an even deeper well. Men and women are scattered around the room, shouting in each other's ear, drinking champagne offered by servants wearing nothing but body paint, not even hair, or peering at the art through the gloom, or simply sitting on the handful of couches, making out.

Cynthia is met by two people: a man painted blue except for his dangling scarlet cock who offers her a choice of champagne, wine or a line of coke—she takes the champagne with a trembling hand and gulps a generous sip, barely tasting it—and a woman in a revealing black dress whose hand brushes her buttock even as she pushes herself against Cynthia's left hip.

"So glad you could make it, darling," she whispers wetly in Cynthia's ear as the servant walks away. "He's expecting you."

She leads her to the back of the room and gestures her through a door painted as a giant vulva. The woman shuts the door behind Cynthia. The music dies to a dull, bass throb. Cynthia leans against the door—she's alone, her senses struggling with the sudden quiet, the dim light provided by flickering candles set around the walls. Her eyes adjust and she takes another sip to steady herself.

The walls are covered with velvet: rich burgundy, black and purple. Had she not had her back to the door, she doubts she'd be able to find it, so expertly do the drapes hang. She takes in a large chair at the far end of the room, a side-table next to it bearing absinthe shining green in the light of an adjacent candle, a silver spoon and mound of sugar cubes nearby. There is the smell of wax and incense, oil paint and turpentine. She finds an easel in the gloom, can make out spots of paint on the bare, smooth timber floor that reflects the candlelight in its highly polished surface.

Cynthia gasps as she realises the walls have long strips of blank canvas attached, all blank bar one. It's her painting, the one she made with Tania. She walks closer so she can see the splotches of breasts and buttocks, the smears where they dragged their pubic mounds across the canvas, the hand and foot prints; feels again those ghostly touches on her flesh, not just from earlier tonight, but from the long years since they'd made this art with their naïve passion.

Movement catches her eye and she gasps again; clutches her champagne glass, now almost empty, tightly by the stem. A figure emerges from the shadows. How had she not noticed him? She stumbles backwards, pushes herself against the door as the man approaches. She recognises him, barely, from his rare appearances in the Times-Picayune and art magazines. The master portrait artist, it seems, does not like his portrait being recorded, at least not by anything as gauche as a camera.

"I am so pleased you were able to come, and that you chose to wear my gift," he says, and his voice forms a melody with the beat in her chest, with the bass that shivers her flesh as it penetrates the wall behind her. She realises, in a detached part of her mind, that she knows this band: Danzig, of all things. Incongruous, but somehow so right as she feels the air thicken between them, feels it grow hot with candle flame flickering in unseen and unfelt drafts. Of course the room would be ventilated, she thinks, abstractedly, or the fumes would overcome him. *Might* overcome him. Because looking at him now, his hand reaching out to greet her as he glides, lion-like with silent, effortless footsteps, she cannot imagine anything overcoming him. At least, not without his approval.

The loa writhes in her belly like a boa constrictor lazily uncoiling; she feels the phantom touch of Papa Legba as he revels in the champagne, the music, her pounding pulse. Her vision narrows to see only Alexander's eyes—"Call me Alexander", "Of course . . . Alexander"—and she hides her teeth behind her hand. His eyes are a serpentine yellow that seem to strip her to the bone. Why have her wear this dress if he could look right through it, she wonders as he extends that hand. Those fingers, seemingly stretching towards her, pale and oh so long and delicate with clear, sharp nails that she imagines—feels—pawing across her naked back, leaving red welts in their passage. Feels them on her thighs, sliding up and around and into her wetness . . .

She blinks, looking for air in the claustrophobic heat, feels sweat on her brow and between her breasts and in the small of her back. She tries to say hello and it comes out as a sigh. She raises her glass but can't find her mouth. His gaze mesmerises; she sees in her peripheral vision his long, black tresses falling in waves across his shoulders, ebon against his pale, porcelain-thin skin that shows a delicate roadmap of blue-purple veins. Thick, black brows in a straight line overhang those eyes; under them, a strong, thin nose and full lips and pointed chin and bright, bright teeth. A flicker of tongue is an unspoken promise that melts her knees. She grips her purse and her glass, desperate for water on her parched lips, her parched tongue.

She senses the strength of his frame, the grace inside that shirt, as red as her dress—as exactly scarlet, she thinks, taken from the same cloth with its elegant lace front and cuffs—and the dancer's balance contained by the tight black pants and the knee-high leather boots that add an aura of aristocracy.

His hand touches hers, removes the champagne glass. His fingers are cold, colder than the empty glass. And then he takes her hand and she feels her warmth flow into him, until his hand is a coal in hers, the heat running all the way to her groin, making her nipples burn, her chest tighten. She leans against the wall, grateful for support.

"Do you recognise the painting, Cynthia?" he asks, and his voice strikes as deep as music, as deep as Danzig.

"I can't believe you've got it," she says hoarsely.

"Come, look closer."

He leads her to the centre of the room. Danzig still plays and her hips sway to the rhythm. Papa Legba is calling for more champagne as he taps his foot in time, making her stomach melt with every beat.

Alexander stands behind her, his pelvis pushed lightly against her rump, his stiffness unmistakable against her buttocks. His hands are on her shoulders, the fingernails glinting in the corner of her vision. She sees again, up close, the familiar splotches and scrapes, dots and smears, and recalls in detailed clarity the passion that drove that painting, the two of them smearing each other with paint of various colours, switching between sex and art with every passing moment.

She leans back against Alexander, feeling his strength support her as his body presses against hers.

His breath gusts hot, flavoured by absinthe's aniseed tang and a heavier, earthier scent. "I would see the delicate brush that created this work," he says.

"That brush is long gone," she tells him, and feels the ache in her belly where her child once was, a vacuum where a rich life should have been. Tears fall unbidden.

"Hush," he says, and turns her to face him. He kisses her tears with hot lips. "I can see the tools remain unblemished, if only you would pick them up. The brush is the instrument but it is nothing compared to the passion that wields it. Life goes on." A look of ineffable sadness crosses his face and she cries a faint 'oh' as something sharp twists in her heart.

She shakes, wishing again for his heat against her, his solidity. The music is louder and her hips and shoulders sway as Legba rises to the occasion, a salve for her insecurity. She remembers Tania, covered in blues and greens, her nipples so tight as she pushed her onto the canvas and ground her hips against Cynthia's, trying she said for the perfect butt print, but content to ride her paint-slick leg and use her yellow-matted hair to make a distorted halo. She remembers Tania, lifting her face from between Cynthia's legs to tell Cynthia that she is beautiful.

Alexander steps back to his easel and gestures to the waiting paints.

"Okay," Cynthia breathes, and runs her hands over her breasts and hips and up her thighs, swirling the slit skirt to one side to the obvious delight of Alexander, whose eyes follow her every movement with hungry obsession.

She reaches up, feeling as though she should be on the banks of the Mississippi, drinking cheap liquor with her buddies under the stars, working up the nerve to dive into the water that claimed Buckley and, far more recently, so many of New Orleans' own. She reaches up and frees the knot at her nape and lets the dress slide. She pries it from her breasts, tweaks her straining nipples, revels in curves she's long ignored. She pushes the silky cloth from her hips, sliding the material down so it pools around her ankles, and steps free, feeling an eddy of fresh air that makes the candles shiver, even as her body goosepimples to the touch. She dances slowly, swaying to that familiar, filthy Danzig beat, her hands on her body, over her head, at her side, as though chasing the notes through the air and making them hers.

Alexander beckons and she teasingly walks to him, aware of her heels tapping on the floor, of the rope of lust that binds her to him. He pulls her in, but at her pace. His hands are smeared in red, so dark in the candlelight. He coats her body, delicately, as she sways and turns, revealing herself to him like a belly dancer before a shah. He coats her with paint that quickly warms, from elbow to knee, and leads her to the wall where she finds a vacant canvas and begins to dance. Slowly at first, and then faster as she channels the music from her youth until it jerks her body uncontrollably. Legba, she can feel Legba, working her limbs, driving her on. She twirls and flails against the canvas, slamming her breasts against it, her pelvis, her hands. She rubs her back against it, a pole dancer, knees wide, eyes locked on the staring, lascivious gaze of Alexander, gratified to see the dew on his parted lips, the bulge in his pants.

The music hits a crescendo and Legba tells her as she gasps her first, small orgasm, that Alexander's all hers.

She sags as Alexander gives a cry, tears open his silky shirt. His chest is smooth and pale and finely muscled. His nipples are dark buds, his hips narrow, his stomach flat. Dark hair tendrils from behind his belt to his navel.

Then he is on her, lifting her, covering her mouth with kisses. Sharp bites release a coppery warmth into her mouth and she turns her head to the side. His mouth finds her throat. Her hands are on his belt, his fly, his cock. He lifts her effortlessly and impales her, driving her against a canvas. She opens her arms and reaches them across the canvas, letting him take her entire weight. The orgasm builds with urgent intensity, as though everything that has gone before has merely been a prelude to this moment. She seizes his head as the spasms wrack her; she grinds against him with savage abandon. His fangs are in her throat and she screams as her passion explodes and she feels, distantly through the white-hot heat that consumes her, Alexander spending himself in her in a series of violent, desperate lunges.

. . . . .

They lie together on the floor, covered in paint, raised on their elbows to best sip the absinthe he has made and take in their newly created artwork.

It is a lurid thing, all black and red, though not all the red is paint. She feels the throb on both sides of her neck where his fangs have parted her flesh; a dribble of dry blood tracks through the oil on her breast, red on red, pale flesh showing through underneath.

She can trace her loss of control through the swirls and splatters, and there the climax amidst the bold strokes of angel wings, where he lifted her and drove her to the peak of passion.

It is, she thinks, a much more mature work than the earlier version she and Tania created. Though that version is also not without its merit. It tells of an earlier time, a more innocent time, though one that might not be entirely out of reach.

"What will you call it?" she asks. The heat of the absinthe runs through her, restoring her, loosening her. With their bodies cooling, side by side, it allows truth, she thinks.

"Maybe *Moon God's Lust*," he says.

"I thought the moon god was a woman."

"Some might say so. *Moon Goddess's Lust* doesn't come off the tongue as well. I guess," he says, stroking her chin, kissing her with a hint of sharp tooth and teasing tongue, "we could make another for the sun god. Though I am not partial to him, if you must know."

She considers his offer. There is another bare canvas yet, on the wall facing the fresh work. How would the third piece balance this new one, and the older, brighter work?

"I'll think about it." She rolls away to avoid his puzzled expression, her action too quick for even him to reach for her. She retrieves the dress and pulls it on, aware of the stains from the paint, that she must look a mess.

He pulls himself into a sitting position, his expression now one of faint amusement. "We work well together," he says. "We could make beautiful art for a very long time."

"We could," she says, finding her purse, then staggering as the dizziness hits from standing up too quickly. Her pelvis aches from his lovemaking, her neck throbs, her lips feel sandpapered. "But I already have a painting partner, and we have a lot of catching up to do."

He laughs. "I find creativity benefits from a broad range of influences." His cock is already stiff as he stands.

She walks quickly to the door, before her body can betray her. Papa Legba is squirming inside her, re-awakened by the absinthe, enjoying the game. She finds the door through the velvet and cracks it open. Alexander stands back, just one step, his hands still by his sides, as the faint grey light of early morning etches the doorway through the distant, darkened windows of the gallery. She hadn't even heard the party end.

Cynthia smiles, eager now to embrace the new day, to wash the paint and sweat and sex from her body, and crawl fresh and clean into bed beside Tania and whisper all that happened into her ear.

"I'll be working from home for a while," she says. "Maybe next time I'll invite you to *my* opening."

He laughs as she steps out and shuts the door. By the time she hits the street, she is wondering what colour dress he's chosen for Tania.

The Dark Season

Heather Albano

ISABEL Derrenford smoothed her gloves. They were perfect—ivory-white, unornamented but of exceptional quality, neatly buttoned—and must remain so. Neat gloves were one of the traits that distinguished a true lady, and tonight every detail of her appearance was important, for she expected to receive a proposal of marriage.

It was high time an arrangement be reached: the London Season was more than half over already.

"We can manage it," her mother had said at the start of the Season. "We must be very careful, after the scandal last year—that girl who was discovered to suffer from seizures after entering into an engagement . . . Families of eligible young men are employing more caution this year, so we must be discreet, but we can manage it."

On the surface, the London Season was a whirlwind of fun for young ladies and gentlemen—four dizzying months of balls and carriage rides and card games and musical performances. The romantic veneer could not hide the reality: it was in actuality much more like a butchers' market, wherein the daughters of the nobility and gentry were paraded before eligible young men and their parents. Should a girl be charming and well-mannered and do nothing to disgrace herself—and of course be possessed of wealth or pedigree, if not both—she could expect at least one offer of marriage before London society dispersed to the country. If the girl failed to secure such an offer, she might return the following Season, and try again, and perhaps once more. After three failed Seasons, however, she would be forever branded unmarriageable.

Isabel had no intention of such a fate befalling her, and in her case, a second Season was utterly out of the question. Her mother's resources could not possibly extend so far. Isabel had only this one chance, and she intended to make the most of it. She meant to walk away from tonight's ball having secured an offer of marriage.

She was labouring under some disadvantages, she knew. Her dark hair and eyes were as far from the blonde blue-eyed fashionable ideal as it was possible to be—inherited from her foreign-born mother, whose birth was another disadvantage. *I heard she has gypsy blood,* Isabel had heard a society matron inform another in a stage whisper, and had clenched her hands and teeth hard in an effort to betray no reaction. It was enough that she had lost the chance of being courted by either of these women's sons; she must not make a scene that would endanger her reputation with the rest.

At least her skin was as fair and fine as bone china, and her father's bloodline unimpeachable. He had died during the many years the family had lived abroad, but there were enough golden-haired, blue-eyed relations in London to remind everyone of who he had been. Though he had not left a fortune, there was a small, respectable sum put aside for Isabel's dowry. And a childhood spent abroad turned some of Isabel's oddities into exoticism.

For the rest, Isabel had been drilled by her mother in all the accomplishments considered necessary for a proper young lady. She could speak both French and German; she could dance gracefully; she could converse politely with a young man and his mother. Her excessively fair skin made it impractical for her to ride in the Row or pay calls under the bright morning sun, but so much of the Season was conducted after dark that her absence during these activities had passed thus far unnoticed. Once darkness fell, Isabel executed her role flawlessly at every ball and salon and musical performance she attended, winning the attention and admiration of many eligible young men.

Tonight was no exception: her dancing card was full. She danced the first quadrille with young Mr de Witt, and enjoyed it greatly, for he was a fine dancer and an agreeable conversationalist. But she expected nothing more from him than the momentary pleasure. He had not a cent to his name, and was in search of an alliance with a girl far richer than she. Colonel Markham led her to the floor for the second dance, but from him she likewise expected nothing. It was well known that he devoted his attentions mostly to Miss Alice King, and although he periodically asked for the honour of partnering another lady, that was merely to observe the proprieties—for while a serious suitor *might* dance more than twice with one girl and still escape scandal, he might not monopolise her attention for an entire evening before a formal betrothal was agreed upon. Colonel Markham was exceedingly proper about all such things: indeed, Isabel had often thought that he did not approve of her.

The Colonel returned her formally to her mother's side when the dance was over, and there young Mr Terrington found her. She had promised him the third dance, and had been glad to do it. He was not strikingly handsome, but his looks were pleasing: his light brown hair fell over one eye in a manner that amused her, and his light blue eyes were guileless and honest. They had spoken often together and he sought two dances with her at every opportunity; she thought he enjoyed her company. And she enjoyed his. Their dance was a waltz, and she leaned into his embrace as closely as she dared. His arm tightened around her waist, and she hoped he might take advantage of the moment. A waltz was not a quadrille, and a couple might sneak away to somewhere private without disordering the figures and being caught—not being caught being the essential point, for it would irretrievably ruin the girl's reputation.

But he made no move to draw her towards a secluded place, for he was, of course, a nice young man. Isabel suppressed a sigh. He would do nothing to damage her reputation, even if she might wish him to. The only thing he did ask was whether he might beg her company for the evening's second waltz.

"Oh, I am sorry," Isabel said lightly. "I am already engaged for the second waltz." She had engaged herself deliberately, hoping that it might kindle within young Mr Terrington a sense of urgency. He must know as well as she did that neither de Witt nor Markham had any serious intentions towards her, but if she could make him believe that someone else did . . .

Terrington did not respond as she wished him to—or, indeed, at all. Isabel tried again, looking up at him: "But I am sure I could put him off this once and be forgiven, if you—"

"Oh, no," Mr Terrington replied. "You must not do that. May I ask who has the honour?"

"Lord Robert Blackwell."

Terrington's arm tightened around her waist again. "Miss Derrenford—" he said. "Isabel—" She looked back up at the use of her first name, and saw the real distress in his pale eyes. "You must not— I wish you would not— I would not be a friend if I did not warn you against spending time with that man. He is not of savoury reputation, Isabel. There is an—an ugly story about his elder brother and a young lady. There is an uglier story about his cousin. I wish you would . . . be careful in your dealings with him. I wish you would not deal with him at all."

"I must dance the second waltz with someone, sir," Isabel replied. *I must secure a marriage offer from someone.* The moment hung there between them . . . but he did not make her an offer, either for the waltz or for anything more permanent. *I cannot wait forever for you to take action,* Isabel thought. *I would rather have you, but I must have someone.*

When their dance was over, she walked away from him as slowly as possible, but he did not call her back.

So she danced the second waltz with wild young Lord Robert. She knew exactly what ugly story had circulated about his lordship's elder brother. He had tempted a girl into a compromising position, so that she had to marry him—for whom else could she marry, after having been caught kissing out in the garden, far away from the indoor propriety of a ball? The story about the cousin was indeed worse: he had persuaded a girl to run away with him, but then refused to actually marry her, so that she—and her family— were ruined indeed.

Lord Robert liked Isabel's vivacity in the same way that Colonel Markham disapproved of it. He told her she was jolly fun, and held her much too close to him while they waltzed. Isabel waited for Terrington to cut in.

But he did not; it became abundantly clear that he would not. Isabel's mother had said that if he truly cared for her, jealousy or a desire to save her from harm would make him speak. The conclusion was as inescapable as it was unwelcome. He must not actually care.

"My dear Miss Derrenford," Lord Robert purred in her ear. "You look unwell. Is it the closeness of the room, perhaps? I wonder if you would not be more comfortable out on the balcony. I am sure you would find it refreshing to stand for a few moments in the clean air."

Any girl who allowed a young man to inveigle her into a secluded place deserved what she got—or so ran the opinion of the town. The girls ruined by Lord Robert's brother and cousin had been too dazzled by the courtship of a rich young nobleman to remember that lesson. Or perhaps they had been distracted by the romance of the idea, or the mischief of it. Isabel, on the contrary, felt utterly businesslike about the experience. She needed to secure a husband. She agreed that the room was indeed unpleasantly close, and the fresh air from the balcony marvellously inviting, and she let him guide her away from the rest of the dancers. There was still, after all, the chance that Mr Terrington might see them leaving and intervene . . . But though she listened hard for the sound of his feet running after her, she did not hear them.

Heavy golden-brown curtains separated the ballroom from the balcony. Lord Robert held one aside and gestured Isabel to precede him—with a bow graceful and courteous, but with a smile that showed his teeth. Isabel stepped out of the ballroom and onto the balcony.

He followed her. She could feel him behind her—a source of warmth in the chilly air—but did not turn at once. She stayed turned away, as though admiring the night, so that he would come closer. She slipped the handle of her fan over her wrist, and unfurled it.

He took a stride that brought him suddenly just behind her, and she turned, covering her mouth with her fan as though startled and dismayed. There was a predatory glint in his eye, reminding her of the way the wolves of her homeland crouched before they sprang. He leaned in, pushing her delicate fan out of his way.

He stopped short when he saw the gleam of the moonlight on her incisors, but her hands were on his shoulders now, and he was not prepared for the inhuman strength of them. That strength—and the teeth—had been the hardest thing to hide, all these weeks of playing at the Season's game. He tried to pull away, but Isabel sank her fangs into his throat.

It was over very quickly, and Isabel blotted her lips delicately on his cravat before releasing her hold. He slumped into the shadowed corner where the rail and window met. He was not dead: the dizziness would pass in a short time, and should anyone find him before that, they would assume an excess of spirits. He was, after all, known to be a wild young man.

Isabel peeped through the curtains, judged that no one could see her, and slipped back inside.

The waltz was not even half over. A roomful of eligible young men still spun about in circles, eligible young women clasped in their arms. Nearer to hand, Isabel's mother stood awaiting her—a tall and elegant figure, most correctly attired in rustling silk. She was a handsome woman for one old enough to have a grown daughter, with her hair still raven-black and her milk-white skin still remarkably unlined. She held in her hand a pair of fresh gloves. Isabel had managed to keep Blackwell's blood from staining her gown, but there were indeed—as her mother had foreseen—tiny red flecks on her gloves. A mother giving her daughter a fresh pair of gloves was nothing unusual: the flecks might have come from splashed punch, an accident that could befall any girl.

Isabel's mother took the soiled gloves calmly. "It is done, then?"

Isabel smiled behind her fan, careful to keep her sharp teeth hidden. Blackwell would recover from the dizziness to hear her voice whispering in his mind. Later, he would discover the other urges that whispered. Soon, he would come to her, and they would be married, and after the Season ended, she and her mother would take him along when they returned to their life abroad. He could live like Papa in the castle, dependent upon her for food, or she would turn him loose to hunt among the peasantry if he preferred. Once he had given her a daughter to raise as her heir, it did not much matter what he chose to do with himself. And there was always the chance that *this* time one of their captured Englishmen would beget a son instead, a son bound by law to inherit his father's lands in Britain.

"It's done," Isabel said. She was aware of a flicker within her mind as, out on the balcony, Blackwell came groggily back to himself. She felt him try to stand; she felt him try to remember; she felt him become aware of the fetters with which she had bound him. He thrashed against them more strongly than she had been led to believe was typical, certainly more strongly than sweet-tempered Mr Terrington could have managed. It was in some sense unfortunate that circumstances had forced her to select a man so unwilling to be subdued . . . but on the other hand, a challenge might be most pleasantly diverting. "It's done. Who else could he marry now?"

The Last Gig of Jimmy Rucker

Martin Livings & Talie Helene

AINSLEY stood in the rain at the red crossing light and waited patiently, despite the light London traffic at 3AM on a Wednesday. It was an automatic reaction, a knee-jerk reflex that was bloody hard to overcome. She even knew she'd look left as she crossed, as directed by the large friendly letters stencilled on the road at her feet. Besides, waiting for the little red man to turn green gave her an excuse to look across the street at The Palais from a decent distance, take it all in. It looked dark and deserted, hardly surprising considering the mid-week hour; live gigs and nightclub sessions ran almost every night there during the summer months, but not so much in winter, and they'd usually be well and truly finished by three in the morning. Even so, the building sent a frisson of excitement down Ainsley's spine. It sat there on the corner, hunkered down like a proud bulldog, the dark painted modern frontage in stark contrast to its main pale body. Its huge domed roof, a delicate green of verdigris in sunlight, was almost jet black in that early morning hour, the halogen street lights not quite reaching that high, and was slick with the mandatory London drizzle. She'd been to many a gig there as a punter, but this would be her first time in a professional capacity. In fact, it was her first time in a professional capacity anywhere. Her first job. And it was at The Palais. The bloody Palais.

She felt like she needed to pinch herself, again. She'd only gotten her diploma from LAMDA a few months earlier, after a couple of years of studying to be a light and sound technician there. Most of the training was theatrical, but she'd focused on live music as much as she could. It was something she'd wanted to do ever since the first gig she'd been to, a family-friendly outdoor concert her parents had taken her to at Hyde Park when she was eight or nine. Oasis had played, louder and more alive than anything else she'd ever heard or seen before in her life, the light show more beautiful than the best fireworks. She'd known, even then, that she wanted to be involved in music, in one way or another. She'd dreamt of being a rock star, bought a guitar, taught herself to play after a fashion, but never managed to get very good at it. But this, this was something she could do, something she *was* good at. Something worthwhile, not like a nine-to-five in a business skirt and jacket, mortgages and life insurance and joyless sunburnt holidays in Tenerife. She'd worked hard, gotten her credentials, and then realised she had no idea how to actually get work in the business. So, with naïve optimism, she'd gone and put posters up at all the music shops around London, just one flyer out of the hundreds on each bulletin board. For the first week, she'd expected the phone to be ringing off the hook. By the third, she'd lost all hope, and the nine-to-five was starting to look pretty bloody attractive after all.

Then the call came, just a few hours earlier. An emergency job. The Palais, 3AM. Pay wasn't even discussed; Ainsley hadn't thought to raise the subject, wasn't even sure how. She'd just agreed without a second thought, not even considering the dangers of travelling alone on London's streets in the early hours of the morning.

And now here she was. The Palais.

Ainsley knew it had been built in Victorian times as a theatre, and had been used as an entertainment venue of one kind or another pretty much ever since, apart from that period in the seventies when it stood idle: dark times that nobody ever spoke of too loudly, like theatre actors and the Scottish play, a superstition rooted deep in the bones of musos and punters alike. But since it reopened in the eighties, it had been one of *the* happening places in North London; smaller than the Apollo or the Roundhouse, yeah, but all the more intimate for that. Ainsley had caught Echo and the Bunnymen there a couple of times, mechanically reliving their eighties heyday, and that Australian band Wolfmother had torn the hall up just the year before. But she'd never been there in circumstances like these. Looking at the dark doorways under the red marquees, she wondered for about the thousandth time in the hours since the phone call if this whole thing was some kind of cruel practical joke, a mean prank played on a green wannabe, maybe by one of her ex-classmates. Or, worse, some kind of trap, laid for a single woman, alone at night, defenceless. She snorted at that thought; she could take care of herself. The small tin of pepper spray in her jacket pocket and a reasonable knowledge of martial arts would see to that. And she could run like the wind if she had to.

A high-pitched beep and clicking noise interrupted her dark thoughts, as the little man on the pole opposite her transformed from red to green. Without thinking, Ainsley stepped off the kerb, looking left just as she'd been reminded to by the almighty road, and walked over to the other side. Before she knew it, she was under one of the red awnings, THE PALAIS written in large white letters across its side. *This is crazy,* she thought again. *This is nuts. It's closed. There's no way I'm getting in.* She stepped up to the door and tried the handle.

Locked.

Disappointment and relief washed over her in almost equal portions, sprinkling down like the rain on the marquee. She was turning to leave when she noticed the Post-It note on the door, flapping in the cold wind.

Ms Fletcher, Please come around the side. J

Ainsley had no idea who "J" was; the voice on the phone had given almost no details apart from the place and time, and not to bring any gear. *"It's all provided,"* they'd said. And Ainsley, in her excitement and inexperience, hadn't even thought to ask. She pulled the yellow note from the door, wondering how it had managed to stay put in the wind and rain—even under the marquee, it was getting soaked—and shoved it into her pocket. Then she stepped back onto the footpath and walked around the side of the building, down an unlit alleyway. There was a door there, barely visible in the shadows. It was ajar.

Ainsley stepped inside, into the darkness, shook water from her shoulder-length dreadlocks. She stood for a few seconds, allowing her eyes to adjust to the low light. There *was* some light to be had, a dim glow from deeper in the building. And something else as well, a sound. Music. An acoustic guitar, unamplified, and a voice without a microphone, natural. She couldn't quite make out the words or the tune, but something about it made her shiver.

Come on, she chided herself silently. *You're in The Palais, in the middle of the night, about to work your first light and sound job. Grow some stones and get in there!*

She took a deep breath and walked towards the light.

Pulling aside a curtain, she could see into the main auditorium. She was at the side, about half-way between the stalls and the stage. She stood there for a moment, blinking. She'd been here dozens of times before, was very familiar with the décor, but it seemed that someone had been very busy remodelling it. Some of it was the same; the art deco sculptures on the walls hadn't been touched, still those vaguely threatening Medusa heads glaring out from all sides. But instead of the two modern bars, one on either side, there was just a single one, more old-fashioned, with posters for booze and fags that hadn't been sold in Ainsley's lifetime. The stainless steel fittings and smoked glass mirrors were all gone, replaced with wooden fixtures and panelling. Even the lighting above the stage was new, or, perhaps more accurately, old; simple spots, unmotorised and unsophisticated. And there on the stage, under one of the spots, was a man on a stool, playing a beat-up old acoustic guitar, just him and his instrument, the single vintage amp behind him unplugged, the mikes unused.

> Well I love to ramble,
> And I've wandered O' so far,
> Lost my mind in the Himalayas,
> Lost my heart in a Stockholm bar.
> My innocence fled me,
> Down in New Orleans,

And in alleyways in Marrakesh,
I almost touched my dreams.

Ainsley recognised the song now, and the man singing it, and also understood why it had given her the shivers. The song was "Sweet London Town", a song from the late sixties by Spirit Level, one of those bands that should have been huge, but had fallen apart just before their big break. Spirit Level had only released the one eponymous album, before the incident that had ended both their career and all but closed The Palais in that one awful moment in 1969. The man singing it had not recorded or performed since.

I rode a caballito,
Down in New Mexico,
Aaaw, those painted ladies,
Nowhere the brush doesn't go.
I've fallen love with Paris,
The tart broke my heart,
I licked my wounds in Amsterdam,
Turning back the clock.
But that great old lady,
Keeps calling me on home,
She's my old lady,
Sweet London town.

Jimmy Rucker still looked like . . . well, like Jimmy Rucker. Ainsley had only ever seen photos of him from the sixties; after sixty-nine, he'd all but disappeared from the public eye, unlike the other remaining band members who'd mostly gone onto other, less stellar projects. Rucker, though, he'd retired, from music, from fame, from everything. Who could blame him? Spirit Level had cost him dearly, more than anyone should ever have to pay. He'd earned his solitude. But now here he was, over forty years later, on the same stage he'd last performed on, singing that song again. Older, yes; some middle-aged paunch beneath the denim jacket, hair thinning but still black and long, tied back in a ponytail, face lined by decades. But still Jimmy Rucker. And his voice . . . sweet Jesus, his voice . . .

Yeah, I love to ramble,
But I sorely hate to go,
I swear there's a compass,
Wired deep into my soul.
Those streets of my childhood,
Where my dreams took flight,
The echoes of a distant past,
Calling me home through the night.

Ainsley was utterly transfixed, feeling as if she was in a dream. Her parents, in addition to exposing her to live music, had also introduced her to Spirit Level; the album, that one perfect album, was one of her favourites. And Jimmy Rucker, the poet-warrior, was one of her earliest and deepest crushes. She still had his poster on her wall, the promotional shot from sixty-eight, standing in a paisley suit beside a gigantic tree, leaning casually against its bark, a small wry smile playing across his lips. She'd known he'd been married at the time of the photograph, and knew of the tragedy that had followed so soon after it, but it still warmed her heart to look upon that young, wise, innocent face. And now he was sitting on stage, and playing to her. Just to her.

She's a great old lady,
She keeps calling me on home.
She's my old lady,
Sweet London town.

Rucker sat there for a while after finishing, just letting the last chords echo in the hall. Then he looked up and saw Ainsley.

"Hey kid," he called, his accent still leaning sharply toward the cockney East after all these years.

"Hey," Ainsley responded automatically.

"How did that sound?" the man asked. "It's been a while; I'm a bit rusty."

Rusty? Ainsley thought in disbelief. "It . . . it sounded good. Great," she corrected himself. "Brilliant, actually, Mister Rucker."

Rucker laughed. "Christ almighty, kid, that's what they called my dad. Jimmy, please. You Ms Fletcher?"

"Ainsley," she responded with a nervous grin. She walked up to the stage, and Rucker leaned down. They shook hands. Rucker's hand was hot and sweaty, a rocker's hand.

"Thanks for comin' at such short notice," he said to her. "I need to do a quick run-through, blow the cobwebs out of the system, a bit of a dress rehearsal, but my usual tech, he had a dodgy goat curry at that Nepalese place, you know the one in Paddington? He's already set all the sound levels and lights up for me, but I still need someone to be here and listen, and he's too busy callin' Jesus on the porcelain phone, if you know what I mean." He winked.

Ainsley nodded, though a pang of disappointment jabbed at her ego. "So, no board work?" she asked, more sullenly than she'd intended. She cursed himself silently for being so damn unprofessional. It's *Jimmy Rucker*.

"Well, there might be a few tweaks here and there, Ainsley," he responded with an understanding smile. "You're here for your ears and your hands, after all. Go check it out." He pointed to the back of the auditorium.

Ainsley turned and started walking away.

"Hey, kid?"

She stopped and turned back. "Yes, Mister Rucker? I mean, Jimmy?"

"Come over here."

Ainsley walked back to the edge of the stage. Rucker reached into his pocket and pulled something out, then knelt down and held it out to her. Ainsley looked at what Rucker had in his palm. Two tiny squares of paper, each with a tiny peace symbol drawn on it.

"Uh, thanks, but no," Ainsley responded. "Call me crazy, but I prefer to work straight. My ears and hands aren't much good to you if they're smashed."

"Aw, c'mon," Rucker wheedled. "It's just a bit of acid. Hardly any, either. Just for a buzz."

Ainsley hesitated, then took one of the squares from Rucker's hand. She knew she shouldn't, but she found himself not wanting to disappoint this man, this legend. She popped it in her mouth.

"Good girl!" Rucker placed the other square on his own tongue, and winked at Ainsley again. It actually creeped her out a bit. This wasn't quite how she'd pictured him, all those years ago, dancing to the music, imagining being on stage with him. She almost laughed at that thought. Reality's never quite as romantic as fantasy.

Turning to walk away from the stage and towards the sound and light board, Ainsley surreptitiously fished the square back out of her mouth, rolled it between her finger and thumb into a tiny spitwad of a ball, and shoved it into her pocket. She hoped she'd avoided the worst of it. Once she'd taken a tab at Glastonbury, and spent the next three hours obsessed by her purple-painted fingernails, how they sprouted from the flesh of her fingers, with that tiny crescent of white flappy skin at the boundaries. Not exactly the best state of mind to be working in, not tonight of all nights. As she walked, she looked around again, marvelling at the job the decorators had done in there. It looked authentically period, like the photos she'd seen of the venue back in the sixties.

"The place looks amazing," she called back over her shoulder.

"Does it?" Rucker replied. "Looks same as ever to me."

"That's what's so amazing." Ainsley grinned, and climbed the stairs up to the second balcony level, where, right in the middle and at the front, the mixing desk sat. The house lights on this level were a little dimmer than down near the stage, so Ainsley reached into her jacket pocket and pulled out the small headlamp she always liked to have with her, just in case. She pulled it on over her dreads and thumbed the switch, the LED lamp coming to life and illuminating the board before her. It was a thing of simple beauty: not covered in whiz-bang electronics, a million different sliders and knobs, LCD panels and readouts like the ones she'd learned her trade on in the Academy. No, this was more basic, more elegant. She immediately understood it, and could clearly see that it had already been set up by someone who knew exactly what they were doing. Until that moment she'd wanted to play with it, fiddle with the settings to suit herself, but there was something about it that changed her mind. It seemed . . . *right*. To its right were the lighting controls, which were even simpler, just half a dozen spots, the footlights at the base of the stage, and the house lights. Ainsley felt like she should have been let down by the lack of nuance—she'd spent hours on much more complex boards during her studies, playing them madly like Manzarek doing a Doors synthesizer solo—but somehow, it seemed appropriate. This wasn't that kind of gig. Ainsley knew that, even though she didn't know exactly what kind of gig it was going to be. She found the switch for the microphone on the desk.

"Mister Rucker? I mean, Jimmy?"

"Yeah, kid?" Rucker called back.

"Is this a solo gig?" she asked. "No support act? No band?"

Rucker shrugged down on stage. "Not sure yet, kid." He grinned. "We'll have to see who turns up." He hooked up his miked-up acoustic to the lead on the floor, and Ainsley heard that distinctive thump and hum as the signal came through the amp. "Right-o, then," he said. "Shall we try another one?"

"That's what we're here for, isn't it?" she called down.

Rucker's expression turned a little strange. "Is it?" he asked. He looked thoughtful for a moment. Then he smiled again. "Yeah, I guess it is. Let's do it," he declared. "Somethin' a little trippier. In honour of the dread lysergic." He turned on the microphone, a big old bastard of a thing perched on its heavy stand. "We set?" he asked into it, and his voice was that of a giant.

Ainsley checked the desk one last time, made sure the faders were all correct for the acoustic. She flicked the footlights on, nice and low, and caught Rucker in a spotlight. Then she nodded, gave the thumbs up.

Rucker nodded in response, and started to play.

A butterfly flutters its wings in China,
A strange little girl rocks my world,
Reading my life in my open hand,
Lifting of veils like Scheherazade wore.
Coming on soft as rain,
Coming on strong as a hurricane,
Butterfly kisses and snow angel wings.

Ainsley closed her eyes, and let herself be carried away on the music. She'd never heard "Butterfly Kisses" played acoustic before. Rucker's guitar was excellent, especially considering he hadn't performed in decades. It almost sounded as if another guitar was accompanying him.

The street is reflecting the sky,
The sky is reflecting the street,

She steps off the kerb of forever,
And crosses an ocean of sleep.
Coming on soft as rain,
Coming on strong as a hurricane,
Butterfly kisses and snow angel wings.

As Ainsley listened, the impression that a second guitar was playing became stronger. And the vocals . . . was that a harmony? She opened his eyes, expecting the illusion to vanish. Her heart skipped a beat.

There was someone on stage with Rucker, in the shadows next to him. She couldn't make anything much out, just a dark shape, an impression of long shaggy hair. Ainsley blinked a few times, rubbed her eyes. No, there was definitely a figure there, holding a guitar. Without thinking, her hand found the switches for the overhead spots, and turned on the one next to Rucker.

Nobody. The light drew a perfect circle on the stage next to the man, revealing nothing at all. Rucker was alone. There were no harmonies, no bass line; just one man, singing and playing his guitar. The illusion burst like a soap bubble. She turned the spot off again. Rucker didn't seem to notice.

My mind unhinges and opens a door,
A white rabbit dash down a corridor,
To the heart of the Temple of Happenstance,
Where Scheherazade reigns in a sacred dance.

Ainsley released a breath she wasn't even aware she'd been holding. It was just Rucker's shadow from the footlights. Well, that and whatever LSD had gotten into her bloodstream before she'd managed to spit the damn thing out. She almost laughed as Rucker finished his song.

Coming on soft as rain,
Coming on strong as a hurricane,
Butterfly kisses and snow angel wings.

"Hey, not bad," Rucker said once he'd finished. He looked satisfied; his eyes slid up and down the length of his guitar in much the same way his fingers had moments earlier. "Like ridin' a bike," he said.

"Or making love," Ainsley murmured, forgetting she'd left her microphone on. The words came out loud and clear, and she immediately regretted it.

Rucker looked stricken for a moment. He was still looking at his guitar, but his eyes went far away. Then he shook his head and smirked. "C'mon, kid," he said. He took the guitar off and placed it on a stand on the stage, next to his electric. Then he pulled a fat hand-rolled cigarette out of his pocket and waved it. "I need some fresh air."

Ainsley came down from the balcony, leaving her headlamp on the sound board, and joined Rucker as he clambered off the stage. They walked back out through the same side door Ainsley had entered through, found themselves in the dark alleyway, in a slight corrugated iron undercroft. Outside, the drizzle that Ainsley had walked through to get from the bus station to here had turned into a downpour. Rain fell merciless onto the ground, pounded on the metal roof over their heads. She looked up the alleyway, towards the main street, and could imagine people lining up out there in the sixties, even in rain like this, to see the latest acts visiting London. Not the bigger bands, but the smaller acts, they'd come here, to The Palais. And this was where Spirit Level played their last set, just after the release of their first—and last—album, right on the edge of stardom. And then . . .

"Why here, Mr Rucker?" Ainsley asked, as Rucker lit his joint and inhaled a lungful of smoke. The man looked at Ainsley, one eyebrow raised. "Why at The Palais? Why now, after all these years?"

Rucker shrugged, and blew out the fragrant smoke into the rain. "Rage Against The Machine said it, hey? 'What better place than here? What better time than now?'"

"Wouldn't have picked you as a Machine fan," Ainsley said with a smile.

"You kiddin'?" Rucker asked with mock outrage. "Kid, I was a shitkicker in the sixties. Protest songs were bread and butter to us. They're just carrying on where we left off."

Ainsley laughed. "Seriously," she persisted. "Why here and now?"

Rucker paused, thoughtful. "It seemed . . . appropriate," he said finally. "Back where it all began. Where it all ended."

"Do you still talk to Richie Tarbuck?" Ainsley asked, curious now.

"Nah, not really," Rucker admitted. "Got a Christmas card from him a few years back. Livin' in Spain now. Given up the synth, workin' as a producer. Probably had his mitts in that naff ketchup song, knowin' 'im."

Ainsley laughed at that. "So, it's just you then?"

"It's never just me, kid," Rucker replied, and the pain in his voice made Ainsley flinch.

"What do you mean?"

Rucker looked out into the rain. "Everyone carries their ghosts with 'em, kid," he said. "Everyone."

Ainsley waited for him to expand on that, but the singer remained quiet, thoughtful. Just watching the rain fall.

"You mean Caitlyn," she said at last. Not a question, a statement.

Rucker nodded. "Yeah, Caitlyn," he replied. It seemed a difficult name for him to speak. "Caitlyn. My Caitlyn." The bittersweet mix of love and pain in his voice made Ainsley's chest hurt. He looked over at her, as if sensing that. "Y'know, you remind me of her a bit."

Ainsley actually laughed out loud at that. "You're kidding. She was beautiful."

"Don't put yourself down, kid," Rucker told her seriously. He looked at her closely. "Anyway, it's not physical. You've got spirit."

"Bollocks," Ainsley snorted.

"You came, didn't you?" Rucker asked. "Alone, at three in the morning, to a deserted music hall? Jesus, kid, I dunno if I'd have the balls to do that. Caitlyn would've, though. She knew no fear." His eyes grew distant for a moment. "But it's not just her, either. It's Dave, of course, and Phil. Fallen comrades. Even Richie, bless the little sod." He took another drag on his joint, finishing it off, then flicked its remains into the rain. "You can't escape 'em, no matter how hard you try. They're always there. And here, especially here."

There was another lengthy silence. Ainsley was about to speak again, to break it, but Rucker surprised her by starting to sing, his voice soft, sweet, clear even through the rain.

So much I never said, girl,
The silences between us,
How you've lifted me above myself,
And made my world spin right.
In the grace of your caress,
You're my haven in the night,
O, kiss me Kate,
Kiss me not goodbye.

Ainsley recognised the song, of course, from the Spirit Level album. It was Rucker's ode to his wife, Caitlyn, which he sang solo on the record. But hearing him sing it *a cappella*, here, in the rain, made her shiver. She'd listened to it a thousand times, pretended he was singing it to her. It was written as a celebration, but here and now it was a lament.

Like a wise woman,
You serenade my childish heart,
With lullabies of starry skies,
Steer me to the shores of dreams.
But do not linger there, my love,
And slip away from me,
O, kiss me Kate,
Kiss me not goodnight.

Something caught Ainsley's eye, movement down the alley, out in the dark, in the rain, silhouetted by the lights of the high street. She looked closely, thinking perhaps a dog had been caught in the downpour, some poor street mutt looking for somewhere dry to shelter. But whatever was out there was too big to be a dog, too tall. It was . . .

It was a person. A woman.

Ainsley almost called out to her, but realised that her voice would never reach her, not through the rain. And anyway, she didn't want to interrupt Rucker's singing. He didn't seem to have noticed the woman himself, so caught up in his song, in his memories. In his past.

My darlin' girl,
I would catch every tear shed over my mistakes,

And string them like stars,
To lay upon your heart.

The woman came closer, down the alley. Ainsley couldn't make out her features, but she was sure she was female. She wore a full-length dress, and her hair was so long it reached her thighs. Still the rain obscured her. She walked mindlessly, like she was drawn to Rucker's voice, a sailor caught by a siren's song. There was something about the way she moved that made Ainsley feel uneasy. It reminded her of visiting her gran in the nursing home, and the old people there who wandered the hallways endlessly, aimlessly, their eyes emptied by dementia. The woman moved like that. And something else, something she couldn't put her finger on at first. Then, as Jimmy finished his song, she realised what it was.

Her hair and clothes looked dry.

O, kiss me Kate,
Kiss me not goodbye,
O, kiss me Kate,
Kiss me not goodnight.

Jimmy stopped singing, and a clap of thunder rocked the sky like God's own applause. Ainsley jumped, and glanced upwards, expecting to see the iron roof above collapse onto them, crumpling under the fury of the storm. But it didn't; it just hung there over their heads, implacable, not bothered one bit by the thunder. She looked down again, into the rain, to the woman.

She was gone, as if she'd never been there at all. There was nowhere she could have run off to, nowhere to hide. The alley she'd been standing in just moments earlier was completely empty.

Ainsley turned to Rucker. "Uh, did you see . . . ?" she began.

"Shh," Rucker hushed. His eyes were closed, and a wistful smile played on his lips. He breathed in through his nose, deeply. "I can smell 'er," he sighed. "The soap she always used. Natural stuff, none of the shop-bought crap. Handmade. Bought at the markets, every bloody week, tuppence a bar."

"What?" Ainsley was confused. She looked out into the rain again, eyes narrowed. The woman had to be there somewhere. But there was nothing; nobody. "I must be tripping," she moaned, eyes closed.

"What, on the tiny bit of acid you got before you spat it out?" Rucker laughed. "Not likely, kid."

Ainsley's eyes snapped open, met Rucker's. "You saw that?"

"I see a lot," he responded with a small smile.

"Ah."

"Don't worry, kid," Rucker said, and put a hand on Ainsley's shoulder. "No offence taken."

"None intended." Ainsley peered into the rain again. "I could have sworn I saw something. Someone," she corrected himself. "A woman."

"Yeah, I know," Rucker said, without any surprise in his voice.

"But . . ."

"Come on," the singer interrupted, and started back inside. "I think we've had enough fresh air. Time to get back to the coalface, hey?" He went in, not waiting for Ainsley, leaving her alone.

She watched the rain fall for a moment longer, her eyes narrowed. Then she turned and followed Rucker.

By the time she made it back up to the control board, Rucker had put his electric guitar on, an old Fender Stratocaster with an amazing painting of a dragon across its face. The guitar was almost as much an icon as Rucker himself. "About bloody time," he said with a grin. "Let's turn it up a notch!"

Ainsley nodded, the thoughts of the woman in the alley already fading into a dreamlike distance. It was just the acid, she was sure. She grinned at that thought; what a bloody girl's blouse. She faded down the acoustic input and faded up the electric, adjusted the levels by pure instinct, then looked over to Rucker, who was standing at the ready on stage, plectrum raised, waiting for the all clear. Beside him on the stage, Ainsley could make out what looked like broken boards, burnt at the edges. She closed her eyes and shook her head, then looked again. The stage was in perfect condition.

What the hell?

Ainsley blinked herself out of the trance she was slipping into. She gave him Rucker a shaky thumbs up, and the man grinned, paused for a moment longer, then hit a power chord that made every tooth in Ainsley's head rattle in its socket. She grinned at the onslaught, soaked it up. It was what she lived for. Rucker looked like he felt the same way.

> *Let's go down to The Crown,*
> *And stir us up a scuffle,*
> *Put your red dress on,*
> *Baby, paint your eyes to hustle,*
> *Drink our blues until they drown,*
> *Or the sky comes tumbling down!*

As Rucker played, Ainsley found herself bobbing her head in time. Even her pulse seemed to synchronise with the beat, pounded in her ears. Boom boom. Boom boom. Boom boom shh shh boom boom . . .

Wait. That wasn't his heartbeat. That was a high hat and bass drum.

At the back of the stage, Ainsley could see movement. A rhythmic flash, something waving up and down in time with the music. It only took a moment or two for her mind to fill in the blanks, draw a complete picture from the sketchy details she could make out. It was a drummer. The shadowy figure was playing along with Rucker; sticks spun in his hands as they found each of the drums and cymbals in turn, moving with deceptive delicacy, picking out the beat. He played with absolute confidence and accuracy, moving as easily as an Olympic swimmer might freestyle down the length of a pool, turning at each end with a natural movement, smooth, effortless.

> *Storm clouds building,*
> *And a hard wind blowin' in no good,*
> *You can sound the alarms,*
> *But they won't save you like they should,*
> *For this world's a-changin',*
> *And the skies coming tumblin' down!*

It should have been impossible to make out much more in the gloom behind Rucker, but Ainsley got flashes, glimpses of detail. A denim jacket with silver studs along the arms. A handlebar moustache stretching from ear to ear, mutton chops at each side. Dark glasses shaped like love hearts. She wondered how much of this she could actually see, and how much her mind filled in from the photographs she'd seen previously of David Guile, the man she was sure sat behind the drums. The man long dead and buried.

Her hand moved towards the spotlight switches again, but something stopped it, a strange feeling. The knowledge that, if she flicked the switch, the man would vanish, the same as the guitarist had earlier, and the woman in the rain as well. And she didn't want him to vanish, not this time. As much as she knew that she was just hallucinating, that the sad history of Spirit Level and The Palais was projecting images into her chemically-altered consciousness, that none of this was real, still she didn't want it to stop. She wanted the music. She wanted the *beat*.

> *Let's go out on the prowl,*
> *For one last night of dancin'*
> *We'll howl at the moon,*
> *Like the ancient lune romancin'*
> *Drink our blues until they drown,*
> *And the sky comes tumblin' down*
> *Drink our blues until they drown,*
> *And the sky comes tumblin' down!*

As the song finished, the drummer seemed to fade away, mist in sunlight. His last beat, a cymbal crash, hung in the air for some time afterwards, joined by feedback from Rucker's guitar. Then it faded as well, and Rucker was alone again, breathing hard, shining with sweat. He wiped his brow with the back of his hand, and grinned up at Ainsley.

"You see that?" he called, panting.

Ainsley was startled. "What?" she asked, thinking of the phantom drummer she'd seen and heard. Then realised she'd turned the microphone off, and switched it back on. "See what?"

"Red dust, man," Rucker said, and shook his hands out like they were wet. "Red dust! That's the rust comin' away. Beeee-yoodiful!"

"Yeah, sure," Ainsley muttered, troubled. "Whatever."

Rucker's smile disappeared, his brows knit. "What's up, kid? Was there a problem with the sound? I thought it sounded dead hot."

Ainsley shook her head. "It's just the acid, Mr . . . Jimmy," she said into the microphone. "I'm seeing things. Crazy things."

"Don't sweat it, man," Rucker told her. "Just go with it. It can't hurt ya. It's just a trip." He leaned into the microphone and spoke into it dramatically with a faux American accent. "*Welcome to a world beyond sight and sound.*"

"Leave it out," Ainsley snapped. She closed his eyes for a moment, tried to get her bearings. She'd never had a trip like this before. "Jesus! This is screwed up."

"Music's like that, kid." Rucker didn't move from the stage. He seemed rooted there, unable to escape. Like it was a Venus flytrap, waiting four decades for its prey to return, to be captured once more, captured and devoured. "It triggers stuff. A melody, a lyric. A drum beat," he said, and nodded meaningfully when Ainsley shot him a glance. "It can take you back to a place, a time. Or it can bring it to you." He gently picked a series of notes on the guitar, and Ainsley recognised it instantly. "Tread Lightly", the song the band had been playing when . . .

"This is it, isn't it?" Ainsley asked, her voice amplified in the hall.

"What?"

"The gig. This isn't a rehearsal at all." Ainsley was beginning to understand, though it wasn't making any sense, not really, except maybe in a drug-addled kind of way. "This *is* the gig."

Rucker nodded. "Time for the last number, kid." He smiled. "You've been a great audience. Couldn't a done it without ya. Ears and hands."

"Mister Rucker . . . Jimmy . . ."

But it was too late. Rucker started to sing.

Like cathedrals in the sky,
Like glass houses
Like granite of the shore,
We are eroded.
At first the loss is small,
So small, it's barely loss at all
It doesn't steel your heart,
Against tomorrow.

Ainsley watched as Rucker played, and around him on the stage, shadowy figures appeared. The drummer in the background, gently tapping the high hat in time with the melody. Dave Guile, dead of a drug overdose not long after Spirit Level had split up, not long after the tragedy in The Palais. To the right, Phil McKenzie strummed a quiet backbeat. McKenzie had died in the eighties, in a car accident in Surrey. He'd been drunk, the papers claimed. And, to Rucker's left, Richie Tarbuck played the synthesizer, swirling melodies around the guitars. This confused Ainsley; Tarbuck wasn't dead, Rucker had said so. Producing music in Spain. Yet here he was, as he was in '69, hair long, fur coat. It took her long seconds to understand.

You were just here,
A moment ago, my love,
A moment ago, my friend,
A moment ago, my brother.
You slipped by me,
Your passing disturbed the air,
That I breathe,
I breathe.

They were ghosts, yes, but not of people. They were the ghosts of the band. The spirits of Spirit Level.

If I tread lightly,
You are just around the corner,
If I move swiftly,
I might catch you,
If I'm oh so quiet,
I can almost hear you whisper,
"Never now, never here, my love."

And now, by Rucker's side, the dust in the air coalesced, twirled in on itself, and formed the shape of a woman, the woman Ainsley had seen in the rain earlier. Her long dress flowed, and bare feet peeked out from beneath its hem. Her arms were wrapped in red ribbons like maypoles, and her long dark hair was loose, free, wild, like her eyes. Rucker glanced over at her, the ghost of his wife, and for a moment he faltered, eyes wide. Then he found the beat again, found the rhythm, backed by his band, and continued.

> *When my love died,*
> *I felt that the world should end there,*
> *The sun rising,*
> *Burned me to the core.*
> *When my friend faded,*
> *The world became so tattered,*
> *Like a threadbare suit,*
> *I wore it.*

Ainsley knew what was coming. Desperate, she stabbed at the controls on the board, tried to cut the sound, the lights, but nothing worked. The board was as dead as the band itself, as the apparitions that played before her. Fear made the flesh on the back of her neck crawl. She didn't want to watch, didn't want to see, but she couldn't look away. She knew that was why she was here.

What's a band without an audience? A tree falling in the forest?

> *If I tread lightly,*
> *You are just around the corner,*
> *If I move swiftly,*
> *I might catch you,*
> *If I'm oh so quiet,*
> *I swear I can hear you whisper,*
> *Never now, never here, my love.*
> *My dreams died,*
> *As all my loved ones left me,*
> *My hope died,*
> *Inside of me,*
> *At first loss was small,*
> *So small, it doesn't follow,*
> *Doesn't steel my heart against the sorrow.*

The spotlight above Rucker wobbled, its beam shifting on the stage. Ainsley didn't need to look up. She knew the coupling was bending, coming away from its anchor. She knew because it had happened before, right here, forty years earlier. That time, Jimmy

Rucker had just noticed it, had instinctively thrown himself aside. Caitlyn, oblivious to the danger, lost in the music, had not. And now, here and now, it was happening all over again.

> *You were just here,*
> *A moment ago, my love,*
> *A moment ago, my friend,*
> *A moment ago, my brother,*
> *You slipped by me,*
> *Your passing disturbed the air . . .*

Rucker glanced upward, saw what was happening overhead, saw the ominous wobble of the spotlight. This time, though, he didn't move, didn't dive aside. Didn't save himself. Instead, he reached out and took Caitlyn's hand, and looked into her eyes, smiling. She smiled back. Ainsley's heart ached at that exchanged look. As the band played on behind them, they embraced, kissed, just lightly.

Then the light fell. The hall was plunged into darkness, and the only noise was the cataclysmic crash as the heavy spot slammed into the stage. It filled The Palais to brimming, echoed in Ainsley's ears. She clapped her hands over both side of her head and screamed.

When she stopped screaming, there was nothing, just a distant peal of thunder from the rainstorm outside. Then the sound of her own heavy breathing, her heartbeat in her ears, and a familiar ringing sensation like tinnitus, like she'd just come out of a gig. Nothing else. She flicked the switches blindly on the control board, trying to get the footlights up, a spot, anything. There was no response.

"Mr Rucker?" she called into the utter darkness around him. Only echoes of her ragged voice answered. "Mr Rucker? Jimmy?" She found himself starting to panic; the flesh on her hands tingled, and sweat ran down her face. She recalled her earlier bravado, the thought that she could take care of herself; that was gone now, wiped away by events unexplained, unexplainable. Her hands continued to scrabble around the control board, until they came across something sitting on it. Her headlamp. She pulled it over her head roughly and flicked the switch. The beam illuminated the control board in front of her.

It was a newish looking Yamaha, the complex array of sliders and displays completely different to what she'd been using just minutes earlier. The lighting board to the right was similarly modern, with directional spot controls and multiple effects. She swung her head around, looked at her surroundings as best she could in the dark. The bars were all stainless steel and smoked glass again, the wooden panels gone. She turned towards the stage, but from up on the balcony, the beam of her headlamp was too weak to reach that far into the darkness.

"Jimmy?" she called again, and made her way down from the second level, confused. The décor was as she'd always known it here, clean and modern and utterly unlike the way it had been in the sixties, the way it had been earlier. As she approached the stage, she knew what she'd see. Nothing at all.

She was wrong.

On the clean stage, no sign of fallen lighting rigs, a figure lay slumped on the boards, face up. The headlamp lit Rucker's pale face with an unearthly glow. He lay right where Ainsley had seen the burnt and damaged section of the stage earlier, the place where the light had fallen forty years earlier, killing his wife, his band and his life with one horrific crash. He looked old, so much older than earlier, his face lined and grey, his hair and beard almost white. His eyes were closed, and a tiny smile turned his lips upwards. There was no spotlight on the stage, no sign of any physical trauma. No Stratocaster guitar.

Ainsley knelt beside the man and felt his neck for a pulse. His flesh was stone cold. He was dead, and though Ainsley was no doctor, she'd have wagered that he had been dead for many hours. She stood up again and looked down at the man who, moments earlier, had been playing a song on this very stage. Then she turned away and stepped back off the stage. She stood down there for a while, her heart racing, tears catching in the corners of her eyes. Her breathing was fast and shallow, and she forced herself to calm down, not to panic. It was the drugs, just the drugs. Her hand found its way into her pocket, felt around for the spitwad of paper that she'd had in her mouth earlier, but found only the post-it note there, the one she'd found on the front door of the Palais. She looked at it with her headlamp. Blank.

"It's over," she said out loud, but instantly knew that it wasn't, not just yet. There was something missing, something undone.

There was still a hushed expectancy in the hall. It took her a few seconds to figure out what to do.

Ears and hands, Rucker had told her. *Ears and* hands.

She turned off the LED headlamp, plunging the hall back into total darkness. The air seemed alive around her, charged, electric. She turned back to the stage, and began to clap. Slowly at first, but getting faster. To begin, it was just her own hands making noise, echoing around the hall, but then more clapping merged with hers, joining in. She felt presences all around her, elbows touching elbows softly. That familiar feeling of being in a crowd, all of a like mind, as dozens, then hundreds of hands all beat a steady rhythm, not just applauding, but calling, imploring. Ainsley put her fingers in her mouth and whistled, as did other around her. They all continued to clap, faster and faster, the rhythms breaking apart into a mad staccato. Feet pounded the boards.

Then, one by one, the footlights slowly came up, revealing five figures on the stage. Ainsley cheered, as did the rest of the phantom audience, their applause and whistles doubling and redoubling in volume. Around them, in the dim light, Ainsley could see that The Palais was once again as it had been four decades earlier. The ghost of a venue.

The spots came on, and there they were, all of them, just as they were in the photos Ainsley had seen, dressed in their colourful sixties clothes, young, shining. Dave Guile twirled his drumsticks, grinning at the crowd like a madman. Phil McKenzie waved, his long, thin guitar hanging low, and the audience cheered louder. Richie Tarbuck, young Richie Tarbuck, hundreds of miles and forty years from Spain, played the opening synth notes of a familiar song. And, at the front, Jimmy and Caitlyn Rucker stood, hand in hand, his guitar hanging unused in front of him, as they greeted the audience warmly, the same man who'd looked down upon Ainsley from her wall for years, the man she'd loved from a distance of forty years, right here, right now.

Jimmy took up his guitar, and he and Caitlyn sang in harmony, smiling, lost in each other's eyes again at last.

Well I love to ramble,
And I've wandered O' so far,
Lost my mind in the Himalayas,

Lost my heart in a Stockholm bar.
My innocence fled me,
Down in New Orleans
And in alleyways in Marrakesh,
I almost touched my dreams.

Ainsley found tears flowing down her cheeks, but she didn't wipe them away. She just smiled and sang along, loud as she could, just one voice in the crowd as they watched the encore together, Spirit Level's final encore, forty years postponed.

But that great old lady
Keeps calling me on home,
She's my old lady,
Sweet London town.

About the contributors

HEATHER ALBANO is a writer of speculative fiction, historical fiction, and roleplaying games. She hails from New England. Her work has appeared in *Aoife's Kiss*, *Spectra Magazine*, *Midnight Times* and (forthcoming) *Electric Velocipede*, and she is an on-staff designer for Choice of Games, producer of award-winning text-based multiple choice games for the iPhone, Android, Kindle, Palm, and web. One of Heather's far-too-numerous projects is a steampunk time-travel novel. While doing research for the part of the novel that takes place in upper-crust Regency England, she came across the line, "Most of the Season's activities took place after dark"—and was struck by how easy it would be for a vampire to blend into such a society. And here we are. Check out her website at heateralbano.com.

· · · · ·

ANNETTE BACKSHALL has just changed seas from the Indian to the Pacific, leaving Perth and thirteen years of firefighting and a pet rosemary bush behind to live and write in Phegans Bay, NSW. She has been an active participant with the Katherine Susannah Pritchard Speculative Fiction Writers Group for about five years, albeit a long distant one now. Annette is pleased to offer *More Scary Kisses*, "Hunting Rabbits".

· · · · ·

As a preteen, LIZ COLEY was hooked on science fiction thanks to alien Tripods, spacetime warping tesseracts, and a Martian maid named Thuvia. Now she writes science fiction and fantasy for teens and adults (lizcoley.com) and posts a photographic blog (phlography.blogspot.com). Prior publications include "Immortals" (*Cosmos* 32), "Messiah" (*FlashMe* online), "Origins" in *The Last Man* anthology (2010), and "The Final Gift", in the upcoming *Strange Worlds* anthology. Her agent is circulating several of Liz's young adult novels in the U.S. When she isn't writing, Liz enjoys singing, photography, tennis, and cooking. She feels fortunate to call Dublin, Ohio home as it is a very supportive community of fellow writers.

. . . . .

ROXANNE DENT resides in the United States. She moved to Haverhill, Massachusetts from New York City eleven years ago. She has sold eight novels and four short stories. She also co-wrote two plays put on by the Firehouse Theater in Newburyport, MA and her screenplay, "The Pied Piper," won First Prize in *Fade In Magazine*. In New York, she belonged to The Sunday Club, an independent filmmaker's club where she wrote and produced her short movie "Valentine's Day," which won the Audience Choice Awards in the Bare Bones International Film Festival. Roxanne belongs to the Essex Writers and Artists Group in Haverhill and is currently working on a full-length Victorian novel.

. . . . .

An interviewer once said of DAYLE A. DERMATIS, "She has so many aliases, you'd think she was a spy!" A dabbler in several genres (and with several coauthors), she's published two novels and more than 100 short stories. She lives in southern California (USA) within scent of the ocean, and she and her husband spend their spare time following Styx around the country (and sometimes out of it), exploring the world on a motorcycle, renovating their 1911 Craftsman home, doing historic re-creation, and lounging in their hot tub. She loves music, cats, Wales, faeries, laughter, and defying expectations. You can read more about Dayle and her pseudonyms at www.cyvarwydd.com.

. . . . .

Melbourne-based writer FELICITY DOWKER is a Ditmar and Chronos Award winner and an Aurealis and Australian Shadows Award finalist. Felicity's short stories have been published in Australian and international journals and anthologies including *Aurealis, Andromeda Spaceways Inflight Magazine, Midnight Echo,* Morrigan Books' *Scenes From The Second Storey,* and Ticonderoga Publications' *Scary Kisses,* among others. Felicity's debut short story collection *Bread and Circuses* is forthcoming from Ticonderoga Publications in 2012. Felicity can be found online at http://felicitydowker.livejournal.com.

. . . . .

*D*ONNA MAREE HANSON lives in Queanbeyan, New South Wales, Australia right next door to Canberra. She has been writing speculative fiction for nearly ten years, with publications in: *Redsine* Magazine, *AntiSF,* the CSFG anthologies: *Machinations, Elsewhere* and *Masques.* In 2010, she had stories in *Belong* and *Scary Kisses,* both by Ticonderoga Publications and two other stories, "Liquid Night" in *Novus Creatura* published by Aurore Wolf and "Warning Buoy" put out by Static Movement. In 2011, so far her stories will also appear in *Dead Red Heart* edited by Russell B Farr. Donna has also edited an anthology, two single author collections and managed a small press as well as running a couple of science fiction conventions. She is currently writing a new novel length manuscript to go with the others she has written as well as new short stories.

. . . . .

*T*ALIE HELENE is a musician and writer, from Melbourne, Australia. She has poetry published in journals including *Voiceworks, Avant,* and *Inkshed,* and Mary Manning's *About Poetry* (Oxford University Press). She is Horror Editor for the anthology *The Year's Best Australian Fantasy and Horror* and was News Editor for the Australian Horror Writers' Association for four years, for which she received Ditmar nomination. Talie is a member of the SuperNOVA writers' group, and is working on her first novel. As a journalist she has been on staff at the UK's bible of extreme music, *Zero Tolerance* magazine, for five years, and her column Waltzing Macabre was a regular in *Black: Australian Dark Culture* magazine. Talie is currently preparing her AMusA in Classical Singing, and has performed with many artists including The Tenth Stage, Wendy Rule, and Eden. You can find out more about Talie's music and writing at www.taliehelene.com.

*P*erth-based writer MARTIN LIVINGS has had more than sixty short stories published in a variety of magazines and anthologies both locally and internationally. His work has appeared in *The Year's Best Australian SF and Fantasy*, and in Australian Dark *Fantasy and Horror*. His first book, the horror novel *Carnies*, was published in Australia in 2006 by Hachette Livre, and was nominated for both the Aurealis and Ditmar awards. He was finally married in 2010, thus earning his formal qualifications to appear in a paranormal romance collection at last. He is, it goes without saying, the paranormal one in the relationship. www. martinlivings.com

. . . . .

*K*IRSTYN McDERMOTT was born on Halloween, an auspicious date which perhaps accounts for her lifelong attraction to all things dark, mysterious and bumpy-in-the-night. She has been published in various magazines and anthologies, including *Macabre, Southerly, GUD, Aurealis, Southern Blood* and *Island*. Her short fiction has won Aurealis, Ditmar and Chronos Awards and her debut novel, *Madigan Mine*, was published by Picador in 2010. Kirstyn lives in Melbourne, Australia, with her husband and fellow author, Jason Nahrung. She is an active member of the SuperNOVA writers group and can be found online a www. kirstynmcdermott.com.

. . . . .

*N*ICOLE MURPHY has been a primary school teacher, bookstore owner, journalist and checkout chick. She grew up reading Tolkien, Lewis and Le Guin; spent her twenties discovering Quick, Lindsey and Deveraux and lives her love of science fiction and fantasy through her involvement with the Conflux science fiction conventions. Her urban fantasy trilogy Dream of Asarlai is published in Australia/NZ by HarperVoyager. She lives with her husband in Queanbeyan, NSW. Visit her website www.nicolermurphy.com

. . . . .

*J*ASON NAHRUNG grew up on a Queensland cattle property and now lives in Melbourne with his wife, the writer Kirstyn McDermott. A journalist and editor, his coverage of Australian speculative fiction has earned him a William Atheling Jnr Award for review and criticism. His fiction is invariably darkly themed, perhaps reflecting his love of classic B-grade horror films and 80s goth rock music. He is the co-author of the novel *The Darkness Within* (Hachette Australia), and continues to beaver away at novel-length manuscripts. A love of travel has resulted in an enduring love of New Orleans and a keen interest in photography. www.jasonnahrung.com

. . . . .

AMANDA PILLAR is a speculative fiction author and editor who lives in Victoria, Australia, with her partner and two children, Saxon and Lilith (Burmese cats). She has had numerous short stories published and is the in-house editor for Morrigan Books. Amanda has co-edited the fiction anthologies *Voices* (2008), *Grants Pass* (2009), *The Phantom Queen Awakes* (2010), and *Scenes from the Second Storey* (2010). She is currently working with Liz Grzyb on the anthology, *Damnation and Dames*, due for publication in 2012. In her free time, she plans on becoming the next Indiana Jones. You can find out more at www.amandapillar. com.

. . . . .

CAROL RYLES lives in WA, is a graduate of Clarion West 2008 and is writing her first novel, a steampunk fantasy, as part of her PhD in creative writing. Her website is at carolryles.com/ wordpress. She loves bushwalking in wild places in winter, but to date has not met any vampires and hopes that she never will.

. . . . .

After 10 years of Florida newspaper journalism, FRASER SHERMAN is now a freelancer writer who has been living in Durham North Carolina (USA) with his fiancee for the past year. He pays the bills with online nonfiction for the ehow website and *Raleigh Public Record* newspaper. He's written three film reference books—*Cyborgs, Santa Claus and Satan*; *The Wizard of Oz Catalog*; and the newest, *Screen Enemies of the American Way*. Fiction remains the most fun, though. He's written short stories for *Allegory*, *Realms of Fantasy*, *Tales of the Talisman* and *Abyss and Apex*, and has a series running on the Big Pulp website.

You can find him at his Wordpress blog, brilliantly titled Fraser Sherman's Blog.

$\cdots\cdots$

*E*RIC IAN STEELE hails from Manchester, England. He is the screenwriter of the sci-fi/action film *Clonehunter*, produced by Pandora Machine and the author of several short films in production across the United States. He has optioned scripts in Los Angeles and Europe. He is also a published fiction writer with stories in numerous anthologies, such as *Terminal Earth*, *In Bad Dreams 2*, *A Glitch In The Continuum*, *Timelines*, *Death Grip 3: It Came from the Cinema* and *Terror Tales* where he was published alongside authors Neil Gaiman and Kim Newman. His superhero the Silver Shadow appears in *POW!erful Tales* and returns in the upcoming sequel, *Beta City*. His work has also appeared in magazines such as *The Random Eye*, *Withersin*, *The Willows*, *Alienskin*, *Chaos Theory: Tales Askew* and *Scifantastic*. His zombie poetry has featured in *Vicious Verses and Reanimated Rhymes*. He is also the author of several unpublished novels which he keeps in an attic locked up in a trunk, and if questioned will continue to deny they exist.

$\cdots\cdots$

*F*RANK SUMMERS (franksummers.com) lives in Texas and writes speculative fiction including stories of humour, urban fantasy, dark fantasy, horror and science fiction. His short fiction has appeared in anthologies, online magazines, and eReader apps for the iPhone. His published work includes tales about werewolves, lonely robots on the moon, zombies in Buffalo Bill's Wild West, UFO sightings over small Texas towns, and time machines and human skeletons buried in the Arizona desert. In the 70s and 80s Frank worked part time as a singing songwriter performing original songs in clubs, coffeehouses, and college campuses as well as on radio and TV. He has been an IT professional for 30+ years. When not writing, Frank enjoys reading, watching movies, and spending time with his wife, two grown daughters and four dogs.

D C WHITE has been writing for several years. His work can be found in several anthologies including the original *Scary Kisses* and *The Killing Words*. Other fiction has appeared in *The Picture* magazine and on the internet. D C lives in Noarlunga, South Australia with his cat Toffee.

. . . . .

about the editor

*L*IZ GRZYB was born in the middle of a thunderstorm in Perth, Western Australia. She is the editor of the acclaimed *Scary Kisses*, Australia's first paranormal romance anthology, and is editor at *Ticon4.com*. Upcoming projects include co-editing *Damnation & Dames* with Amanda Pillar and *The Year's Best Australian Fantasy & Horror* with Talie Helene.

Acknowledgements

"Berries and Incense" Copyright © 2011 Felicity Dowker.

"Matchmaker" Copyright © 2011 Dayle A. Dermatis.

"Snake Charmer" Copyright © 2011 Carol Ryles.

"Philomena and the Blond God" Copyright © 2011 Amanda
  Pillar.

"Dances with Werewolves" Copyright © 2011 Frank Summers.

"The Protector's Last Mission" Copyright © 2011 Nicole R.
  Murphy.

"3AM" Copyright © 2011 Eric Ian Steele.

"Miss Luella's Magic Shop" Copyright © 2011 Roxanne Dent.

"The Sword of Darcy" Copyright © 2011 Fraser Sherman.

"Frostbitten" Copyright © 2011 Kirstyn McDermott.

"The Dark Night of Anton Weiss" Copyright © 2011 D C White.

"Phantom Lover" Copyright © 2011 Donna Maree Hanson.

"Hunting Rabbits" Copyright © 2011 Annette Backshall.

"Marriage of Convenience" Copyright © 2011 Liz Coley.

"Resurrection in Red" Copyright © 2011 Jason Nahrung.

"The Dark Season" Copyright © 2011 Heather Albano.

"The Last Gig of Jimmy Rucker" Copyright © 2011 Martin
  Livings & Talie Helene.

Thank you

The publisher would sincerely like to thank:

Elizabeth Grzyb, Felicity Dowker, Dayle A. Dermatis, Carol Ryles, Amanda Pillar, Frank Summers, Nicole R. Murphy, Eric Ian Steele, Roxanne Dent, Fraser Sherman, Kirstyn McDermott, D.C. White, Donna Maree Hanson, Annette Backshall, Liz Coley, Jason Nahrung, Heather Albano, Martin Livings, Talie Helene, Angela Slatter, Lisa Bennett, Terry Dowling, Simon Brown, Jonathan Strahan, Peter McNamara, Ellen Datlow, Grant Stone, Jeremy G. Byrne, Sean Williams, Garth Nix, David Cake, Simon Oxwell, Grant Watson, Sue Manning, Steven Utley, Lew Shiner, Bill Congreve, Jack Dann, Stephen Dedman, the Mt Lawley Mafia, the Nedlands Yakuza, Shane Jiraiya Cummings, Angela Challis, Kate Williams, Kathryn Linge, Andrew Williams, Al Chan, Kaaron Warren, everyone I've missed ...

... and you.

www.ingramcontent.com/pod-product-compliance
Lightning Source LLC
Chambersburg PA
CBHW031941240626
47153CB00003B/819